The AUKUS Affair

Robert Ferraro

The AUKUS Affair

A Conspiracy of Spies

Robert Ferraro

Copyright © 2024 Robert Ferraro
All rights reserved.
ISBN: 9798323883073

This is a work of fiction. Names, characters, places, and incidents either are the product of the author's imagination or are used fictitiously. Any resemblance to actual persons, living or dead, events or locales is entirely coincidental.

DEDICATION

For Paula, forever my Child Bride

Robert Ferraro

CONTENTS

Prologue   3

Chapter 1 The Morning Meeting 9

Chapter 2 The Pacific Strategy   17

Chapter 3 The Counterattack   22

Chapter 4 Unwelcome Visitors   34

Chapter 5 The Young Rebels   41

Chapter 6 The Counterspies   48

Chapter 7 *WNOW* Makes News   54

Chapter 8 Where is Chen Lin?   62

Chapter 9 A Secret War   73

Chapter 10 The Intern   77

Chapter 11 In It Together   86

Chapter 12 The Mole Digs In   93

Chapter 13 Closing the Circle   105

Chapter 14 The Truth Will Out   115

Chapter 15 Deadly Measures   131

Chapter 16 A Federal Case   143

Chapter 17 Gabe Gets a Tip   156

Chapter 18 Collateral Damage   167

Chapter 19 Going on Offense   172

Chapter 20 Operation Neptune   187

Chapter 21 The Russian Connection   193

Chapter 22 A Loose Thread   200

Chapter 23 The Triple Offensive   208

Chapter 24 Mission to Guangzhou   225

Chapter 25 A Very Dead End   231

Chapter 26 On the Pearl River   236

Chapter 27 The Final Phase   247

Chapter 28 River Run   255

Chapter 29 Whampoa   267

Chapter 30 A Rookie Error   274

Chapter 31 Sail East Go West   283

Chapter 32 New Beginnings   290

Epilogue   298

Acknowledgements   301

Author Profile   303

Robert Ferraro

PROLOGUE

Saturday morning broke clear, the wind calm. For two sailors the sunlit dawn promised a benevolent day without impending storm or shipboard drama. Aboard their small sloop the sleepy morning was exceptionally hushed, almost soundless except for the slight lapping of wavelets against the boat's hull. It was the kind of early July day you could imagine on the nearby land birds were twittering, insects chirping and suburban dogs yawning awake.

Peaceful certainly, but for the two sailors now on the final leg of a race around Long Island the morning was entirely too quiet. Sailing west on the Long Island Sound in the waters between New York and Connecticut, they were almost becalmed. What little wind there was blew from the south, tumbled over the tony East end of Long Island and, obstructed by the land and objects ashore, weakened further. The sea barely ruffled. The boat loafed and wallowed languidly allowing the early morning sun to warm the sailors' backs. It was a welcome warmth after the chill of a night spent on the open ocean. They were well past the halfway point of the race, but the young couple still had a hundred miles to the finish line, and at this pace crossing it could take another twenty-four hours.

Devlin and Marina McCarthy were alone on their thirty-foot boat. They had left their two kids with Marina's mother to allow a long weekend together. While this springtime sail was ostensibly a race, the organized competition was for them just a way to add purpose to a shakedown cruise; preparation for what they hoped would be a longer summer trip to Maine. It made their approach to this sailing contest fairly lackadaisical.

Devlin was at the wheel when Marina climbed from the cabin below into the cockpit carrying the first coffee of the morning. The petit brunette had her hair pulled back into a ponytail held together with a scrunchy. She was wearing an oversized white tee which did double duty as a pajama top, tan shorts, and light blue canvas boat shoes.

"See anyone?" Marina asked while doing a three-sixty scan. She squinted down to the water glinting in the morning sun and up to the few fleecy fair-weather clouds hanging motionless in the still air. In the distance she noted a fishing boat making its way toward Plum Island, *probably to work the rips there* she thought, otherwise as far as she could see they were alone.

"Nope, nobody," answered Devlin taking a steaming cup from her. He stood, leaned across the wheel and gave her lips a light pecking kiss then sat back again into the stern seat. She slid to his left, along the port side, so that her back rested against the transom coaming, her legs stretched out in front.

"Sun feels good," she said. Then after a pause, "I guess we fell behind last night when we sailed south looking for better wind."

"Maybe. Whatever. We are all by our lonesomes now," Devlin said with a grin, "not that I mind that much." His lanky frame, he was a good head taller than Marina, was still dressed in jeans and a hooded gray sweatshirt against the dampness of the evening watch.

She leaned against him, her head against his shoulder, her right hand resting on his leg. With his free arm he pulled her close, lifted her face and they kissed more passionately. Married ten years and this, an anniversary cruise of sorts, found them in their mid-thirties with two children and almost as physically affectionate as teenagers.

"We're not far from your dad's place," Marina noted as she looked across the water to the Connecticut shore about ten miles to the north.

"Uh huh," Devlin agreed. "New London is there, right up the Thames River," he said pointing.

They had rounded Montauk Point at the eastern tip of Long Island in the early hours of the morning, its famous lighthouse guiding them in from the open ocean. They were now just west of Fishers Island. It was the skinniest part of the Sound, where the north shore of Long Island curves upward toward the Connecticut coast. The seaway in that area is called The Race because of the swift tidal currents swirling through the narrow gap between the two land masses. The couple had been lucky to arrive in The Race on an incoming tide; the ineffectual wind meant if the tide were ebbing, they would have to drop anchor to keep from drifting backwards. Despite the wispy breeze the rushing current was boosting them westward at about three knots, a little more than three miles an hour. Not much but it would have to do until, hopefully, the wind picked up. With a modicum of breeze their boat, *Coastie,* could average better than seven knots.

Coastie got its name from Devlin's occupation, he was a Coast Guardsman and captain of one of its cutters based in the Port of New York. Devlin had bought the boat before marrying Marina, and while she would have liked to have it named for her, *isn't that what most men did?* She had to accept it was a fait accompli. Besides, the name was well known in these waters and assured special treatment if they ever needed to call on the Coast Guard.

Like Devlin, Marina also had a job which put her near New York's waterfront; she was a linguist and interpreter at the United Nations whose iconic glass-sided building sits alongside Manhattan's East River. From her office window Marina would often spy her husband's cutter patrolling the river or transiting from Hell Gate between the Sound and New York Harbor. That would usually prompt a teasing text message to him about some perceived infraction or poor seamanship. Knowing she was watching he would leave the wheelhouse and wave to the UN's faceless green façade in reply.

Devlin's career choice was a family affair. His father Liam McCarthy was also a sailor, for the U.S. Navy, though no longer seagoing. Liam was now a respected naval architect for a civilian firm, General Dynamics' Electric Boat Works in Groton, Connecticut, a town across the Thames from New London. Electric Boat was where America's nuclear submarines were built; not at all far from *Coastie's* current position.

Devlin was still looking toward Connecticut when he felt the boat take a slow roll to starboard. Just as he shifted his gaze forward to see what was causing the roll he cried out, "Marina, hang on!" Despite the windless day and the otherwise flat calm water, he saw two giant seas rolling towards them from his left, the port side of the boat. Before he could swing the bow to angle into them, the rollers struck beam on. *Coastie* lurched sideways the mainsail boom driven down to within feet of striking the water. Devlin clutched the wheel and its bolted-down mounting to keep from being tossed onto the starboard lifelines. Marina, caught off guard slid sideways and was thrown hard into him. Both cups of coffee went flying. The boat, which had been knocked down onto its right side then careened to the left as it slipped off the back side of the wave, only to be hit by a second roller. Again, the boat leaned wildly, swinging again right, then left. From below came the sound of loose gear being flung about and rattling onto the floorboards.

The two sailors were shaken but not hurt.

"What the hell was that?" Devlin cried as *Coastie* righted herself and the two big rollers moved past, diminishing in size as they headed toward the Connecticut shore.

As suddenly as the waves had erupted, all was once again quiet, the sea flat as if never disturbed. Marina, collecting herself, stood and looked toward where the waves had apparently originated. Her eyes widened at what she saw, clutching Devlin she gasped, "Oh my God," and pointed to a towering black steel structure rising slowly from the sea only yards from their port side. Various antennae poked from its top, otherwise it was totally smooth, without obvious seams or hatches. Water falling from its sides and sinister black tower foamed white, hissing as it spilled over the emerging hull and back into the sea.

The ominous cylindrical boat, now obviously a submarine, looked like a mammoth torpedo, long as a football field. Other than the wake it had created, it slid through the water like a menacing apparition. The boat made no discernible sound as it sped away at what Devlin estimated to be better than twenty knots.

On the side of its superstructure painted in white were the letters SSBNX. Devlin knew enough about Navy nomenclature to decode its meaning; it was an experimental ballistic missile nuclear submarine. And that submarine was probably one of his father's new creations returning to the U.S. Navy's submarine base in nearby Connecticut.

CHAPTER 1
May
THE MORNING MEETING

Eight a.m. and the conference room at New York's WNOW-TV newsroom was crowded with the usual morning gaggle, twenty-five producers and reporters all clutching coffee cups and seated around a long oblong desk. An all-glass wall looked out over the newsroom. At the head of the table sat the wiry, disheveled overnight assignment editor clutching his night's work, a list of stories he called The Daily Gist. Everyone had a copy. Some stories were labeled *Onworking* with the names of reporters and producers already assigned. Others were listed *Possibles*, news that had broken overnight, or which various reporters were pitching for coverage that day. For a reporter, getting airtime was the daily goal and they competed with each other for that exposure. The best way to ensure getting on the air was to find a story the news director couldn't resist, and then own it.

The Executive Producer gave a nod and Manny Rizzo the overnight editor kicked off the meeting, "Not much to report overnight, couple of fires, no fatalities, some stringer footage, that's it. But we do have plenty going on dayside." He listed a Mayoral press conference on the homeless, an anti-police protest march in Brooklyn, a transit employee strike threat, a new anti-rat initiative, and finished with a few light, "kicker" items to end the newscast.

After those around the table voiced their opinions and made suggestions on possible story angles, the executive producer decided which reporters would cover which stories. He was about to adjourn the meeting when Rizzo added, "Oh yeah, I checked in with Stu Simpson down at DCPI to see if he heard about anything not yet on the wire, and he said the Commissioner might have something interesting to say later today." DCPI, the Deputy Commissioner of Public Information, was the police department's public relations office.

"Like what?" asked Jim Butler the Executive Producer.

"Don't know. He couldn't say anything more, said he didn't know anything more; but Simpson's always been straight with me. We should send someone down to One Police Plaza to nose around."

Butler looked around and his gaze landed on Roger Barnes, a new hire who was usually stuck with saccharine features; stories that sometimes didn't make air at all, or if they did only after he had been "big footed," replaced, by a more seasoned reporter.

"Barnes you up?" Butler barked.

Startled, the young man nodded yes and was ordered to go to Police HQ and find out what the Commissioner's office was being so coy about.

***

Roger Barnes, who at 24 had been hired from a New Haven, Connecticut station, a farm team of sorts for WNOW, was desperate for a break. When he arrived in New York he had been assigned to cover the United Nations as a regular beat, but dig as he might there was precious little news that came out of there that interested his local news audience. Barnes had to fall back on covering food fairs, flea markets, and amateur art shows. For a local reporter anxious to make his "bones," his reputation, the U.N. was Siberia. For the rest of the world it might be a crisis center, but in this town it was almost invisible. For any truly big, Big Apple crisis, ground zero was at One Police Plaza.

After a quick cab ride from the newsroom on the West Side down to Chambers Street at the foot of the Brooklyn Bridge, Barnes entered the police department's fortress-like brick building. He was met by uniformed officers, showed his press pass, emptied his pockets, and went through a metal detector. Collecting his phone and watch he took the elevator to the NYPD Public Information office on the sixth floor. The space, furnished with metal industrial-style desks, exuded the bland aura and casual indifference of a bored, overworked bureaucracy.

"Hiya doin' Stu Simpson around?" Barnes said to the seated officer on duty.

"He's gone for the day. Works the overnight," said the cop, a portly woman in uniform who looked to be in her fifties. Barnes introduced himself and told her he was trying to get some information on the Commissioner's upcoming press conference.

"What press conference? There's nothing on his schedule," she said.

"Funny, Stu told our assignment editor there was something in the works. Could you check?"

The officer sighed, mumbled something about the Department's byzantine chain of command and went to see her supervisor. She came back looking a bit quizzical. "Well, you're right, but it's not here," she said, "the Commissioner will be making a joint statement over in Chinatown. A joint statement with the FBI. It seems whatever it is, it's their gig."

"The FBI?" repeated Barnes, his voice up an octave.

"Yeah," she said handing him a slip of paper with a street address. "Go figure, we're the last to know."

"I guess the Feds big-footed you guys," Barnes said with a laugh as he thanked her and left to walk the couple of blocks to Chinatown. As he walked, he pulled a mobile phone from his jacket pocket and called the assignment desk, now manned by Noah Goldman the dayside editor. "Hey Noah…"

"Yeah, I know," broke in Noah, "We heard it from the Feds, I was just about to call you, Jimmy Bell's mobile crew is on its way down. They'll meet you at the corner of Pell and Doyers. Got it? Pell and Doyers. Give 'em a half hour and set up for a live shot."

"What's up? NYPD was apparently blindsided as well."

"This is a Fed sting. Something about a Chinese government spying operation or something weird like that. FBI says it'll be an outdoor briefing in front of the building at 22 Doyers."

"No shit!"

"Yeah, sounds big but that's all I got on it," said Noah. Then the words that made Barnes's day, "And if this pans out, I think you got the lead spot in the newscast." To lead the newscast, going live with the biggest story of the day, a fantastic break! Unless of course they big-footed him again.

"Noah, tell me straight, is Butler going to give this to Gabe?"

Gabe Breslin was a legendary street reporter with years covering the cops; he had deep sources in the Department. "Nope, Gabe is out of town today. If this turns into something big, missing it will really burn his ass. It's all yours Barnes my boy." Barnes had to grin at the frustration that was sure to rankle Breslin. As he raced the last few blocks to Pell Street Barnes said to himself, *Screw that prima donna. He's had the PD beat to himself long enough.*

While quick-stepping through the crowded streets Barnes rang his longtime girlfriend. Li Hana, was a Taiwanese who worked in the UN's video production department, more formally known as its WebTV Service. She was responsible for providing video of UN meetings and producing segments touting the worldwide work of its peacekeeping and social service outreaches. For the UN, WebTV was a part time news service and full time PR agency dedicated to making the member nations feel they were getting their money's worth. Li acted as a producer and occasional on-camera talent. She was a slim, athletic-looking twenty-one-year-old with long, raven black hair. She usually coiled it into a bun which, when unraveled and draped on a pillow, drove Barnes into raptures. Only a year out of Yale but with a restless, dynamo personality, Roger teased she would be a Tiger Mother ... if she were ever to be a mother.

Hana answered as soon as his name popped onto her phone. "Hi Roger, you coming to visit, taking me to lunch?"

"No, I finally have a story that might make the top of the program. Something big is going down in Chinatown. I don't know what it is yet, but I might need your language skills."

"Chinatown? The only thing you guys ever cover there is the New Year fireworks. What's up?"

"Should know soon. I'm on my way to a press conference now, the Feds are involved. I just wanted to give you a heads up to watch the top of the Six.

***

Hana was still in her office at six o'clock. It was a spacious office for someone as young and inexperienced as she, but the large office was typical of the UN where they were generous with perks, if not pay. She settled into her swivel chair, clicked the TV onto WNOW News and immediately after the opening animation heard the anchorwoman, Gloria Herrera, say, "Good evening, and welcome to all the news that's happening NOW! We begin tonight with a reported Chinese invasion of New York. No, not military, it is a stunning revelation from the FBI about an alleged Chinese government plot to spy on and intimidate U.S. citizens and residents. According to the Feds the Chinese have established what's being called their own, quote, "Police Precinct" in the heart of Chinatown. The FBI alleges it has been manned by Chinese government spies. Our reporter Roger Barnes is on the scene at the corner of Pell and Doyer streets. Roger."

The control room cut to Roger live.

"Gloria, I am standing in front of 22 and a half Doyer Street. It is a nondescript five story walkup in the heart of Chinatown which officials say was where this spy ring was headquartered. A ring whose job was to recruit spies, to intimidate and harass activists opposed to China's government, to silence their critics and possibly even engage in sabotage."

The screen then turned to pre-recorded video of the building exterior with Roger's voiceover narration. The camera zoomed into one apartment in particular.

"According to the FBI, an apartment on the third floor of this building was dubbed a Chinese Police Precinct and two men, now fugitives, were operating from here. They are currently the subjects of a nationwide manhunt."

The chief of the Bureau's New York office Bill Roscoe appeared onscreen. "We have been observing this operation for some time and intercepted various communications from those involved to American residents of Chinese descent. They often try to manipulate these innocent people by threatening harm to relatives still living in China."

Roger's narration continued over footage of Chinatown street scenes. "The FBI says their goal was to blackmail members of this community into assisting China's Ministry of State Security, its espionage service.

Once again on camera Roger said in a standup, "FBI agent Roscoe also said this sort of operation is not unique to New York or indeed the U.S., but that there are hundreds of similar so called 'Police Precincts' in cities around the world. The government hopes that by exposing this cell of spies it will inspire some of those victimized to come forward. The NYPD says such activities are definitely not welcome, nor legal in New York."

New York's Police Commissioner appeared on camera and said, "The NYPD is the best police force in the world. We don't need nor want any such phony 'precincts' in our city, threatening our people. And take it from me, the fugitives who worked out of this building will be found and brought to justice."

Roger came back live on camera.

"Gloria, what exactly these alleged Chinese government operatives were up to, who they were pressuring and to what end, has yet to be revealed. One thing is sure, this is just the beginning of what will prove to be a far-reaching investigation by both Federal and local law enforcement. Reporting from Chinatown this is Roger Barnes."

Roger wrapped his live shot on a determined high, vowing *I'm going to own this story.* This was the chance he had been waiting for; like a bulldog with a bone, he would clamp down on it and not let go. There would be plenty of follow-ups as the investigations proceeded and he intended to lead all the reporting on them. But first, *I'll recut the tape for tonight's News at Eleven, and then celebrate with Hana.*

Their celebration was a simple meal at a bar not far from Hana's apartment in the East Thirties. It was one of the last quiet nights they would get to enjoy for the next month.

CHAPTER 2
The Previous January
THE PACIFIC STRATEGY

The story Roger was hoping would jumpstart his career had its origins almost six months earlier and three thousand miles away, in London. Its conception took place during a January summit meeting of the NATO nations helping Ukraine defend against a Russian land invasion. While most of the world's attention focused on the war and the assembled chiefs of state, secret side negotiations were being held in a nondescript basement space at the British Prime Minister's office, 10 Downing Street.

In attendance and seated around a small round table was the U.S Secretary of State, Britain's Foreign Secretary, and the Australian Minister of Foreign Affairs. It was the Australian who had called the meeting, and purposely requested the setting be intimate; in a space small and confined. Also, as he requested the three men were alone, unaccompanied by staff members.

"Thank you for agreeing to this meeting," said David Whitaker the Australian. "I asked for your attendance because my government has made a decision which will undoubtedly have some negative diplomatic consequences, and I don't want you to be blindsided."

The Brit and the American glanced at each other concerned that, despite Whitaker's warning, they were indeed about to be blindsided by something unpleasant.

The Australian continued, "I know you are up to your asses dealing with Ukraine and a land war in Europe, but I want you to shift your focus for a moment to the Far East, where our principal concern remains China and its aggressive expansion in the South China Sea."

These long-term allies had been watching for two decades as China enlarged several coral islands and atolls in the South China Sea, militarizing them with airfields, anti-ship and anti-aircraft missile systems, lasers and signals-jamming equipment. The Chinese air force was also getting more aggressive, routinely harassing planes flying in international air space. The three nations were concerned that the Chinese military was slowly but inexorably turning the South China Sea into a Chinese lake; eventually they'd have the capacity to choke-off all trade through it at will.

"Right, our concern as well," said Bruce Addison the American Secretary of State. "Which is why we have reinforced our assets in the region." The United States had been adding substantially to its Pacific naval forces not just because of the threat to international trade, but also because it feared the Chinese were preparing for an invasion of Taiwan, which the U.S. was obligated by treaty to defend.

The British Foreign Secretary, Malcolm Benedict concurred, saying they too had shifted warships to the Pacific to defend its Commonwealth allies. But Whitaker, unsatisfied, pressed on.

"Your assurances of coming to our aid are of course welcome. We recognize that we cannot successfully defend Australia alone. But given that, we have concluded that we need more modern, robust weapons systems than we currently possess." Benedict and Addison shifted uncomfortably. Where was the Australian going with this?

"We are already all over the area, patrolling with ships, planes, satellites, drones," said Secretary of State Addison. "What else are you looking for?"

Whitaker responded, "It's not enough for us to hunker down in a defensive posture. We can't allow the Chinese to keep building their forces unchecked. We need to blunt any plans they might have for territorial expansion with an offensive capability we just don't have now."

"Well," interrupted Benedict, the British Foreign Secretary, "you are buying three new attack submarines from the French. They will go a long way to extending your offensive reach."

At the mention of the submarines the Australian minister clasped his hands and rested them on the table, he leaned forward, bent his head down and sighing, shook it side to side.

He then looked up directly into the British diplomat's eyes and said, "You are half right there, Mister Secretary. The right weapon, but also the wrong one."

The American and British diplomats looked at each other and said simultaneously, "What do you mean?"

"I mean the ninety-billion dollar deal we have with the French is for the wrong sub. I want to scrap it."

"What???" the other two blurted in surprise.

"We want to switch our buy from the French attack submarine to the next generation American ballistic sub, the ones replacing the Ohio Class." He turned to face the American Secretary of State, "The ones you are calling the Columbia Class. We want them, and the missiles they carry.

My government wants the Chinese to know that any attack on us will mean instant Armageddon for them."

"But David," said the American, dropping all formality, "the French will be furious. This sub purchase is a longstanding agreement of huge economic consequence to them, and their defense industry."

"It is of greater importance to us that we buy the system we need, whatever the diplomatic uproar it causes. We are determined to initiate in the Pacific a version of MAD." Whitaker was referring to the policy of Mutually Assured Destruction which kept the Soviets at bay during the cold war.

"We want to do the same now against the Chinese," he said with finality.

***

It took months of negotiations after that London meeting, but a trilateral security treaty binding the three nations was signed; it was called the AUKUS agreement, an acronym for Australia, the United Kingdom and the United States. A key provision was that the U.S. and U.K. would assist Australia in acquiring the nuclear-powered submarines it wanted.

As predicted the French were livid, they called the pact, "A stab in the back." even pulling their ambassadors from the U.S. and Australia. It was a futile, symbolic protest which was short-lived and quickly sputtered out.

However, there was a much more violent reaction brewing, the results of which didn't take long to materialize. The Chinese government denounced AUKUS as "A return to a Cold War mentality," by the West. For China, the threat of

Australia patrolling its coast with an invincible class of nuclear submarines heavily armed with ballistic missiles was intolerable.

And China was not alone, Russia joined in the condemnation, advocating a Sino-Russian strategic military partnership which would catch the U.S. between two antagonistic nuclear superpowers.

Like chess players moving powerful pieces across a board, the opposing governments would be shuttling weapons across latitude and longitude lines, probing, feinting, threatening, all looking for tactical dominance. It was inevitable that this global escalation and repositioning of offensive weaponry, though conceived as a way to keep the peace, would ignite an espionage war aimed at achieving technological dominance.

CHAPTER 3
May
THE COUNTERATTACK

That Spring, shortly after the AUKUS agreement was announced, the Ministry of State Security in Beijing made its first counter move. It sent an urgent message to Ma Bai, a diplomat at the Chinese Mission to the United Nations; he was ostensibly the head of the Mission's communications department. In reality, Ma controlled all espionage agents of the People's Republic of China, the PRC, on the East Coast of the United States.

Ma Bai stood facing the wall-to-ceiling window of his spacious 20th floor office looking out at the East River. The morning sun was climbing over the nearby landscape of Queens and shone directly before him. On one wall a photo portrait of President Xi Jinping looked down at him, on the other walls were posters depicting Chinese cultural and natural wonders, the Great Wall, the Li River in Guilin, and the Pillars of Zhangjiajie. In his right hand he held a slip of paper with a newly deciphered message. Ma read and reread the text. The action order was curt and simply stated, yet breathtaking in scope. *"You are ordered to initiate an operation to uncover all possible information relating to the construction and capabilities of the new Columbia Class of American submarines."*

The order was straightforward, but Ma knew it was probably —except in the imagination of some Beijing bureaucrat— nearly impossible to successfully carry out. He might be able to nibble around the edges of such a high value target, but getting detailed information about its construction, much less its capabilities, would require a well-placed mole. Something that couldn't be developed overnight.

But an order was an order, and as was his proactive manner he immediately decided where he had to start. As he gazed out the window his eyes followed the East River down toward lower Manhattan where, beyond the latticework of the Williamsburg Bridge and lost in the jumble of aging eastside tenements, was the Chinese "Police Precinct" on Doyer street.

Ma Bai pocketed the note and decided he would contact his man there today, but not until he first arranged a meeting with a friendly colleague at the U.N. Rather than using his cell phone, which he feared might be monitored by the FBI or the CIA, or both, he picked up one of the U.N.'s internal phone lines to call Vladimir Ivanov, his counterpart at the Russian delegation. They made an appointment to meet in the delegates' dining room.

The spacious restaurant faced east along the width of the U.N. tower and, like Ma's office, was bright with morning sun. An exterior patio wrapped around the dining room whose glass walls reflected the sunlight and gave expansive views both uptown toward the 59th Street Bridge and downtown to New York's sprawling harbor. The two men pushed open the dining room's glass doors and carried containers of coffee outdoors. They sat on cushioned settees along the patio perimeter, the edge of which was bordered by nautical-style wire rigging. Their seats were in a corner, distant from anyone else. Out of earshot they could talk freely.

Ma got right to the point, speaking Russian he said, "Vladimir, we have great interest in learning more about the Americans' new Columbia Class of submarines. We have begun to research them ourselves, but I would like to hear what you might be able to tell me about them."

Ivanov hesitated a moment considering how much of what he knew he should share. Since what he knew was very little, he decided to be truthful, "We don't know too much, as of now. From what we hear the design is still undergoing revision. I do know they are supposed to carry more ballistic missiles than the current Ohio Class, and run even quieter." Ivanov gave a slight shrug, "That's it. So, as I say what we know is not much."

"How will they compare to your Akula Class?"

"The Akula is good. A match for anything the Americans have now. They are quiet, dive fast, can take significant punishment and survive. But how they will compare with the Columbias we don't yet know. Especially when it comes to payload."

"Are you actively pursuing more information?"

Ivanov smiled, "We do our best." He sipped his coffee and added more seriously, "We are not happy with what we don't know."

"I understand," said Ma, "neither are we, and so I must do something about it."

"Let me know if I can help. Of course I will share what we ourselves uncover."

The two men stood, and as they reentered the building Ma said, "I will keep you informed." But despite the collegial words and proffers of cooperation, neither man fully trusted the other. And neither did their governments. Theirs was a marriage of continually suspicious convenience.

Once back at his desk Ma dialed the number for the "Precinct." He felt no need to hide the call since that phone number was well known in the Chinese community. The Doyer Street office had been promoted long and loud as a place meant to assist neighborhood residents in their dealings with the American government, so it was entirely reasonable that someone from the Chinese Mission would be calling. The allegedly innocent nature of the Precinct might have been a widely publicized pitch for the benefit of American ears, but even the least political of Chinatown's population knew this small office in an upper story of a decrepit sixth-floor walkup tenement, was a front for the infamous Chinese Ministry of State Security. A place to be avoided.

Ma's call rang only once before it was answered by Zhang Wei the director of the office. From his caller ID Zhang saw who was calling. Surprised and a little rattled he popped out of his chair and, almost comically, snapped to attention and took the call standing. "Hello Mister Ma Bai," he said, "so good to hear from you, how can I be of help?"

Ma snapped, "Meet me this afternoon, one o'clock at the usual place."

"Yes sir, understood. Must I prepare anything?"

"No."

Without another word Ma clicked off. He had chosen *Forlini's* Italian restaurant off Canal Street for their meetings because, though it was near the Precinct and in the middle of Chinatown, it was unlikely many, if any regular patrons spoke Mandarin.

Ma buzzed his driver and was soon seated in the backseat of a black sedan on the FDR Drive threading its way downtown through midday traffic. Exiting the Drive at the Brooklyn Bridge off ramp, he had the driver stop on Chinatown's bustling Elizabeth Street. Ma had purposely left early for the meeting. He wanted to lunch at the Oriental Palace, a favorite of his, before meeting with Zhang. They would not eat at *Forlini's,* just talk. Italian food did not agree with him.

In the cavernous Chinese restaurant strings of fluorescent lights cast a brilliant light that vanquished all shadows. Red wall hangings festooned with gold lettering promised patrons health and long life. Plastic Ibises standing one-legged shared wall space with long-toothed dragons exhaling tongues of fire. Ma sat at a corner table next to a fish tank with live carp swimming lazily, awaiting their turn in the fryer. As he sipped a bowl of hot and sour soup, Ma reflected with irritation on the task he would ask Zhang to initiate. He was not in a good mood, nagged by doubts of his colleague's effectiveness. Ma believed Zhang had gained his position only through his family's political connections and so treated him with a mix of disdain and condescension. *I must oversee him closely,* Ma thought, *this project though ill conceived, is too important. I need him to succeed.*

After his brief lunch it was a wary but determined Ma who strolled from Elizabeth Street through the three blocks crowded with fish mongers, vegetable stalls, and dim sum shops to *Forlini's* on Baxter Street. The place was a popular hangout for the cops, lawyers and reporters who worked at the nearby courthouses. Forlini's long mahogany bar and plush red leather banquettes could have been designed by the producers of a Hollywood mob movie. And Ma believed it was more than likely some of the men inhabiting the space at this time of the afternoon were of that criminal persuasion.

In an era of gastronomic innovation, *Forlini's* cuisine was a red sauce throwback, and the clientele here loved it that way. It was considered by the criminal courts' judicial combatants to be neutral territory; even so, conversations were hushed, and everyone minded their own business. Legal deals might be consummated here, but the atmosphere was subdued, not boisterous. No one came looking to make new friends or cruising for a casual hookup.

Ma pushed through the frosted glass doorway to find Zhang waiting and seated in his usual spot, a curved banquette for two known as a deuce. A cozy corner perfect for couples who might be enjoying an illicit rendezvous. Behind Zhang a window faced onto the street, its opaque white curtain muting the pale afternoon light. The curtain provided privacy, and the traffic sounds from the street created a buzz of white noise to cover their conversation.

As Ma approached, Zhang who was silhouetted by the backlit window, half stood and bowed a greeting, "Ninhao, Maxiansheng," he said with a broad, if forced smile. Ma grunted a reply, and both sat huddled close around the small table.

Zhang was sitting with a beer and a dish of cashew nuts, no food. He knew his boss's routine. A portly waitress appeared, Ma signaled for a beer for himself and, as was his way, immediately got to business. "Zhangxiansheng, I am going to need someone of substantial technical expertise, an engineer of sorts, for a new project. It will involve some prior knowledge of ships, or ship building. Preferably military ships. This is a rather urgent need."

Zhang was used to Ma's brusque manner, but even so was taken aback by the intensity of his demeanor and by the unusual specificity of this request. Zhang's primary duties to date had been countering anti-regime critics among the Chinese diaspora, but he was also charged with nurturing scientific or technical talent, people who could help transfer industrial knowledge back to China. Industrial espionage was an ongoing priority. Even so, this nautical engineering request would likely demand time-consuming research, not something he could quickly provide.

"W,w,w,well, Mister Ma," he stuttered, "I will immediately see who we have under observation who might be good for this purpose. It is a unique expertise you are asking for."

Ma had decided to use a psychological gambit that had worked for him before. Knowing well the fear he inspired in subordinates, he would use that fear to ignite a cognitive firestorm. Ma said, "True, a very special expertise. But I want you to join me in a little exercise Mister Zhang, just to humor me."

"An exercise?"

"Yes, a quiz of sorts," Ma said, with no humor at all in his voice. "I know you have dozens of scholars and professionals on your list of potential recruits. From them I want you to give me a name this minute. Do not think too hard about it, whichever name with a nautical expertise first proposes itself to you. Let your unconscious speak."

Zhang panicked. This was craziness. A white fog seemed to suddenly envelop his eyes. It was as if his brain neurons short-circuited. If asked, he would be lucky to be able to give his own name. Zhang twisted in his seat. The room dissolved into a blur of moving shadows and hazy light as his vision narrowed. He tried to focus on the request. *Where would a name...who could possibly...* Then as if from a celestial gift, he saw the graphic characters of a name flash in his mind and blurted the words aloud.

"Chen Lin," he said. Ma stared at him unblinking, then slowly asked, "Who is Chen Lin?" Gathering himself Zhang said, "A student at Columbia University who has led anti-Xi, pro-Taiwan protests and was involved in other anti-regime demonstrations."

"What is your interest in him."

"His parents live in Guangzhou. I am sure by enlisting their help I could convince him to give up his traitorous activities."

"Yes," said Ma with a thin smile. "With his family in China I am sure you can convince him. But what else about him made his name come to mind?"

"I, I don't... Yes, I do know. He is a graduate student at Columbia. He already has a degree in Naval Architecture from the Stevens Institute." Zhang looked up smiling, suffused with relief at his recollection. "That must be why I thought of him."

"Stevens what?"

"The Stevens Institute of Technology. It is an engineering school in New Jersey. He is now pursuing graduate studies at Columbia."

"He is a naval architect you say?"

"Yes."

"What sort of ships?"

"I really don't know," Zhang said, still stunned that a name that made some sense popped into his mind and out of his mouth.

"Put together a dossier on him as soon as you can. Call him in immediately. Understood?"

"Certainly."

"An excellent start, now please take your time and look carefully among your biographies to see if there are others you can recommend. In case Mister Chen does not serve."

"Certainly, Mister Ma."

"Good work, Mister Zhang."

"Xiexie, xiexie," thanked Zhang with repeated nods of his head.

Ma, smugly satisfied that his little psychological pressure game worked, finished his beer and once again exhorting Zhang to swiftly come up with more candidates, called his driver to bring the car around to the front of the restaurant. He and Zhang exchanged formal bows of goodbye, then he left; and left a still nervous but mostly relieved Zhang to relax with another beer.

It was good that Zhang was able to enjoy those few moments of apparent triumph, because after he paid the bill and walked the few bustling blocks to Doyer Street he was greeted with a confounding sight. A crowd had gathered in front of the building housing his office; a portable podium placed on the sidewalk was festooned with microphones behind which uniformed police officers were standing, flanked by men in plain clothes. One of the officers was speaking to a gaggle of reporters and cameramen assembled in front of the podium. They had just begun shouting questions to the man at the microphone.

Zhang slid to the back of the crowd pretending to be just another local onlooker curious to hear what was said. From the questions it didn't take long to ascertain that his office, and he himself, were the focus of the gathering. The third-floor office had been raided, his records confiscated, and according to the officer speaking, a manhunt was underway for the men who worked there. Apparently, the office had been under observation for some time. The authorities knew all about its clandestine activities, and that the Chinese government was behind them all.

Alarmed and thoroughly disoriented Zhang turned away and keeping his head bowed, walked slowly in the direction of Canal Street where he disappeared into the crowd of shoppers. He dared not go to his apartment on Mott Street. He made his way west to the subway station on Lafayette Street where he boarded a crowded car and took the Number 6 train north. At Grand Central Station he exited onto 42nd Street and walked briskly, head bowed down toward the East River and the U.N. building. He needed to get out of sight quickly, and in his current frazzled state of mind he believed it was the only place he could find even a temporary haven. He sat on a bench in a small park on First Avenue across from the U.N. and called Ma on his encrypted office phone.

"Yes, Mister Zhang how can I help you," said an annoyed voice, obviously unhappy to be getting this call, at this time, and from this person.

For once Ma's disapproval had no terrifying impact on his subordinate. Zhang was too distressed to be concerned by Ma's imperiousness. He spoke in staccato, "The police have raided my office. It is closed. All equipment and documents confiscated. The press was there. A mob of them. On the street when I returned after lunch. Cameras and everything. I guess it will be on the news tonight."

"Where are you?" Ma said, himself now rattled.

"I managed to get away without being seen. I am in the park across the street on First Avenue."

"Are you sure you were not followed?"

"Yes, absolutely. And the park is deserted. I am alone ... I think."

"Get into a taxi as soon as you can and go to the Mission. I will call ahead and get you a room. Go right now!" Ma hung up without waiting for a reply.

Zhang had forgotten all about the Mission; it was as if his mind were a jigsaw puzzle and its disarranged pieces were only gradually coming back together. The Chinese Mission had its residences in a building it owned ten blocks south of the U.N. on East 35th Street. By the time Zhang caught a cab and made his way there, Ma had done as promised, a room was waiting for him; a room that, of necessity, would become his home and office for the foreseeable future.

As Chinese property the Mission building was a safe haven, enjoying all the privileges and immunities of a foreign embassy. Zhang was on the run, but untouchable. In this building he was secure from arrest and could disappear from the American authorities while still mostly free to work. That is, free to do what Ma had ordered him to do: pursue Chen Lin, a Columbia University graduate student.

Chen Lin, innocently immersed in a materials science doctoral program, would soon be visited on campus by a couple of Chinese government officials practiced at subtly twisting arms.

CHAPTER 4
UNWELCOME VISITORS

Zhang Wei wasted no time. That very afternoon, with authority from Ma, he commandeered an office complete with computers and secure phones, and demanded two State Security operatives based in the Mission report to him.

It was still daylight when the two men were dispatched to pay a visit to a Columbia University graduate student. They were given no details other than to inform the student he was invited to a meeting at the Chinese Mission to the United Nations where he would be informed of some news about his parents in China.

Chen Lin, a slight man in his early thirties was a bookish student, serious and single minded in his pursuit of a career as a naval architect. He hoped a further degree in materials science would open doors to a promising future in the evolving field of alternative ship construction techniques. Chen was holed up in his dorm room studying when interrupted. To date he'd never had any occasion for contact with the Chinese Mission, or Embassy, and so he was immediately alarmed when he received notice that two men from the Mission were asking to see him. Because of his public participation in various anti-regime demonstrations, he surmised this visit was going to be unpleasant. He was not disappointed.

Chen encountered the two emissaries in the featureless lobby of his apartment building. The student and his two visitors found seats in a corner of the institutional looking lobby. With its bare white walls, fluorescent lighting and faux redwood doorman's desk it had the aura of a budget nursing home, or low-end office suite. His guests, dressed in inexpensive looking blue suits, sat stiff and erect, perched at the forward edge of a small couch's plastic covered cushions. He, tense and suspicious, sat in a wing chair facing them across a glass coffee table. Despite the ominous undercurrent their manner was not overtly threatening; there was no obvious sign of the clenched fist hidden in the innocuous cloak of words in which it was wrapped. But Chen knew better.

"Mister Chen, thank you for agreeing to see us without any previous introduction or communication," said one of the men with stilted formality. "We are here to invite you to meet with Mister Zhang Wei at the Chinese Mission regarding some news about your family."

Alarmed, Chen Lin asked if any of his loved ones were ill or had been injured. "Unfortunately, we are not informed of the reasons they might have come to the attention of the State," said the man with a small solicitous frown. "But," his face brightened, "we have been instructed to tell you they are all fine physically." His mouth cracked into a brief mechanical smile which disappeared as rapidly as it had formed. It was like a lightning flash across his countenance which conveyed nothing to Chen but icy indifference. "It must be some administrative issue, as is usually the case," the emissary added, waving a limp hand dismissively.

"When must I report?" Chen asked with a catch in his voice.

"Tomorrow morning will be fine. It is not especially urgent. You need not worry." He lied, knowing full well Chen would be frightened enough to want to find out what was going on as soon as possible.

Chen was given contact details and instructed to meet Zhang Wei at the Mission's residence, rather than at the U.N., at nine a.m.

The meeting would be as disastrous as Chen had feared. Sitting bleakly on the subway as he made his way downtown his face was drawn, his eyes blank, unfocused, his thoughts turned inward. Now, facing the consequences of his rebellious student activism, he bitterly regretted his idealism; he was a fool to risk his and his family's future for some democratic dream. The entrenched Chinese autocracy would not be shaken by some placard carrying students half a world away. In the subway car around him other passengers were going about their everyday business, most pecking away at their cellphones or listening on earbuds oblivious to the agony he was enduring. He envied them, resented them, and wallowed in his misery.

It was 8:45 when he walked into the Mission building, his mouth dry, his hands moist with nervousness. He had told no one, not his friends, nor his girlfriend, nor did he message his parents about the meeting he faced. He was astute enough to know his fate had probably been sealed already. He had spoken out forcefully against the Xi regime, gambling that he would be anonymous and unimportant enough to escape revenge. He had lost that gamble. Even before confronted with the government's accusations, he had been humbled, surrendered his spirit and was mentally defeated. He glumly concluded he would protect his family;

it was their lives he had risked; he would do whatever the regime wanted.

"Mister Chen Lin please be seated," Zhang began with a neutral bureaucratic tone, "do you know why you have been summoned?"

"Something about the condition of my family."

"Well, yes and no. Your family is fine: mother, father, all together in Guangzhou," Zhang said. A not subtle way of letting Chen know they were in the crosshairs. "The real reason you have been asked to come is because of your non-scholastic university activities."

"Meaning?"

"Come now Mister Chen," Zhang said with a glare, "you know what I mean. For the future benefit of you and your family we expect you will cease all further contact with the anti-China hooligans at Columbia. Their activities are a criminal assault on the welfare of the People's Republic and could be cause for reprisal."

Chen had to admire how swiftly any pretense of cordiality had been dropped, the knife blade drawn and pointed. Resistance was futile. He dropped his head and said softly, "I understand fully and will quit all protests."

"Good," Zhang said, "that is a good beginning."

Chen raised his head, "Beginning?"

"Yes. It is good that you will commit no future crimes, but it remains for you to expiate for the damage you have already caused."

"Expiate?" Chen said confused. "What does that mean?"

"It means you must perform some service for your country to erase the traitorous label which stains your family."

Traitorous! He is threatening my parents and me with prison, thought Chen. His previously obsequious surrender to Zhang began a rapid morph into anger.

"What sort of service are you talking about?"

"That is something we will work out together," Zhang said with a conspiratorial smile.

"Tell me Mister Chen, how are your studies progressing? Are you still studying for your doctorate in materials science?"

These bastards already know everything about me and my family, thought Chen. "Yes," he snapped.

"Very good. And you anticipate a career designing a new generation of naval vessels? Is that right?"

"Not necessarily military ships. I'm not certain where I might end up working."

"But of course, you will return with your new skills to China, and your family?"

Chen knew there was only one possible answer to that question. "Yes, of course," he lied.

"And your course of study, it ends soon, is that right?"

"A year from now, next June."

"How are you spending your summer? Visiting your family in China perhaps?"

"No," Chen said trying to disguise his anger and frustration. "It is expected that I will serve an internship at an American shipyard."

"Have you chosen or been admitted to one yet?"

"I've submitted a number of applications. Nothing certain."

Zhang then instructed Chen to submit the locations of his potential internships to him, "For support and guidance."

Chen, without a choice, reluctantly agreed.

"Excellent."

Finally, Zhang the insecure, timid government functionary could relax. He knew he had just the person Ma Bai needed, and that Chen Lin would do whatever he was asked to do. Feeling self-satisfied Zhang then abruptly dismissed Chen.

"That is all for now. I think you understand there will be no more student foolishness. I will be in touch soon with what additional support will be required of you. Thank you for agreeing to visit." Zhang stood and without shaking hands gestured to the door. "Goodbye."

As soon as he was alone Zhang called his boss and proudly filled him in with Chen's nautical qualifications, and on his successful recruitment. "Excellent work Mister Zhang," said Ma Bai who felt he had to constantly stroke Zhang to bolster his self-confidence. "I suggest you encourage the young man to accept a position appropriate for our needs."

"Yes sir!" Said Zhang, with a complacent smile. Not even a full day had passed since he received this difficult assignment, and he had already successfully found and recruited an agent. All that remained was to mobilize him.

Zhang then went back to making himself at home in his new room at the Chinese Mission, oblivious to the fact he had just created in Chen Lin an implacable enemy.

The student who had been a fearful, quivering jumble of nerves on the trip to the meeting, was now furious and bent on vengeance. There were only two things he would demand of himself, first to get his family out of China, and second to punish the Xi regime in the most damaging way possible.

CHAPTER 5
June
THE YOUNG REBELS

The reporter Roger Barnes finally had a story which he could make his own, and rather than bigfoot him the news desk was going to give him the time to develop it. Immediately after his Chinatown Precinct report aired, he began to research the Chinese government's spying initiatives. With his girlfriend Li Hana's help, Roger started by identifying and listing the groups which had been targeted by the Xi regime, many of which were student organizations. Over lunch at a restaurant on Mott Street Hana translated some of the reporting which had largely been done by New York's Chinese language newspapers.

"I'm amazed we haven't heard about any of this until now," he said to Hana. "The Chinatown papers have been all over this precinct story for months."

"I guess the NYPD needs more Chinese speakers in the ranks. I told you, the only coverage we get is during Chinese New Year."

"Well to be honest, we've been a little gun shy of pointing out Chinese problems ever since the Covid Pandemic was blamed on China," responded Roger. "Having the White House label it 'China's Flu' encouraged this country's xenophobes. Too many innocent people were being physically attacked and threatened by would-be patriots."

"The U.S. *has* gone a little paranoid," Hana said with a shrug, "but in this case it's not American nut jobs, but the Chinese government which is threatening innocent Asians."

Roger collected his notes, sweeping them up from the tabletop. "Something tells me this FBI bust is just the tip of the iceberg," he said as they finished their tea. The two walked out onto the crowded street, and as a stream of people washed past, they pecked a kiss goodbye. Hana turned East and returned to the United Nations, he went in the opposite direction and caught a subway back to the station. Once there he reported to the assignment desk.

"Noah, I've got some good leads on this Chinese spy story. No need for a crew yet, but I'm going up to Columbia University to talk to some student activists."

"Alright, but let me know what you get," said Noah. "The boss wants something to air soon, if not he'll bug me to put you back on the street."

"What, to do another bagel eating contest?"

Noah threw up his pudgy arms in mock surrender, "Hey, if the boss says it's news, it's news."

From the office Roger walked to Columbus Circle and took the West Side Number 1 subway to 116th Street. Exiting the underground, he strolled Broadway and entered the Columbia campus through the large iron gates which face the wide avenue. He purposefully hadn't notified anyone in the school's public information office since he wanted to remain anonymous, at least for now. He was young enough to pass for a student and thought he'd get a better sense of campus activity if he just nosed around on his own.

In front of the classic dome of the Low Library he stopped at the Sundial, a meeting point where students posted flyers touting upcoming activities. Among the tattered remnants of past events, he saw one calling for a demonstration by a group calling itself The Chinese People's Freedom Front, the CPFF. He jotted down the contact information, walked over to the library steps and sat down to make a call.

"Hi is this Fu Muchen?" he said brightly, trying to sound youthful and non-threatening. A male voice gave a cautious reply in the affirmative. "Good, my name is Roger Barnes a reporter for WNOW News, I got your name from a flyer on campus, and I'd like to speak with you about the CPFF." The caution in the listener's voice disappeared. Roger got an immediate and enthusiastic response, and within an hour was seated in the West End Bar on Broadway, a favorite of Columbia students, meeting his first informant.

The two young men sat in a booth along the north wall of the bar and ordered a couple of pints. Fu Muchen was slightly taller than Roger, slim with straight black hair which hung uncontrolled over his forehead, and which he had constantly to flick away from his eyes. Those black eyes looked intently at Roger and together with his compressed lips signaled a no-nonsense directness. Despite Muchen's eagerness to talk he was irritated, annoyed that it had taken so long for a member of the white media to finally come talk to him. "To what do we owe this belated interest in the Chinese People's Freedom Front," he asked.

Roger had decided to avoid saying anything about the raid on the Precinct in Chinatown, opting to see if Muchen would bring it up, and then gauge his reaction. But Fu Muchen quickly settled the issue. "I guess you want to talk to me because of that police raid down on Doyer Street."

"Well, yes at least for starters," Roger said with a smile, amused at his own naïveté. "I'm here because I have seen news stories about how your group has had some dealings with that peculiar office."

"Peculiar is right. Peculiar but not funny. Deadly serious is more like it."

"How so?"

"Threats, intimidation, demands made with lots of not-so-subtle muscle being flexed. The Mafia has nothing on China when it comes to making offers you can't refuse."

"Can you be specific? I mean what offers, the who, the what and the why?"

"Sure. Why the hell do you think we have been holding these demonstrations and protests. Our only protection is to go public but so far, we've gotten zero support from guys like you.

"Well, help me change that."

The student disregarded the invitation, still intent on scolding the reporter for what he felt was the news media's incompetence. "You say you've read about our protests. Where? Certainly not in the New York Times. The only time you guys show up is if we are dancing with dragons or some shit."

Roger laughed, "You sound like my girlfriend. She's the one who read me the coverage in the Chinatown newspapers."

"She's Chinese?"
"Taiwanese."
"That counts."

Roger told Muchen about Hana, about her feelings toward the Xi regime, and how she had been helping him understand the pressures put on Chinese Americans. That broke the ice, and Muchen began a detailed tutorial on the widespread intimidation and espionage activities of the PRC.

Muchen went on to describe a classic protection racket: Do what we want, say the government agents, or we will hurt you, or those you love. And no one doubted they meant what they threatened. A surveillance state as efficient as China knew who, and what mattered most to these students. What screws to turn, what buttons to press. And what the regime wanted was nothing so trivial as money. Of course, the agents demanded all public criticism of the Chinese regime must cease, but beyond that they wanted nothing less than these young well-placed professionals create a corps of operatives which would infiltrate American industry, then steal and pass along proprietary information. They were to be agents of industrial and military espionage.

"First," Muchen told Roger, "You've got to understand we, the students, are only a small part of what interests the Chinese government. Sure, they want to mute our voices, shut down our public criticisms of the totalitarian state, but their goals are much more ambitious."

"Such as?"

"They want to steal as much intellectual property as they can: business, government, military anything that could be useful. The Chinese government even has a formal name for this thievery. They call it 'The Thousand Talents Program.' That's really what China cares about. Our protests are an annoyance, but we are small potatoes."

"You may be small potatoes but you're all I've got right now."

"True enough. We students are basically insignificant, but we can point you in the right direction."

Muchen slid sideways in the booth, his back rested against the wall, his legs lifted prone on the bench as if taking possession of the space. His posture was a way of asserting physical command. He was determined to use Roger, and he knew exactly how to use exclusive access to bait a reporter.

"I can give you access to the people you will need to tell this story, but to do it right you will need more than two minutes on the nightly news. It deserves an hour documentary."

Roger bristled at the young man's arrogance. "Why don't you tell me what you have in mind and let me figure out how it could be presented."

Far from being chastened Muchen said, "It's just, Roger, that this story is bigger than you imagine. It can make your entire career."

That was a bait too delicious for Roger to ignore. He had to bite, but did so resentfully.

"Big words Muchen, but you're beginning to sound like an overhyped press release. What specifically do you have in mind?"

"I can introduce you to men and women who have been propositioned, threatened, and asked to turn over sensitive information to Chinese agents. Others who have courageously refused and paid the price. Or have seen their families pay a price.

"And they will talk on camera?"

"That depends on you and your powers of persuasion. Not me."

Muchen agreed to assemble some members of the Chinese Peoples Freedom Front who would be willing to be interviewed either on background or, if Roger could convince them, on camera.

They finished their beers and the two went their separate ways, Muchen back to campus and Roger back to base.

Before he scheduled interviews with any of Muchen's people, Roger wanted to set up some face-to-face meetings with a triumvirate of U.S. law enforcement: first with the Feds, specifically the FBI, then the head of the NYPD's head of counter terrorism, and finally the U.S. Attorney for the Southern District of New York, whose Criminal Division's National Security Unit would be the lead prosecutors on such cases. Since the U.S. Attorney of the Southern District is a major political player, he is someone who will always talk to the press. On camera.

Just as Muchen had bitched journalists had failed to pursue this story, now Roger thought, it was his turn to hold law enforcement's feet to the fire.

CHAPTER 6
June
THE COUNTERSPIES

The day after his meeting with Muchen, Roger went down to Manhattan's Federal Plaza where he had arranged an interview, on background only, with William Roscoe, Chief of the FBI's New York Bureau. After initial pleasantries, Roger got to the point.

"Chief, I've just had my ass reamed by a student at Columbia for not covering their protests over the heavy-handed actions of the Chinese government. I'm guilty I guess, but you guys have apparently known all about China's machinations for some time. What can you share with me that didn't come out at that press conference in Chinatown."

"Yeah," Roscoe said cautiously, "This intimidation has been ongoing for some time and pretty much under the radar. I've already laid out to you much of what we are prepared to talk about at this time. To reiterate, there is a sophisticated and wide-ranging espionage and intimidation effort going on in many sectors and we are actively investigating."

Roger had expected to be fed this kind of ambiguous verbiage. Now that he had graciously swallowed the pablum, he wanted some meat.

"Well, why don't we start with some names. You wouldn't give us any yesterday, who are the suspected perps?"

"Like I said at the press conference, we are keeping most details close to the vest. We'd like to apprehend the guys before giving anything away."

Makes no sense, thought Roger, we could help flush them out, but it's no use pressing him on something he's not going to give. "Do you feel confident these people, whoever they are, are still around. That you can nail them."

"Oh, absolutely. They won't get far." Roscoe gave a condescending smirk and wouldn't elaborate.

"What about victims," Roger asked. "All these people you say are being leaned on? Who are they, I'd like to talk to them."

"Look Roger, this is an ongoing investigation. What I don't want is you TV guys screwing it up. When we have something definitive to say, we'll say it. I don't want to say anything, or identify anyone, prematurely."

Roger was getting dizzy, walked like a circus pony around a ring to nowhere. It was obvious this was a wasted trip; he wasn't going to get anything on the spy ring or any leads to its victims. After a few more "no comments," he thanked the Bureau chief and left.

Next stop, the NYPD. Roger walked the two blocks to One Police Plaza and then rode back up to the sixth floor. The Commissioner was unavailable, but the head of the counter terrorism force agreed to meet. Other than the Feds, New York's anti-terror cops were considered the best in the country. Joseph Mitchell ran the department. He was formerly a reporter, sympathetic to their needs and could usually be counted on to give straight dope and speak on the record. But he also threatened to be another dead end.

"Sorry Roger, I'd like to help but the FBI is handling the investigation. We're just doing some housekeeping. Shutting down the so-called Police Precinct, looking into who rented the office, that sort of thing."

"You mean you've got that? The name of the renter?"

"Sure, it's public information. Some guy," he rummaged through papers on his desk, "some Chinese guy named Zhang Wei."

Roger's face revealed nothing, but his heart started racing, "How do you spell that?" he said scribbling.

Mitchell then told him, "This Zhang guy lived in an apartment on Mott Street. No answer there, so we're getting a warrant tomorrow to bust in and check it out. We're also looking into how he paid his rent. Following the money."

Finally, a crack in the investigative stonewalling. "Cool, might lead somewhere," Roger mumbled in a whopper of understatement.

"But I wouldn't bet on finding him," Mitchell added with a laugh. "He's probably already on a slow boat to China."

"Or a fast jet. Or maybe he's been plucked up into one of their spy balloons and is floating somewhere over the Atlantic," Roger joked.

But it was Roger who felt like he was floating on air. He had enough to do a short piece for tomorrow's news. The identity of one of the Chinese working in the infamous Police Precinct. That would be good enough to satisfy his boss, infuriate the FBI, and make Gabe Breslin green with jealousy. A Trifecta!

But first he needed to lock in the Prima Donna, Richard Giordano the U.S. Attorney for the Southern District. He would get him on camera to say just about anything at all. Just having his face in the story would add weight to the report. There was no doubt about his appearing on camera, as the joke went: 'The most dangerous place to stand in New York was between a TV camera and the U.S. Attorney.'

Roger phoned the assignment desk. "Noah, I need a crew down at St. Andrew's Plaza this afternoon, got anyone free?"

"Don't tell me you got that schmuck Giordano lined up?"

"Yeah, he's quote, 'squeezing me in' for a couple of minutes," Roger joked. "Like there's ever anything more important to him."

"When he finally becomes Mayor, he'll hire you to be his PR guru. What you got?" Noah continued, "I hope it's something good because the boss is getting antsy about you. He has a Kindergarten parade in the Bronx for you to cover if you're not doing anything."

"Tell him I'm going to have a spot for tomorrow's six on the hunt for one of those Chinese spies. I got a name, and a location."

"Sounds good. Why you talking to Giordano? There's no prosecution yet."

"Why do you think?"

"Because he'll talk on camera?"

"Exactly!"

"Schmuck!"

Roger's crew set up their camera and lights in a conference room adjacent to Giordano's office. Through the wall they could hear him berating one of his attorneys for trying to take all the credit for a recent high-profile arraignment. "Don't forget who the star of the show is here," he was shouting. The camera operator, a slight young woman with a ponytail of long blond hair rolled her eyes and made a 'he's crazy' gesture, twirling a finger near her temples.

When Giordano strode in, he went directly to the head of a long mahogany table and sat where a microphone had been placed. He smiled.

"How you doing kid? What's your name, haven't seen you here before, where's Gabe?"

"Uhm, I'm Roger Barnes. Gabe Breslin is out of town."

"You want to talk about that Chinese Precinct scam, right."

"Right."

"Well, you know the investigation is still ongoing. We don't get to put our two cents in until we have some evidence for the grand jury."

"Right, but I want to get some general reaction from you about what sorts of laws would apply to something like this. You know alleged intimidation and personal threats."

"Yes, also likely spying and even sabotage," Giordano offered.

"Exactly," said Roger and told the camera woman to start rolling.

Giordano waxed enthusiastically about how his office would approach such a case if it were presented to him. And just as Roger hoped, he indicated he would likely bring RICO charges against whomever was accused. Racketeer Influenced Corrupt Organization charges were a favorite form of prosecution for Giordano. He made his reputation charging Mafia members with the statute, and he subsequently found he could indict almost any group of ner'-do-wells with it.

"The way I see it, if the people behind this so-called Police Precinct were working in cahoots to intimidate people it would be a criminal conspiracy and chargeable under RICO."

Bingo! Roger had his sound bite. All else was just blather. Now to write the next installment in this story.

CHAPTER 7
June
WNOW MAKES NEWS

Roger had a good story, but not good enough to lead the newscast. *Lousy luck.* The top spot went to a report about a local U.S. Senator accused of accepting kickbacks. Roger was frustrated when he was bumped from the lead for what he considered just another case of political malfeasance. *What's new about that?* But he did make it into the first section of the newscast and that was good enough. Anything before the first commercial break was prime.

From the anchor desk Gloria Herrera introduced him as having 'Breaking News,' and an 'Exclusive' report on the investigation into China's den of spies in New York. A little hyperbole couldn't hurt.

"Roger Barnes is live now in a secret spy nest, the actual apartment belonging to one of the alleged suspects. Roger..."

"Gloria, WNOW has learned exclusively that this apartment on Mott Street was home to one of the suspects, now a fugitive, in that infamous ring of undercover spies working out of what was called a Chinese Police Precinct ..."

Using file footage from his original story Roger recapped the Doyers Street raid and went on to describe once again what was known of the espionage operation. He then named: "The alleged ringleader, Zhang Wei, who lived in this very apartment." He went on to describe how the NYPD's anti-terrorism unit got a warrant for access to the man's home and found a picture of the suspect there.

"This is it, a photograph of a smiling man who looks to be in his forties, posing with wife and son in an Asian park, complete with pagodas."

Back on camera Roger said, "The U.S. Attorney, Richard Giordano told me what sort of crimes Mister Zhang Wei could be charged with, if and when apprehended." That was followed by Giordano's RICO soundbite.

"Investigators also told me they are following the money, specifically Mister Zhang's rent money, to see who else might be involved in this alleged conspiracy of intimidation and espionage." Roger then signed off saying he would, of course, keep on the story and report any developments; making it very clear to the boss he had no intention of being bigfooted off this gravy train. It was a story which promised to keep giving for some time to come.

Reactions to the report came fast, and often furious. The FBI's Roscoe was livid, "What the fuck was the NYPD doing giving out the name, location, and picture of a prime suspect?" Someone they hoped might lead them to others.

Mitchell of the NYPD was getting blasted by his own brass for blabbing to a reporter about the still developing investigation. Gabe Breslin also let Mitchell know he was pissed for not being notified of the upcoming warrant. *What was Mitchell doing feeding tips to this new kid instead of him?*

And although Roger didn't know it, across town at the United Nations someone else was seething mad. Ma Bai saw the news report and slammed his fist on the desk, for a moment losing his usually unflappable demeanor. But he quickly composed himself. *That fool Zhang was stupid enough to rent an apartment under his own name!* Once again, all Ma's concerns over Zhang's competence resurfaced, *How dumb can you get?* Happily, none of Zhang's income could be traced back to the UN Mission. He was paid directly by the Ministry of State Security through a shell company innocuously called the Organization of Brotherly Comfort. Thankfully, Zhang was now safely hidden away in the Mission building on 35th Street. Trapped in the building was more like it. Now that a photograph of Zhang's face has been made public, he was more a prisoner than an effective agent.

The sudden glare of publicity meant Ma had to work fast, and ruthlessly, to contain the damage and keep his various operations safe. Particularly, the one in which Zhang was most directly involved, spying on the new Columbia class submarines. First, one way or another Mister Zhang must disappear. That was a relatively simple problem to solve. Second, he had to prevent the ongoing investigations by both law enforcement and journalists from penetrating his network. That would be more difficult and might require some more extreme, measures. Well, one step at a time.

Not all reaction to Roger's story was negative. His boss, Executive Producer Jim Butler was delighted. He liked the new kid and didn't mind at all if there was a certain amount of rivalry and competition for Gabe Breslin. It would ease the pay pressure from his star when contract time rolled around. Especially true if Roger's story came with some legitimate "Exclusives." Lord knows, they had been touting as exclusive some stories that he knew were anything but. He was sometimes derided as an ossified old timer always complaining that: "Hype is taking over this goddam business."

Also cheering Roger was a certain young woman who watched his report from an office at the United Nations, just floors away from Ma Bai.

"Very nice going Mister Barnes," Li Hana cooed into the phone. "You think this story is going to get you an Emmy?"

"First, I hope it keeps me employed," he laughed, "and away from back-of-the-book features. The Emmy can wait … but not too long."

"You doing a recut for the Eleven O'Clock news?"

"Yes, but the producer wants me to wrap it live on set, so I've got to be here."

"Why don't you come to my office for dinner?" Hana said. "We can order from the cafeteria, and you can return to the studio after we eat."

"Sure, see you in a bit."

Another person delighted to see that the Precinct story had not faded away was Fu Muchen. He called a fellow student, and member of the CPFF, Wu Yao. "You see that story on WNOW News about the Police Precinct guy?"

"Yes. Is that the same reporter you spoke with the other day?"

"The very same. I guess he is serious about following this story. He seems legit, I want to gather a few people who will agree to speak to him. You okay with that?"

With her approval Muchen made a few other calls and then texted Roger. "Saw your story today. Not bad. Call me to schedule a meeting."

Muchen was in his room, a small spartan space with a single bed, chest of drawers, and a battered desk by the window. The dormitory building was located off campus, one of the many buildings Columbia owned in the neighborhood. While bare bones, the room did have a decent view. Without craning your neck too far, Riverside Park and even a sliver of the Hudson River could be seen. The sun was just setting beyond the river when Muchen's phone rang.

"How you doing Fu Manchu?" Roger quipped.

"You think that's funny?" Muchen shot back, annoyed at the silly, purposeful mispronunciation he had had to endure repeatedly in New York. Roger blanched; he'd taken a liberty he was not yet permitted. Their partnership, such as it was, could be derailed right then and there.

"Oh man, stupid of me. I apologize for being such a dunce," he said backpedaling fast.

"Yeah, for a man with a Chinese girlfriend you really are brain dead."

"Sorry, sorry, sorry. Call me Roger Rabbit and we're even."

"A rabbit has more between his ears than you."

Muchen laughed and Roger breathed a sigh of relief. To keep the defused momentum going he quickly said, "I'm available to meet with your friends any time you say. Just name it."

"I'd feel better if the reporter finally taking us seriously had better sense; but since you're all I've got, you'll have to do."

"Ouch, I deserved that. Give me the where and when and I'll be there."

Muchen said his place was too small in which to shoot video, but one of his friends lived with her boyfriend in an apartment with a fair-sized living room on Broadway. She was a student in the Journalism school. Her boyfriend was also a student, and both were anti-regime activists.

Roger was aware that at work he was riding a wave of goodwill after his exclusive naming of Zhang Wei, but he also knew he needed to keep delivering or Butler was sure to add Breslin to the story. Maybe Butler wouldn't cut him out completely, but Roger had no interest in sharing the glory. Profiling some victims of the Chinese Precinct's pressure was one way to keep momentum, and keep the assignment all to himself. Roger desperately needed the meeting Muchen was setting up, and he needed it on camera. Background-only interviews would just not do.

He laid it out plainly to Muchen, "Let everyone who's coming know I'll have a camera with me. This has to be on the record. There's no other way to tell this story."

"Understood. And that's what we want too. However, some of my people might want their faces obscured, or voices distorted."

"No problem, we can shoot them in silhouette, only their hands or feet, whatever. I'll protect their identities."

They agreed to meet the next evening in the apartment of Wu Yao and her boyfriend, a young naval engineering student named Chen Lin.

Roger's earlier televised report from Zhang Wei's apartment made some interested viewers like Ma Bai angry, some like Fu Muchen happy, and at least two others simply terrified. The one most directly involved, and most fearful, was Zhang. His name and face were now publicly exposed; as an undercover operative he'd become useless. Not only useless, but his very existence had become a liability which could be an embarrassment for China, and therefore a potential death sentence for him.

Zhang spent most of his career putting the screws to powerless people, but the screw had turned. Now he was the one pinned, squirming and fearful for his life. All it would take is one word from Ma and he, and the problem he presented would disappear. Zhang Wei needed to find some way to make himself irreplaceable, and he had to find it quickly.

The other person suddenly put in a precarious position was Chen Lin. He not only knew who Zhang was by name, but he had seen him in person and knew precisely where the U.S. authorities could find him. This knowledge meant Chen was no longer just an annoying student, someone who could be turned and used, he was now a threat to Zhang and all those for whom Zhang worked. It didn't take great perspicacity for Chen to see that though he was a threat to those people, he was a threat that could easily be neutralized. With terrifying immediacy, he understood that he and everyone he loved was now in mortal danger.

As strange as it seemed these polar opposites, Chen and Zhang, the manipulated and the manipulator, were now both dependent on each other; their lives and the fortunes of their families hung on the success of whatever project Ma demanded they undertake. It was an assignment by which both might be saved, and in which both would be trapped. They were like two scorpions in a bottle, facing each other with deadly stingers poised to strike. A very personal version of Mutually Assured Destruction.

CHAPTER 8
WHERE IS CHEN LIN?

It took all the next day for Muchen to assemble his friends and convince them to tell their stories on camera. He managed to corral five, including Wu Yao in whose apartment they were meeting. Unfortunately, her boyfriend had begged off saying he had an important meeting with one of his Columbia professors.

Yao's home was decidedly more comfy than Muchen's spartan space. She had it almost completely furnished with a cozy bedroom, a fully equipped kitchen, and a living room with couch and easy chairs around a low coffee table. Framed family photos were on a desk along one wall and heavy curtains hung on the two windows overlooking Broadway. They helped mute the lights and noise of the busy avenue. Unlike barebones student housing it was as if Yao were already preparing a marriage nest for herself and Chen Lin.

Muchen was already there when one by one the other guests climbed the four dimly lit flights and drifted into Wu Yao's apartment. It was seven in the evening, a half hour before Roger had been told to arrive. Muchen wanted some time alone with his friends to encourage them, and ease some of their fears.

Yao agreed to have her face shown on camera, as did Muchen and one other. The others did not.

"I'm sorry Lin couldn't make it," said Muchen. "Who is he meeting?"

"I don't know but it probably has to do with his application to General Dynamics," said Yao. "He's really hoping for that internship. It's the top of his list."

"Still, this is really important, a big opportunity to get some publicity."

Yao just shrugged, "He knows, but getting that internship has him totally preoccupied."

The six students then discussed the points they wanted to make when the TV camera rolled. Each had an incident in which they were threatened or intimidated for their involvement with the Chinese People's Freedom Front. And a couple even had fake charges leveled against them by anonymous online actors. Muchen advised them to keep their answers to Roger's questions short and direct, and keep their energy up as they spoke. "I just don't want you to put anyone to sleep!" he joked.

Roger arrived with a camera operator, the same young woman who had worked with him in the U.S. Attorney's office. The duo was soon joined by Roger's girlfriend Li Hana.

Muchen greeted her with a jab at Roger, "What's a smart, attractive girl like you doing with this numbskull roundeye."

Enjoying his impudence Hana shot back, "I just can't seem to find any Asian men who know how to treat, or appreciate, a smart, attractive woman."

"Still, you could have chosen one who knows which end of a chopstick to pick up."

"True, but at least he doesn't ask me to walk five paces behind him."

"Now that's ..."

"OK, OK," Roger broke in, "enough. We've got work to do."

While the camerawoman arranged the seats, set up her tripod, and adjusted the lights Muchen took Roger and Hana aside.

"Before we start Roger, let me give you a little background on what you're getting yourself into. As you know the Ministry of State Security has very long tentacles, and its members are very good at hiding their muscle behind meaningless verbiage. Take for example, "The Thousand Talents Program." He went on to explain that the innocuous sounding initiative was in truth a program to entice college professors and other professionals to share their expertise, and their discoveries, with China.

"You name the discipline, and it is targeted: optics, chemistry, physics, biology, information technology, the whole gamut of academic and intellectual property. Professors are constantly being solicited with both bribes, and threats."

"And the Chinese police precincts that have been uncovered, I assume they're often used to facilitate this espionage?" Roger asked.

"Sure," said Muchen, "but get your terminology straight. In China these 'precincts' as you call them, are formally known as 'Chinese Overseas Police Service Stations.' Basically, they are just outposts of the MSS, the Ministry of State Security." With Muchen's help, Roger's understanding of the serpentine world of China's intellectual espionage was deepening.

Once they began videotaping, each of the students Roger interviewed described a different experience. One told how his protest activity resulted in thugs visiting his parents' home in China. "They were publicly humiliated in their village. Blamed for what the officials called my betrayal."

For Wu Yao the attack was personal. A fake email was sent to her department head at Columbia complaining that she was a prostitute. "The note said I saw men in my apartment and should be removed from the Journalism program." Worse, she said the email contained an attachment, a falsified photograph of Yao purporting to show her naked on a bed. The chairman of the department called her in and sadly agreed she was the victim of a vicious attack. "Probably because of my protest activities. I begged him not to go to the police because I was terrified those responsible would post the pictures on social media." Something which, happily, did not occur.

Another student, who refused to be seen on camera said, "Someone sent the head of my department a letter, in my name, saying that I wanted to withdraw from the program in which I am enrolled. It caused me much trouble to straighten out." These were all blatant, heavy-handed attempts to warn the students to stop their embarrassing protests, and keep their mouths shut.

Muchen said most of the students involved with his group had suffered some form of harassment, but interestingly, there had been no attempt to recruit any of them as spies. At least not yet. "They could always be approached later, when employed and with access to sensitive information."

Once Roger finished his interviews and sent the camerawoman back to the station, he, Hana, Muchen and Yao went to the West End Bar to discuss next steps.

The four of them settled into a booth. "Here's what I am going to propose to the News Director tomorrow," Roger said. "Rather than trying to get all these individual stories into one report, I want to do a series. Five nights, one student's story each weekday night."

"Do you think he will agree to that?" Hana asked. "That's quite a commitment."

"Not only do I think he'll go for it, but I'm also going to ask for an advertising push. Promos we can run during the day to sell the series."

To Roger's way of thinking, this would cement his hold on the story. No more worries over being partnered up, or replaced. *And*, he thought, pushing personal ambition momentarily aside, *the story truly warrants extended coverage.*

"You looking for a Pulitzer or something?" Muchen teased.

Roger gazed upward as if pondering the possibility, "An Emmy would do. For now." Then turning to Yao he asked, "I thought you had a roommate, and we were going to meet him tonight?"

"Yes, my boyfriend, actually. I did expect him to join us, but he had a last-minute meeting come up."

"Too bad. What's his name?"

"Chen Lin."

"Is he a member of the CPFF?"

"Oh yes," said Muchen interrupting, "one of the founders. I'm sure he'd love to speak with you."

"Send me his number, I'll give him a call tomorrow."

"Sure."

"Does he have family in China?" asked Hana, "I mean family he might worry about."

"Yes," replied Yao, "in Guangzhou. His parents. He is hoping to get them to emigrate to the U.S. someday."

"No siblings?" asked Roger.

"No, our parents were forbidden by the State to have more than one child. A prohibition that for economic reasons the government now regrets."

"Well, good luck to him in getting his parents out," said Hana. "Just as with the rest of you, I'm sure the government is happy to have them available as hostages if they'd ever want to put pressure on him for something."

Yao just looked at her sadly and shrugged, "Yeah, maybe Lin's parents will manage to get out in time for my wedding."

Hana jumped right in, "Oh, you're engaged? What's the date?"

Yao smiled, embarrassed, "No, I am getting a little ahead of myself. Nothing formal yet." She held up her left hand to show a bare ring finger. "We think next year, after we graduate."

The foursome then discussed Roger's idea of highlighting one student's story each night. They parsed what sort of intimidation each faced, and in what order their stories would be most effectively told. Roger wanted to illustrate the various ways the Chinese government pressured members of the academic and professional communities to show how pervasive and unrelenting were the coercion and the badgering. By spreading the reports over a number of days he could build momentum, create a cumulative effect that would drive the point home. Discussing the stories with the others, he'd already begun to mentally outline his series.

Roger finished his beer and touched his girlfriend's arm, "Let's go Hana, I want to begin planning this. Muchen, I'll call you tomorrow and let you know if my series idea flies with the powers that be." If his bosses bought the idea of a multipart report, he wanted to be able to begin airing it before the end of the month. With their go-ahead he would start writing tomorrow.

***

Chen Lin had been truthful when he said he was busy that evening. As he told Yao it did have to do with his internship; but his meeting was not with a professor nor Columbia's internship coordinator, it was with Zhang Wei at the Chinese Mission.

When the two men met the atmosphere was even more tense than at their first encounter. Now both had reason to be fearful. Zhang had the riot act read to him by Ma Bai, who told him he was to consider himself imprisoned in his apartment in the Mission building. He could not show his face on the street for fear the NYPD would arrest him. Ma promised he would have Zhang evacuated when the time came, *if I haven't killed him first.* He also demanded Zhang immediately activate this Chen person since his skills and potential were too valuable to risk losing. According to what they learned, Chen made several internship applications and was waiting to choose from his acceptances. But Ma was making the choice for him. He told Zhang the only potential internship he must accept if offered would be from the General Dynamics Electric Boat Division.

When Chen arrived for the meeting, it was a newly chastened and subdued Zhang Wei who said, "When do you expect to hear about your internship applications Mister Chen Lin?"

Chen was distraught, torn between fear and fury. "Any day now," he said. "The program requires I begin working no later than July." He mumbled the words almost to himself.

"You are not to accept any appointment until you have heard from General Dynamics. Do you understand?"

Chen nodded disconsolately.

"Do you understand?" Zhang said again, loudly. "Answer me!" He was under enormous pressure and the strain was making him lose control. Not one who enjoyed a surplus of self-confidence Zhang was now almost begging Chen to help him out of his dilemma. For his part Chen could see no way out, he either did what he was told, or risked the safety of his family. "Why are you so interested in that company? Why do you want me to go there? What do you want me to get from them?" His mind was reeling, he was blabbering.

"First get yourself hired. Then you will be told."

"What if I am not offered a place there? It is not guaranteed."

"Pray on the graves of your ancestors that you will be accepted. Nothing else will be tolerated." Zhang tried to sound stern and forbidding, but his voice cracked, and the word 'tolerated' came out as a squeak.

The meeting between the two harried men ended with almost as much uncertainty as it began. Zhang's position was hanging by a thread, and Chen was about to begin a duplicitous existence he was not prepared for. And that existence was complicated by the presence of a lover who knew nothing of the hazardous journey on which he was about to embark.

Chen boarded the subway uptown, the painful screech of the metal wheels seemed to pierce his brain, scrambling all thought. During that agonizing ride home, a clear conviction came out of the fog of his fear and confusion. It was a decision about Yao. She must never know what he would really be doing that summer. Instead of returning to her apartment he went directly to his dorm room, anxious to avoid contact with her or any of his friends.

Early the next morning Chen's phone buzzed him awake. Suspicious of the unknown number he let the call go to voicemail.

"Hello, Chen Lin this is Roger Barnes from WNOW News. I met with your friends Fu Muchen and Wu Yao and they gave me your number. I'd really like to speak with you about an upcoming report I'm working on." Roger left his number and requested Chen call him back as soon as he was free to do so. Chen groaned to himself *Oh no, this is the last thing I need. Why the hell did she sic him on me?* He knew what this had to be about, and just days ago would have been happy to be asked to speak to a reporter. Not anymore. He would ignore the invitation.

As soon as he dressed Chen called Yao, "Hi honey," he said in as bright a voice as he could manage. "I just got a call from that reporter Roger Barnes. You know anything about that?"

Yao explained about the meeting and the upcoming series of reports Roger was preparing. "I guess he is hoping to speak to you too," she said. "Oh, and how did your meeting go last night? Anything new?"

"Yes, meeting with my adviser went great, but I must tell you he told me to lay low until I get an internship offer from someone. He says to avoid anything controversial, especially concerning the Chinese government."

"Really, why?"

"He says all these companies do business with China, and they want to avoid anything, or anyone, that might create a problem for them with the PRC."

"So, you don't want to speak with the reporter? It's exactly the kind of publicity we have been working so hard to get."

"I know, I know. But the timing is all wrong for me. I'm going to keep a low profile until I lock something up for sure."

Yao was disappointed but bought the story he was spinning. "Okay honey, you do what you think is best."

Roger tried to reach Chen multiple times that weekend. Frustrated by not getting a response he called Yao to see if she knew where he was and why he was not answering his calls. She told him her boyfriend was in the middle of arranging for his internship and he was sorry but insisted this was not a time to get publicity which might hurt his chances. "Maybe he'll change his mind when he finally locks in a position," she said. Roger thought Chen's concern unwarranted but shrugged it off and went about preparing his series of special reports.

It turned out to be a TV news series which would create a furor, inflame an enemy, and put Roger's own life in danger.

CHAPTER 9
A SECRET WAR

Roger wasted no time in presenting his idea to Steve Wills, the News Director at WNOW. In his pitch for the series, he described "Five terrific stories of Chinese government arm-twisting and attempts of intimidation at one of America's premier Ivy League campuses." He then outlined the elements he would include in his reports. "I already have interviews with the students and can get corroborating emails, letters and other intimidating communications from their professors and family members."

"What about government agencies, anything from them?" asked his boss.

"I think I'm ahead of them, at least with this group of students."

"Exclusive?"

"You bet," Roger said, knowing how that word made his boss salivate.

"Video?"

"Well, there isn't much video that's dramatic in the way of action, but the stories are shocking enough to carry the narrative. I do have a fake video used to accuse a girl of prostitution. The video is doctored to show her face on a woman who is naked in bed with some guy." That got his boss's face to light up, which he quickly turned into a frown. "Terrible!" he lied, immediately thinking of how that video could be used to promote the series.

"I also have some home video shot on cell phones in China. It shows one student's parents being harangued by neighbors. The 'People's Republic' was behind a campaign of harassment."

"You have anything about the students being asked to spy, or steal proprietary information?"

"No," said Roger, "at least not yet. I am sure though I will find some if I keep digging. The fellow who heads their protest group talks on camera about spying and industrial espionage, but I don't have any smoking gun yet."

The News Director called Jim Butler, the Executive Producer into the office, "Jim, we have a good exclusive spin-off of that Chinese Precinct story. Roger says he can quickly work it up into a series of special reports. I want to take him off the daily rotation for a couple of weeks to get it done."

Butler wasn't too pleased to lose a general assignment reporter for an extended period but really had no choice. "Sounds great." he said with fake enthusiasm, "Really milking this thing, Roger?" Butler teased.

Roger laughed, "You're going to love it, Jim. And if you're down a reporter maybe you can induce Gabe Breslin to get his overpriced ass back to work. You know how he loves street fairs and church bake-offs."

"Don't be a wiseass Roger," scolded Wills, the News Director. "Breslin can write circles around you; and he knows more about this town then you'll ever learn."

"I'm joking, I'm joking!" Roger said, embarrassed to have been slapped down and shamed for impertinence.

Turning to Butler the News Director said, "Jim, tell PR to work up promos for this series, I want to title it, 'A

Secret War.' And have them make sure the world knows it's all 'exclusive' to WNOW."

    As soon as the promotional videos started running Roger began getting more leads. Students from other schools including New York University, Fordham, and Queens College were willing to share their stories. There was particular interest from Queens, the New York borough with the highest Asian population of any county in the country. It wasn't just civilians who were contacting him; the FBI wanted to talk to him, as did the NYPD. He had dug up a viper's nest, and many viewers imagined spooks were now crawling over the city like King Kong over the Empire State Building.

    Chinese community activists were of two minds over the sudden notoriety. On the one hand they welcomed having the hostile intrusion of the Chinese government exposed. On the other they feared a wave of uninformed, bigoted, anti-Asian sentiment. Something which could, and had in the past, incited violence against innocent people.

    However, when the full series began to air the reaction was for the most part, positive. The expose' caused outrage focused mainly on the autocrats in China. The only truly angry response came secretly from Ma Bai at the United Nations. It was directed at the one person he blamed for all the negative publicity, Zhang Wei.

    "Because of your ineptitude this reporter finds out where you live and even your real name," Ma said angrily into the phone. "And as if that is not bad enough, he is now making heroes of the very students you were charged with keeping silent. I just hope for your sake his investigations don't go any deeper."

The threat rattled Zhang who was already terrified he'd be sent back to China, and to a very uncertain fate. "This reporter only has stories of common political mischief against the students. Nothing serious Ma Bai. I am sure the publicity will soon die down."

"It better. If this Roger Barnes gets any closer to me, it won't go well for him."

"A member of the American media, he is almost untouchable, isn't he?"

Ma didn't answer. Instead, he said, "What about the mission with Chen Lin? That remains our most important priority. Isn't he a member of that group at Columbia?"

"Yes, but he is under my direct control and will not speak with the reporter or anyone else."

"You sure?" Ma said with exasperation, not believing Zhang ever had anything under control.

"Yes, I am sure," Zhang said with a confidence he didn't truly feel. "And there is some good news about him."

"What."

"He has been invited to meet with someone at General Dynamics about his internship application."

Relieved to finally hear something positive from Zhang, Ma moderated his tone. "And when might that be?"

"This Friday, just in a couple of days."

"I hope for his sake he is accepted."

CHAPTER 10
July
THE INTERN

July 1st was an auspicious day at the US Navy's Submarine Base in Groton, Connecticut. The prototype Columbia Class submarine, designated SSBNX, had just returned from its inaugural test run and was tied up at one of the base's many berthing areas; a long, cavernous indoor space at the water's edge. The giant barn-like structure kept the top-secret sub from prying eyes ashore, and also from spy satellites looking down from above. The lofty interior space echoed with the clanging of metal hatches thrown open, the shouts of dockhands hauling lines, and sailors hurling good natured insults.

    The mood was celebratory, congratulatory. This billion-dollar weapons experiment was proving its worth, and one of the men most responsible for it, and getting the loudest back slapping congratulations was Captain Liam McCarthy. He was the principal designer; the naval architect who led the various teams tasked with creating the sub's nuclear propulsion system, its ballistic missile armament, hydrodynamics, noise suppression, defensive measures and torpedo systems. Captain McCarthy was a retired naval officer, now working for the General Dynamics Company's Electric Boat Division; the main builder of American submarines.

McCarthy exited the boat's main hatch, walked off the gangway, down the dock and through a metal door which opened into a warren of office suites. He was not a tall man, rather short and stocky with muscular arms and legs and a thick middle which was getting thicker as he aged. He was right-sized for submarine service. Approaching sixty his hair was well gone gray, and he now needed glasses, but his long active military service left him still robust and without any chronic medical issues. Though as common for men his age he did pop a daily blood pressure pill.

"Good morning, Margaret," he said with a broad smile to the Ensign assigned as his assistant. "And a good one it has turned out to be."

"Good morning, sir, all went well I hear."

"Yeah, better than well. All the principal systems are checking out fine, so now we can get to work on those little add-ons that have been requested." He added with obvious understatement.

"Good," she laughed, "so we won't be any more behind schedule or over budget than normal. Are you heading home?"

"Yes. I'm getting a little long in the tooth for these all-nighters. I'll nap until three this afternoon then return for a couple of hours to write up my report."

"Remember, you have an interview scheduled for four o'clock."

"Oh right, I almost forgot."

She picked up a folder and handed it to him, "Here's the info on the fellow. Oh, and your son called a couple of hours ago."

"Devlin? What did he want?"

"He said he was sailing through the Race at dawn today and one of your boats made a sudden appearance. I gather its wake tossed their boat around a bit. He was with Marina."

"Well, I'll be damned! That *was* us out there at that time. There sure would be hell to pay if I swamped my own son and his wife."

"They are sailing in some kind of race," Margaret said, "probably still out there somewhere."

McCarthy took a personal cellphone from his jacket pocket and called his son.

"Hi dad," Devlin said on seeing the caller ID. "You have a successful trip this morning?"

"I gather you got a good look at us."

"A little too good. Maybe you should look up when surfacing."

"Not a bad idea. I'll mention it to the captain," he said facetiously. "How are you, and what were you doing out there so early."

Devlin explained about the Round Long Island Race and that he and Marina were taking it as an opportunity to tune their boat for a longer excursion during the summer.

"And the kids?" Liam asked.

"With Marina's mom in Connecticut. She'll pick them up tomorrow. I've got to report back to work in the morning."

"Come visit soon with Marina and the kids. I'll fill you in on things here. The new bambino is growing fast,"

Liam said, referring to his latest submarine project as a baby.

The two had an easy, relaxed relationship. Both were seamen and both proud of each other. Devlin was an only son, and Liam a widower. They depended on each other emotionally, especially so since the death of Devlin's mother Kathy three years earlier.

Both expressed their love, then clicked off.

"OK Margaret, I'm outta' here." Liam said buttoning his service jacket.

"Don't forget the interview for the new intern," she said pointing at the folder on his desk.

"Oh, yeah. Shoot."

Before leaving, Liam picked up the folder and opened it to read the cover letter, "So what's his name again?" He took a second then closed the paperwork and dropped it back onto his desk.

"Oh yeah, Chen Lin, kid from Columbia."

***

Chen arrived at Liam's single room office promptly at ten minutes to four. Ensign Margaret Cronin welcomed him, introduced herself and invited him to wait in a chair placed against the wall nearest the door. The office space was broad but bare bones, two metal desks separated by an architect's easel stood in front of two windows on the opposite wall. Blueprints of some sort were piled on the easel. The only personal effects were some family photos arranged on a nearby bookshelf. One picture was of a young couple, a man in a Navy officer's uniform, the woman holding a young boy by the hand. *Must be Mister McCarthy,* thought Chen. *Wife and child.* He was surprised by an unexpected emotional response to the simple, almost hackneyed scene. An involuntary twinge of guilt over his own duplicity perhaps.

"He should be here shortly," Ensign Cronin said. "He was out all night and has been catching some shuteye."

"Partying?" Chen said with a nervous laugh, "I hope he's not tired and irritable."

"Not quite," she replied also laughing. "But don't worry, Captain McCarthy is quite a lovely guy and really enjoys helping students. No need to be nervous."

Chen noted his damp palms and realized he was more wound-up about this interview than he had anticipated. He was an accomplished graduate student who had won honors in naval engineering at Stevens, his undergraduate school, and had every reason to be confident of acceptance for the internship here. But that was conscious reasoning, his subconscious managed to cast unwanted shadows from the back of his brain and cloud his thoughts.

He smiled weakly and said, "Well, this is a pretty important internship for me, a lot riding on it, so …" He threw up his hands letting her finish the thought as she walked back to her desk.

Chen sat quietly ruminating over his predicament until he heard footsteps in the hallway. McCarthy burst through the door, looked straight to Ensign Cronin and blurted, "The boss is back! Make believe you're working!"

She laughed and threw up her hands, "You caught me. But before you say something you'll regret say hello to Mister Chen Lin."

Liam, caught momentarily off guard, swung around to see to whom she was pointing, gave a start of surprise, and then with a wide smile welcomed the young man.

Liam's brief discomfiture helped Lin relax a bit, both sharing a moment of humorous discovery. Lin was surprised to see a vigorous looking man, handsome in a weathered way, with broad athletic looking shoulders and an erect posture. Lin couldn't help comparing him to the flabby desk-bound professors more usual in the university. His face was ruddy, almost florid in its Irishness which enhanced his beaming smile. Lin immediately liked the man.

Liam's quick appraisal of his new intern was more guarded. Chen appeared to be in his mid-twenties, was slim, not short but well under six feet tall and slightly built. He had raven black hair slicked back which seemed to emphasize his straight nose, a trifle large for his face, and his myopic eyes which were magnified by thick glasses. It went without saying that he was smart; he wouldn't get the interview if his scholastic record was not impeccable. At first blush he seemed good natured and apparently with a sense of humor. And Margaret seemed to like him. Always a plus. Liam motioned for Chen to take his chair and move it to sit across from him at his desk. After initial pleasantries Liam got to the point.

"You're studying materials science, why do you want to spend time at this outfit?"

"I am especially interested in the development and use of carbon fiber in the construction of submersibles," explained Chen. "I think there could be a future in the use of carbon instead of steel in shipbuilding and I am hoping to get a better sense of the dynamic stresses and loads you encounter at sea."

"Carbon. The saving in weight would be significant, I'll grant you that," replied Liam. "But when it comes to submarines, we have a long history with steel and trust our numbers."

"Exactly, that's why I want to explore carbon further. Compare its structural qualities to what you know and trust about steel."

Liam was quiet for a moment then nodded. "Okay, I doubt carbon would work but I would be interested in what you come up with. Who knows you might be on to something."

Liam then outlined what would be the parameters of Chen's responsibilities. He would be given a specific section of exterior hull on which to work but would not have access to the sub's operational systems, nor even the complete exterior profile. His authorization would be strictly limited, and his work monitored.

Chen Lin understood the limitations. They then turned to practical matters: where he would live, *employee housing on the base,* when he could start, *scheduled for in a week.* "Actually," said McCarthy catching himself, "I could use you as soon as you can get here. Can you start as soon as this coming Tuesday, after the Fourth of July weekend?"

"Sure, the sooner the better. I'm totally free. No strings," Chen said with a smile, especially happy to quickly put some distance between himself, Zhang Wei, and his friends at Columbia. He couldn't bear facing his compatriots now that he was betraying them.

Liam's interview with Chen was brief but had gone well. Most of the deep vetting had been done in earlier perusal of his transcripts before he was even invited to visit. The interview was more a meet and greet than decisive to acceptance. From his academic record Chen appeared to be a serious student, and a creative researcher. But his persona did seem a little intense. *I don't know how this kid will get on with the rough and tumble enlisted men*, Liam mused. But Chen Lin had the right qualifications for the internship, and the appointment was only for two months. *So, he'll be fine.* He certainly seemed competent, and while apparently an introspective type, a lot less of a goofy fuck-up than many other students McCarthy had accepted over the years.

From Chen's professional perspective, he would be entitled to get college credit for the time he spent at Electric Boat, but the real value of an internship for any student was the experience, and especially the contacts. A recommendation from Captain McCarthy would be invaluable when it was time to job hunt.

"Okay Mister Chen, I think you will work out fine here and the experience should be at least interesting if not especially fun. But tell me, what are your plans after you get your doctorate. Do you want to teach?"

"No, Captain McCarthy, I expect to find shipbuilding work, perhaps at Bath Iron Works in Maine."

"Not bad, but if you like working on nuclear propulsion you might consider staying right here. Is your family in the area?"

"No sir, they are still in China, in Guangzhou. I will bring them to join me as soon as I graduate."

"And that will be?"

"Next June."

"OK great. By the way, since you are a civilian you can forget the 'sir' stuff. Just call me Liam."

"Yes sir. Uh, Liam. Oh, and you can call me Lin … if you want of course."

"Sure Lin. So, Margaret will process the paperwork, get you a place to bunk, and I'll expect you here next Tuesday at eight a.m. sharp."

Their thanks said, Lin shook hands and left. It had been almost too easy. Without special security clearance he would be doing mostly grunt work, copying architectural drawings designed by others. But he was in the door and, despite discomfort over his duplicity, getting access to more restricted material would be his priority. His focus must always be on the safety of his parents.

CHAPTER 11
IN IT TOGETHER

Chen Lin didn't have much time, a weekend to be precise, to pack his clothing and prepare for his summer at the base in Groton, Connecticut. Moving out of his dorm would be simple, he had nothing there other than textbooks, a computer and clothing. The only important personal items were a few family pictures which he would take with him. *My movable shrine,* as he jokingly referred to them.

He would take the train up from Grand Central on Sunday. Margaret had already arranged for his room and clearance at the naval base, all he had to do was show his Columbia I.D. and he would be admitted.

The hardest part of the move would be his separation from Wu Yao. He called her while still at the station in New London waiting for his train back to New York.

"How did it go?" She blurted, "You get it?"

"Yes, fooled them again," Lin said with a laugh. "The chief designer actually thinks I won't screw things up for him."

"Oh honey, that's great," she said and gushed a few minutes more about how smart he was, besides being handsome, and of course how lucky he was to belong to her. "I want to hear all about the meeting as soon as you get here."

On arrival in Manhattan, Lin went straight to meet Yao in her apartment. This would be the longest separation they had to endure since they began dating a year earlier; the need to be apart was something both regretted.

Yao was a student in the Columbia "J" School, Journalism, and had secured an internship at the New York Times for the summer. They expected she would visit him in Connecticut as often as possible over the next two months. Although not formally engaged, both were anticipating marriage and excited that his graduation was less than a year away.

His current and future personal and professional prospects should have put Chen in an exultant frame of mind; however, the intense pressure laid upon him by Zhang had its effect, and despite attempts to pretend to Yao all was going well he was obviously troubled. His behavior was artificially buoyant, something even a person not as observant and loving as Yao could see. He was too loud in his greeting, spoke too fast, blathered uncharacteristically about the people he met and the access to advanced ship designs he would have.

"This is going to be great for me, for us, with these Navy credentials I should be able to get hired most anywhere I want." Lin went on to describe Liam, "Great, great guy. Irishman. Big bear of a man, almost broke me in two with his hug." Margaret was, "A real sweetheart, taking care of all the paperwork and stuff." And the base, "Like no marine installation I've ever seen, armed guards everywhere."

Yao was taken aback, delighted with what Lin was telling her, but unsettled by his frantic, almost distracted behavior. If she didn't know better, she would think he was on drugs. Finally, she had to slow him down.

"Lin, are you okay?"

"Whattayamean?"

"You seem so hyper? Is something bothering you?"

Lin took Yao's innocent question as an accusation.

"Why if I am very happy do you immediately think there is something wrong?" he snapped. His voice rose, "You are getting paranoid, always looking to see if I'm hiding something."

Yao recoiled in shock; her hands began to tremble. She was now positive something was seriously wrong. Those words, this behavior was so out of character. She was stunned.

"Lin, I don't know what happened in Connecticut, but something did. If you can't tell me for some reason, okay I'll respect your privacy, but just don't lie to me and say nothing is wrong."

Lin doubled down with his denials, trying to calm her. Speaking in a voice he thought slow, firm and relaxed, but was in fact tight with tension he said, "Everything ... went ... well ... in ... Connecticut. As I said, they liked me, and I liked them. And the work should be really interesting. I'm just excited is all."

That did it. The obvious contradiction between his reassuring words and his agitated manner cemented her suspicions, and her apprehensions. Overwrought, she began to cry.

Then the most startling thing, something that might happen only between two young lovers. Moving quickly to sit next to her he said in anguish over her tears, "Please don't." And then this always serious, supremely imperturbable man lost all composure. He turned so they were face to face, and they fell into each other's arms so emotionally agitated they clung together in both confusion and relief. At this point there was no more dissembling, the truth had to come out or there would be no future together for them.

"Yao, everything I've told you about Connecticut is true. There is no problem there. The trouble is right here."

Wiping her tears Yao said, "Here? With me?"

That brought the first legitimate smile to Lin's face. "Never, never think that. You are my joy. No, I am being punished for protesting the Xi regime."

Lin, then explained that he was being pressured by the Chinese authorities to take this internship. For what exact reason he didn't yet know, though he could imagine it would involve some sort of spying on the work being done there.

Yao understood immediately, it was the sort of manipulation all too commonly faced by their compatriots.

"Have they mentioned your parents," Yao asked, already knowing the answer.

"Yes, of course."

"The bastards!"

"Ironic, isn't it? Here I have been marching around telling people to stand up against Xi's agents, and now I'm forced to do their dirty work."

"Have your parents been directly contacted?"

"I don't know, don't think so. But it was made clear to me that either I cooperate, or they will pay."

The two sat side by side in dejected silence.

Yao spoke first, "What do we do now?"

Lin gave her a startled look, "We? I don't know about 'we,' but I am going to do as I'm asked. At least for now."

"Lin sweetheart you are not alone, we are in this together. If nothing else, you need someone you can talk to, or the pressure will ruin you. And me. Not to mention the risks you are taking of getting caught." He was too dejected to reply, so she continued. "This is all a shock so let's not do anything hasty. I agree you must do whatever they ask, at least for now, then we can plan a way out."

"You're more positive than I am," Lin answered. But he was already feeling a bit better. She was right, having someone with whom to talk did give him some relief. "Unless I can get my parents out of their clutches, I am just a slave. A robot. They push a button, and I do whatever they order me to do."

Yao leaned back in her seat, thoughtful. After a long moment she said, "Well dear Lin, I don't know how we will do it, but I think you have not only just diagnosed the problem, but also the cure."

"What do you mean?"

Allowing herself a smile Yao said, "The only reason they have a hold on you is because your parents are in China. That's the problem, So, the cure is simple, we must get them out."

"Yeah right. Simple!"

"This is all premature but remember, my parents run a travel agency. They lead groups of tourists from China to all parts of the world. There must be something they can do to help."

"Honey, it's bad enough that I put my parents in trouble, the last thing I want to do is expose your parents to those criminals. That would just make things twice as bad as they already are."

"I'm just saying we are not powerless. I don't know how we can get your parents to safety; I'm just saying it is what must be done and can be done. Somehow."

Once again morose, Lin thought of the job he was starting in a few days. He had not even considered the risk he was running of spying and getting caught until Yao mentioned it. Now, the thought of the shame and ruination he faced if that were to happen sank him into despair. Everything he hoped to achieve, his profession, the life he looked forward to with Yao. *All would be lost, and for what?* he thought. *To save my parents, that was what.* But then a counter thought; what could the Xi's government actually do? They surely won't kill his parents. *It would cause an uproar.* His mind flipped from one contingency to another: one hopeful, one pessimistic, until he was lost in a miasma of doubt and anxiety.

Yao responded to his troubled expression. "Lin, we have to keep this simple. Let's not get lost in a lot of 'what ifs.' You know what you must do in the immediate future, and that's enough for now. We have a couple of months to work something out, and we will."

Yao's firmness, loving support and optimism was contagious. Lin rallied enough to say, "You're right. At the moment Zhang Wei thinks he is in control of me, and for now he is. But he is a hunted man, frightened for his own safety; and what he doesn't know and can't possibly know is what we plan to do. Of course, neither do we," he said with a relieved laugh, "but that's only temporary."

CHAPTER 12
THE MOLE DIGS IN

It was a heady time for Chen Lin. He arrived at the U.S. Navy Submarine Base New London, on a Sunday, the day before the Fourth of July, and spent the holiday weekend walking around the base getting acquainted with his new home and its surroundings. Chen had taken the Amtrak train from the Moynihan Train Station on West 33d Street in Manhattan, then a cab from New London to the base. He quickly realized he would need some personal transportation because the base, even though located in a populated area, was not well serviced by public transport. He would either have to rent a car or be forced to take Ubers everywhere.

Chen entered the base through the Pass Gate where his Columbia ID was checked, and thanks to Margaret's efficiency, he was issued a Navy pass. He was then directed to a center for visitor housing where he was assigned a room in a building with a view west over the Thames River. It was a striking view. Standing at the window he could see across the water to the campuses of Connecticut College and the nearby Coast Guard Academy. Looking downriver was the city of New London proper on the west bank, and Groton on the east. It was down there at the General Dynamics facility in Groton where the submarines designed by Liam and his staff would be assembled. But the exact process of design, fabrication and assembly of these war machines was something he was yet to learn.

Looking out of his window he could see more than twenty long groins projecting into the river from north to south, many of which had the sleek black hulls of sinister-looking submarines tied alongside. Staring at the subs there was something ominous about the blankness of their external aspect, their smooth windowless hulls with no portlights, no outward sign of a human's conscious control. It reminded Chen of the implacable, deadly indifference of a shark, which seeing prey would decline its head, bare its teeth, strike and kill. Killing machines is what they were. Chen could not conjure a crew of living, breathing sailors working, laughing, swearing and fighting aboard, as on surface ships. From his vantage the submarine appeared a blind automaton, a drone of the sea which could, without a shudder of conscience unleash its firestorm unseen, turn, and disappear into blackness.

Suddenly depressed he sought relief; he called Yao. "Well, I made it," he said with excitement. False merriment and anxiety mixed in his voice.

"Good. How are you feeling? You okay?" she said with concern for his mental state. Duplicity was not a strong suit for someone with his ethical upbringing.

"Yeah, okay. Stomach a bit in knots but I'll get over it." Gazing out the window he said, "My room has a very interesting view. Grass, trees, houses, and submarine conning towers!"

"What did you expect chickens and cows?" she said laughing, trying to lighten the mood.

"Man, I wish you were here," he said weakly.

"The word 'cow' make you think of me?" she said in mock horror, determined to cheer him up. It worked.

"Actually, I wouldn't care if you mooed, I miss you already."

"How about I come up next weekend? We could visit something fun up there. I'll go online and see what's around."

Chen leapt at the thought, and they made plans for her to take the train up on Friday. It was only about a three-hour ride, and she could easily make it home for her Monday internship duties at the Times.

After unpacking, booting up his computer, arranging multiple chargers for his personal electronics, and checking out the kitchen and bedroom accommodations, *bare bones dormitory,* it was still early in the day. He decided to walk down to the riverside.

At the southern end of the base, near the Navy's submarine warfare museum, he strolled past the world's first nuclear submarine, the *Nautilus*. It was docked in a special exhibit space and available for tourists to visit. He considered that would be an appropriate first introduction to this place, so signed up for a tour of SSN 571 for the following day.

It wasn't exactly a disappointment when on Monday morning he joined about fifty people threading their way through Nautilus's innards, but Chen had seen enough films about older submarines; there were no real surprises in what he saw. Cramped quarters, nothing extraneous, everything functional. There was the nuclear reactor amidships, that would be the same, torpedoes of course, but missing were the ballistic missile tubes of a modern submarine. Still, he thought it worthwhile to poke around even an antique version of what he would be working on. His new boss might even appreciate his having made the pilgrimage to an icon of the submarine service.

Sure enough, on Tuesday morning as they shook hands Liam McCarthy said, "So, did you visit the *Nautilus*?" Chen Lin grinned at his own prescience, "As a matter of fact, I did." Then signaling an informality he was beginning to feel he teased, "I thought I should see what you were working on when you started here."

Liam laughed, "Whoa, I'm not that old! But you're right the *Nautilus* is something of a relic now."

"Like he is," chimed in Margaret smiling. She came over to shake Chen's hand. "Welcome, and I hope this experience works out well for you." Chen was shown to a desk with an architect's table. "This is all yours," she said.

Liam invited Chen to join him in the Commissary for coffee and a welcoming chat. They discussed the status of the new Columbia submarine, issues the shakedown cruises were exposing, and the remedies under consideration.

"I am concerned about an increase in vibration at the base of the forward planes once speed goes over 25-knots," he said. "I'm going to be looking into that and will share the numbers, and my thinking with you."

"Thanks," said Chen, "but not knowing the design parameters, I'm not sure how much I can usefully contribute."

"I just want a fresh pair of eyes to look at the calculations. Don't be afraid to speak up. If you see something you think I might have missed, let me know."

"Sure thing."

"I'm not expecting anything novel from you, just that you help back me up. Understand?"

Chen agreed that was a good way to begin his internship. Liam would use him as needed; if trusted, more responsibility would come his way.

Back in the office Chen made mental note of where the various design records were kept. Margaret would open a wall safe each morning and bring out whichever drawings Liam requested for that day and return them in the evening. Everything was secured, but because they were a nondescript office in the middle of a navy base, no other special precautions were taken. An unauthorized person could never figure out where in this vast space the classified drawings were, or how they were secured. In a sense it was a secret in plain sight. So, on his very first day Chen had already made an important discovery. How he would use that information he had yet to figure out.

As the week progressed Liam and Chen tried various pitch and contour combinations on the diving planes to see how they changed the hydrodynamic forces transmitted to the hull. A scale model of the Columbia was tested in the tank at the Navy's Surface Warfare research facility in Bayview, Idaho. There, they found the convex curve at the top of the diving planes created a swirl, the force of which was passed to the hinges attached to the hull. By altering the shape of that curve and adding small winglets at the end of the planes, similar to those seen on commercial jets, the swirls dissipated, and the pressure on the hinges reduced. It was a major breakthrough in a persistent problem that the computer simulations had missed. Liam was ecstatic. His buoyant mood propelled him to invite Chen to celebrate.

"Hey Lin, what are you doing tomorrow night," Liam asked as they were leaving on Friday afternoon. He had begun using Chen's given name.

"Well, my girlfriend, my fiancé really, is joining me and we are hoping to do some touring tomorrow. To see some of the sights here."

"I'm asking because my son Devlin and his wife are coming for a visit, and I thought you might join us for dinner. Both of you of course."

"That sounds great, but let me run it by Wu Yao, that's her name."

Liam thought for a second then said, "Here's what I suggest. You and Wu Yao spend the day in Essex, it's a beautiful old town on the Connecticut River not far from here. Good shopping for your lady too. They even have a steam train that will take you for a picturesque ride along the river. Then we can meet for dinner at Essex's Griswold Inn. Been here since 1776."

"That sounds good, but I'll need to rent a car. I don't have one."

"Don't worry you can Uber there, not expensive, and I'll drive you back."

Chen said he would run it by Yao and returned to his room. It turned out to be an easy sell. "Essex? Sure, it is one of the places up there I've been reading about." Yao said she would take the train up that evening, and they could leave first thing Saturday for Essex. Yao was pleased at the prospect of a weekend getaway. So was Chen, despite some misgivings inspired by a nagging conscience.

***

Liam had neglected to tell Chen that his son and daughter-in-law were arriving in Essex by boat. After sailing up from Greenwich, Connecticut, *Coastie's* home port, Devlin and Marina took a mooring at the Essex Yacht Club which was located just a short walk from the Griswold Inn. Waiting for them in the hotel's main dining room were Chen and Yao. They had just returned from a trip up the Connecticut River aboard a local tourist boat.

The wooden walls of the dining room were covered with a collection of rare prints depicting the ornate steamers which had called on Essex over the century and a half of their heyday. Yao was studying one of the paintings when Devlin and Marina entered. They stood at the entrance to the room trying to decide which of the diners might be the couple they were to meet. Just as they focused on the only Asians in the room, Liam stepped in from behind and gave his son a pat on the back.

"You made it. How was the trip?" he asked.

"Oh, hi dad. Easy," answered Marina turning to give him a peck on the cheek. "Steady southwest breeze all the way."

The three joined Chen and Yao with Liam doing the first introductions. Chen introduced Yao calling her his fiancé, which was a surprise to her; he didn't usually make their relationship so definitive to strangers. It prompted a broad smile and shy blush which captivated both Devlin and Liam. Marina, who was almost ten years older, felt an immediate fondness for the young woman and greeted her in Mandarin. Both Yao and Chen were taken aback until Marina explained she was an interpreter at the United Nations and fluent in the language.

    Conversation during dinner varied from discussion of life on a Navy base, to Yao's impressions of The New York Times, to Devlin's experiences patrolling New York Harbor, and also how Marina balanced her career with mothering two young children. "Having my mother nearby was a godsend," she said. Avoided was any discussion of the work Liam and Chen were doing in Groton. This was just as well, because any reminder of Chen's double life agitated Yao, while distracting him almost to the point of incoherence.

    Chen had successfully bifurcated his mind so that he could thoroughly enjoy devoting himself to the solution of naval design problems essential to the creation of an attack submarine, and simultaneously hold as his ultimate mission protecting the lives of his parents by spying for China. But talking about his work on Columbia would force him to dissolve that psychological barrier and exacerbate his mental confusion.

    After dinner the five of them retired to the bar, a cozy dark space with no music that night. Perfect for conversation. Liam picked up a basket, loaded it with popcorn from an ancient popper, and treated everyone to an Irish coffee.

Over the drinks Yao explained her ambition was to complete her journalism courses, get a Green Card for permission to remain and work in America, and make her life here with Chen Lin. "We met a year ago, right after we started at Columbia," she said, "we have been dating since."

"Marriage within the year," explained Chen, "is what we both look forward to. And for me a career at an American shipbuilder." That was as close as he got to describing his work, before adding, "It is very important for me to have my parents join me in this country."

Yao interrupted, "My parents are also still in China. They have a very successful business, a travel agency, and I'm sure they will stay there. They are fortunate, can travel freely and would be able to visit us often."

"But we anticipate having many children," Chen said smiling at Yao, "and I want them to be able to know my parents as well."

"Will it be difficult for your parents to emigrate from China?" Marina asked, "Relations between the two countries can be difficult."

"That might be a problem, but I am hopeful of working something out," Chen said soberly. "You are right though; it is not a sure thing." To lighten the mood Yao said, "My parents might be able to have Lin's parents leave China by joining a tour to the West."

"But that would put her parents at some risk and is not something I want to consider," Chen said.

Marina touched Yao's hand and said, "We certainly wish you luck working that out."

It was Devlin's turn then to describe how he and Marina first met. It was when she was a student at Connecticut College, and he was a Cadet at the nearby Coast Guard Academy. "Marina was a member of her college's sailing team, and I sailed for the Academy. We met after a competition, started dating and have lived and sailed together ever since."

Marina said they were going to continue sailing east the next day and spend a day on Block Island before heading home.

That gave Devlin an idea, "Why don't the two of you stay with us on the boat tonight? We will drop you off in New London before sailing on to Block."

It was a surprise invitation to which Chen stuttered an answer, "Th, th, thanks. but we have no experience with boats, much less sailing," he said honestly, and looked at Yao not sure how to respond.

"No problem," Marina said with a dismissive wave of the hands. "Devlin and I will do the sailing; you're just along for the ride. Please come."

Yao grinned, nodded and squeezed Chen's hand; she was anxious for any positive distraction. "Let's go Lin, it will be something new for us, an adventure."

"We don't have any extra clothing, not even a toothbrush," he protested weakly. He felt he had to demur for form's sake, but secretly hoped their unpreparedness really wouldn't matter. Sailing sounded like it could be fun.

"A few hours in yesterday's clothes won't kill you," responded Liam joining the conversation. "You can shower and change when back at the base." So, it was decided the four young people would journey to the Thames River together.

A sense of almost parental affection for the young couple had grown in Devlin and especially Marina. They were established with careers and kids, but not so much older than Chen and Yao that they couldn't remember what it was like to be preparing for marriage. The excitement and uncertainty of what lay ahead. Spending the night together on *Coastie* would allow them all more time to get to know each other.

It was after nine when they left the Griswold; the long summer day was coming to an end, but there was still enough light in the sky to paint the village in soft pastels. Liam headed back to his car for the short drive to the naval base, leaving the two couples to stroll down Main Street and toward the docks of the Essex Yacht Club. A Club launch took them to *Coastie's* mooring where they clambered aboard and settled into the cockpit to enjoy the sunset.

It was an idyllic scene, the sun sinking low in the west lit the clouds from below, turning them a vivid purple. The river echoed the sky, coloring everything around them with an impressionist's palette. The first stars were beginning to shine in the darkening east, while on the water ducks cruised in single file, and black cormorants flopped forward with a splash as they dove for fish. On *Coastie* Marina fired up the propane stove and brewed a pot of espresso to which she added sweet anisette liquor. "Then we add three coffee beans to each cup for good luck. It's an Italian custom," she said referring to her heritage,

Taking a cup, Chen seemingly lost in thought said quietly, "I could use some of that good luck." Devlin looked at him noting his apparent disquiet. "Well, couldn't we all?" he added solicitously, wondering why Chen, who seemed to be doing very well for himself, had suddenly turned so introspective.

But that lasted only a moment, after which the four sat quietly enjoying the coffee, the night and each other. The conversation was muted. Except for the shadow from China deepening over Chen and Yao, they were just four young people enjoying each other's company and preoccupied with where the vagaries of life would lead them.

There was almost no wind to disturb the boat, or the course of their thoughts, just the subtle river current flowing toward the ever-changing sea.

CHAPTER 13
CLOSING THE CIRCLE

Roger Barnes was getting antsy. His series of reports on the Chinese Police Precinct had generated a lot of buzz, but little else. There were no arrests and no apparent follow-up with the members of Columbia's student activists. From what he heard none of the students, or any of the many others who had come forward, had been seriously or permanently impacted by the heavy-handed bullying they had received. And apparently the Feds were not going to do much of anything.

"The good news is we put that Chinatown Police Precinct out of business," FBI chief Bill Roscoe told Roger in a follow-up phone interview. "The bad news is we have no idea where the guy, or guys running that operation went. We only have one suspect, and there are no new leads. It's totally dried up." Sure, he added, investigations into similar cells would continue, but the spotlight had moved out of New York.

This was unacceptable for the ambitious Roger; he needed to keep this story percolating or there would be no Emmy at the end of it. Where to go next?

"Go back to Columbia," Hana said to him after listening to him moan and complain one time too many. "Those students are your best bet to find someone who'll attract the Federal prosecutors, and that means your slimy friend Giordano the U.S. Attorney. And where he goes, goes the spotlight."

"You make me sound like a publicity whore," Roger said.

"Well?"

"Well, you're right. But only up to a point."

"And where might that point be?"

Offended by his girlfriend's perceptive observation, Roger said, "Come on, you know this is a legitimate story. There really are bad people out there harassing students, stealing intellectual property."

Hana gave a dismissive grunt, "Sure, and you can't help it if pumping up the story advances your career, right?"

Roger had to laugh, he threw out both hands in a gesture of mock helplessness. "No. Like it or not, I have to take what comes, even if it makes me rich and famous."

"Then, as cops on TV like to say, get off your ass and go knock on some doors."

Problem was, the only door Roger had to knock on that might harbor someone who could help, had the name Fu Muchen on it. He called Muchen's mobile.

"Yo, Muchen it's me Roger."

"Yo yourself. What's up? Doing any follow-ups to that excellent series of yours, the one that I made happen?"

"You're still not dead, so I guess you weren't as much a threat to the Fatherland as you thought."

"Motherland. Fatherland went out of favor when the Third Reich went kaput. And just give Xi some time, his henchmen may be slow, but they grind exceedingly fine."

"If anyone can jam their grinder it's probably you."

"You flatter me. But to what do I owe this call?"

"I need a lead."

Roger went on to explain that he'd hit a dead end, couldn't find anyone who could move the story forward and he didn't want it to die. What he didn't say was he needed this story, which had given his career a boost, to keep on giving.

"You told me when we first met, you could supply me with people who have been pressured to provide sensitive information to China. So?"

"Well, maybe I did overpromise a little."

"Bait and switch?" Roger said, peeved at what he perceived as a runaround.

"Look, I do know guys who have been approached and refused to cooperate, but they won't talk. And there are some who have already been publicly exposed and locked up. But they're old news."

"I need fresh meat. Can't just rehash old cases no one cares about."

Fu Muchen had an idea. "Remember Chen Lin, the boyfriend of Wu Yao, the one who missed our meeting? Maybe you should reach out to him."

"Why him?"

Muchen went on to explain that he hadn't heard from Chen ever since he begged off joining their interviews. He didn't know why but Chen was avoiding his old protest comrades. He could just be busy, but maybe he was being pressured to lay off such activity.

"Besides, according to Yao he's got a hot new internship which could make him vulnerable."

"What do you mean hot internship?"

"He just started work at General Dynamics' Electric Boat Division. Where they make nuclear submarines."

"What!" Roger almost shouted. "What's he doing there?"

"Beats me. But if I know my mainland brethren, they will find him an irresistible target. It's at least worth checking out. Ask him. See if he's been approached."

Roger still had Chen's mobile number in his contacts and called it immediately after hanging up with Muchen. No answer. He left a voicemail, "Hi, this is Roger Barnes from WNOW TV News. Sorry we never got to meet for an interview, but I'd like to follow up with you. If you can, please call me back on this number. Thanks!"

Roger had been placed once again on general assignment in the newsroom. As part of the reporters' daily rotation, he was assigned "day-of" stories. If he wanted to research something else, a pet project, it had to be on his own time. A trip to New London to talk to Chen might not lead to anything, but his gut told him it was worth a shot even if he must sacrifice a day off to find out.

Roger had a clear-eyed sense of his own strengths and weaknesses. He knew, and had even been told by his current boss, that he wasn't the most talented of writers, much less, a dogged investigative journalist. He was more expert and valued as a producer, able to package the elements he gathered, the video and audio, into a well-told, entertaining story. He also had an undefinable ability to charm people into sharing their most personal fears and hopes on camera. He elicited good sound bites. And he was empathetic, perceptive about people, which is why people trusted him, and why he trusted his gut feelings.

He was not movie star handsome, but was well built, conventionally attractive, and laughed and smiled easily. When appropriate. Moreover, unlike those frantic, hyperventilating reporters who seemed to be shouting all the time, he spoke in a confident, relaxed manner. It was an easygoing virile style that made both young women and matronly moms react warmly to him. That "nice boy next door" attraction to its women viewers was one of the reasons he was hired by WNOW.

Roger had developed his style, his on-camera persona, while working at the New Haven television station. It was because of that Connecticut experience that he was familiar with the submarine base on the Thames River, and the Electric Boat facility. And also why he was on friendly terms with the public information officers at both locations. If necessary, he'd have an easy time getting access to either site.

But first, he had to hear from Chen Lin. The manner in which Chen responded just might be indicative of … of what? Roger didn't know, but hearing what Chen said, and how he said it would inform his instincts.

It didn't take long for Roger's voicemail message to elicit a response, but the response was not at first directed to him. Instead, as soon as Chen listened to the message he called Yao at her desk at *The Times*. He was panicky, "I can't believe it, that TV reporter from New York just called. He wants to meet me. He didn't say why other than to follow up on that series he did." Chen added with a moan, "Man, I do not need this now."

Yao was also apprehensive, but she tried to reassure him, "Oh, that's no big deal. I've met Barnes and he seems a regular guy. Just tell the truth, that you have this internship for a couple of months and will then return to Columbia when it's over. That's all you need to say."

"You don't think he's suspicious of anything?"

"Why would he be? Your name didn't even come up during his filming here. Besides the police precinct story seems to have disappeared. No one is talking about it anymore, not even Muchen."

"I guess you're right. I just feel so exposed, like there's a spotlight shining on my face, and everyone is staring at me."

"Your imagination is working overtime. Try to be realistic Lin. Let's face it you are basically invisible to everyone there. Just a student, another summer intern soon to be gone and forgotten."

Her logic had its effect, Chen felt she was right; he was being hypersensitive. Calmed by her reassuring words he decided to return Roger's call. To deflect the reporter's interest and satisfy his curiosity he would answer whatever questions as truthfully as he could, without revealing the Chinese government's gun to his head. Then he would ignore any further inquiries, at least until after he'd accomplished what he had to do.

Chen Lin had worked hard to make it to America. At the South China University of Technology in Guangzhou, he matriculated in the School of Material Science and Engineering. He had been awarded the college's top academic prize, which made him eligible to study abroad.

His success was a matter of great pride for his parents. His father was a minor government official in Guangzhou.

Chen was an only child, born during the single child restrictions the government placed on parents to reduce the country's population. As the sole male child of modest parentage, he carried all his family's hopes for an honorable present, and prosperous future. Chen was determined to reward their ambitions for him with a successful career, and more importantly to them, many grandchildren. He could achieve both goals by living in the United States instead of returning to China. He naively anticipated doing what the Ministry demanded and then being free of it forever. The fact his guilt might mean perpetual servitude to the Xi regime never entered his mind. For right now, his main concern was to get this reporter off his back as quickly as possible.

"Hello, Roger Barnes?"

"Speaking."

"This is Chen Lin. You called?"

"Thanks so much for getting back to me. I got your name from Fu Muchen who suggested we talk. He thought you might be able to help on a story I've been working on."

Chen told Roger he had seen the series of reports which had already aired, liked them, but really there was nothing further he could add. "I am just starting an internship in Connecticut and must concentrate on my duties here."

"Yes, of course. I understand you are at Electric Boat, congratulations. It has to be a plum assignment for you. I don't want to be a distraction, but I am traveling to

Connecticut this week to visit some old friends (he lied) and would really appreciate just a few minutes of your time."

"No, really. I would find that very inconvenient. I will be happy to meet with you once back in New York, but not until then."

"Just a short get acquainted meeting?"

"No, I'm really not available while working here."

Chen's reluctance to meet piqued Roger's interest and made him more determined to see him face to face. But he felt it would be better to back off for the moment.

"Well, I'd rather see you sooner, but okay if you insist, I'll see you in the fall." He said this with not the slightest intention of waiting that long.

Chen, relieved, relaxed a bit and before saying goodbye added brightly that his fiancé mentioned how much she appreciated Barnes's reporting and had enjoyed meeting him. Roger saw an opening and dove in, "She was a delight, and seems to have survived that concocted prostitute story well. Courageous woman, you are a lucky guy."

"Yes, I am. Thanks again. See you in September," Chen said, anxious to get off, ready to hit the phone's red button.

"Just one thing," Roger jumped in quickly, "Wu Yao seemed very nervous when speaking of you. As if she were concerned for your welfare." Roger was inventing as he spoke. He had heard enough to know he was being blown-off and decided to give Chen a jolt. "That's one of the reasons I wanted to talk to you. You are okay, right?"

Chen gave a nervous laugh and said, "I just saw her this past weekend. We're both just fine. No nervousness. It must have been your imagination. Thanks for your concern, but now I really have to go. Talk soon. Goodbye."

"Sure. Glad to hear there's no reason for worry. Bye."

Whoa mama! What is going on with that guy? Roger's mind was made up. He called Hana immediately after clicking off with Chen.

"What are you doing this weekend?"

"You want to take me to Paris?"

"Yes. But first to Connecticut."

"New Haven? Pepe's Pizza? So romantic."

"Nothing so pedestrian. Join me on a trip to New London."

"Connecticut's Cote d'Azur. I'm thrilled. What for?"

"I'll fill you in tomorrow."

Roger booked a Metro North train to Greenwich, Connecticut for the next morning. It was where his parents lived, and he wanted to pick up his car which he left parked in their garage. He thought keeping a car in New York was expensive *and more trouble than it's worth.*

While Roger was making travel plans his pointed jab at Chen Lin triggered another hurried communication from Chen to his fiancé.

"Yao, what did you say to that guy Barnes? He just called and said you told him I was scared, or worried about something."

Yao was taken aback, "I don't know what you're talking about. I never said any such thing. As a matter of fact, I haven't spoken to him since the filming when we said nothing about you at all, other than that you had a meeting that night."

Silence, as they collected their thoughts. Yao spoke first, "He must be on a fishing expedition, just seeing if he could get anything new out of you."

"But why? If he doesn't know anything, why is he suspicious of me?"

"Not necessarily suspicious, perhaps just probing. How did you leave off with him?"

"Told him I was too busy to meet with him until I got back to New York in the Fall."

"How did he react to that?"

"He said okay, he'd see me then."

"Good. In that case don't worry about him. By that time this will all be over and done with."

"I suppose you're right," Chen said in what was more a wish than an expectation, "In two months, this terrible business will be history."

Perhaps, but unfortunately for Chen he didn't have two months, not even two days, until he would have to face his inquisitor.

CHAPTER 14
THE TRUTH WILL OUT

Roger entered his parents' home through the kitchen and yelled a greeting, "Mom, dad, anyone home?" His mother called from the living room for him to join her. She rose from the couch where she'd been reading the news on her iPad and gave hugs to Roger and Hana.

"Where are you going that you need your car?" she asked.

"Your son is hunting for a possible interview in New London," answered Hana.

"For that Chinese story you were working on?" she said to her son.

"Yeah, might be nothing but I have an itch I want to scratch. Where's dad?"

"At the hospital."

"Okay, give him our love. Don't mean to rush but we have to go. I want to get to New London by midafternoon latest."

In the garage Hana remarked on the cleanliness of the workspace and the number and variety of tools. "Wow. Looks like a racing mechanic's shop."

"I love to tinker with the car," Roger said, "it's an old diesel model, and keeping it pristine is a hobby."

The thirty-year-old Beamer started right up, and they made a quick exit. By noon they were on Interstate 95 cruising along the New Haven waterfront, the Yale campus just a few blocks away.

"Boola, boola, go Bulldogs," they chanted laughing.

The trip to Connecticut was something of a homecoming for both Roger and Hana. They had met as students at Yale, though both arrived there via widely different paths. Roger was born in the exclusive town of Old Greenwich, the only child of a prosperous orthopedic surgeon affiliated with the Yale Medical Center; his mother a nurse, then stay-at-home mom. The proverbial silver spoon meant he attended private schools and, given his father's position, his admittance to Yale was almost a birthright. There he distinguished himself as a history and political science major, which led after graduation to a starting position as a go-fer in a New Haven television station's news department. The Yale degree, plus his ambition and work ethic, propelled him quickly to field production, and then a reporter's position.

It was not unusual for someone with Roger's background to be hired away by a station in a bigger market, but it was more likely for an Ivy leaguer to be recruited by a network rather than a local station. The networks liked to think of themselves as more sober and intellectual than the local stations where "If it bleeds it leads," was the daily mantra. In the WNOW newsroom they said a reporter going from local to network was "Moving from the whorehouse to the cathedral." That was true even of reporters lucky enough to work in New York, the number one market in the country.

Local reporters didn't cover the White House or big international stories, but Roger liked local news because of the deep knowledge it provided of the politics and the people of a town. That's why he accepted the offer from WNOW-TV. However, his parents did expect that sooner or later he would exchange his station's blue blazer uniform for a sober suit and tie and get promoted into the cathedral.

That potential boost in status was also very important to Li Hana's parents. Her father had been the head of engineering at a Taiwanese computer chip manufacturer when he was recruited by Intel, and then stolen away by Google to work in its Artificial Intelligence division. The Li family had moved from Taiwan to Vancouver, to Seattle, and finally to New York where Yao's father was employed at Google's massive headquarters on the West Side of Manhattan.

Like Roger, Hana was also an only child, her mother a couture-dressed social doyenne and a member of some of New York's most desirable cultural Boards including the Metropolitan Opera, and Whitney Museum. Hana's parents were not at all pleased by her relationship with Roger. There was an element of snobbishness, even racism, in their perception of him as an unintellectual "roundeye," who, despite his Yale degree wouldn't amount to much. Her mother particularly scorned his work as a television reporter. "What are these meaningless stories he spends his time doing. Foolishness. Not really news at all. And what does he earn? A pitiable salary." Both parents felt he was not good enough for their daughter whose pedigree and education should have landed her a more desirable mate.

Though a dutiful daughter, Hana didn't obsess about their opinion; but did secretly believe Roger should aspire to become at the least a respected network commentator. If she decided to stick with him, she was determined to see that he did.

Neither Hana nor Roger suffered from a lack of ambition.

When the couple began dating, Roger's parents were similarly concerned about their cross-cultural relationship. But that concern evaporated on their first meeting when on arrival Hana presented Roger's mother with a beautiful bouquet of flowers. Roger's father was the most impressed with her show of respect. Leaning over to whisper to his wife he said, "What a classy thing to do. She was obviously very well brought up." From that moment, Hana could do no wrong in his eyes.

Driving past New Haven, Hana decided to call him from the car, "Hello Mister Barnes, it's Hana. We're passing not far from the hospital and just wanted to say hello."

Always charmed by her he said, "Why thanks Hana, delighted to hear your voice. I gather you're going to New London."

"To the Naval base there. Your son has some business. But just for the day."

"If you finish early, stop at the house on the way back and we'll have dinner together. We've no other plans."

Roger chimed in as he drove, speaking loudly so the car's microphone picked him up, "Hi dad, we should be able to make dinner, I'm not sure my meeting will even come off. I'm going to try to ambush some guy into talking to me."

"On camera?"

"No, no, just trying to beat the bushes to see what might pop out."

"Well, good luck, and drive safely you two. Hope to see you later."

After signing off Hana said, "Ambush? How are you going to manage that, you can't jump out of the bushes and surprise him since you don't even know what he looks like."

"Why, with your help of course."

"Uh oh. I thought I was just along for the ride. Why don't you fill me in on what supporting role you've obviously already scripted for me."

Roger told her that Chen was refusing to see him, and so he needed her to help flush him out.

"You want me to bird-dog him?"

"Like a pointer."

Roger explained his plan. Hana would call Chen, pretend to be doing a story for UN television and ask to meet him.

Her response was swift and emphatic. "Hell no! I'm not going to lie to the guy and risk my own credibility."

Frustrated, Roger pushed, "You don't even have to meet him. I just need to get him into the open. I'll take it from there."

"No way."

"I'm just doing what you suggested, knocking on doors. Besides it is the only way to confront him without causing even more grief."

"What do you mean?"

"Look, my only other option is to go to his boss, this McCarthy person, tell him why I want to find Chen and what

I'm researching. That suspicion would probably kill his internship with the Navy. Put at risk his whole career. This way it's just between me and him."

Hana saw Roger's point. There was enough reason to suspect Chen, and that suspicion had to be pursued. She also knew Roger had too much invested in the story to let it die. Hana agonized silently for a few moments but eventually agreed to play along. "I don't like it at all, but I guess it is the lesser of two evils."

Using her own phone, and with substantial reluctance, Hana dialed Chen's mobile. It was early Saturday afternoon; Chen was walking by the river enjoying the day off when the call came through. Seeing an unfamiliar New York number he was inclined not to answer, but curiosity got the better of him. He touched the green button, and tentatively asked, "Hello, who's calling?"

Hana, speaking Mandarin, gave her name and explained she was a reporter for the United Nations Web TV service and wanted to speak with him for a story she was researching. It was about mainland Chinese students studying in the United States.

"I got your name from the Columbia University director of internships, and yours sounds like such an exciting choice." But the last thing Chen wanted to do was talk about himself, or his internship to an international audience; he immediately declined her offer to meet. "I'm very sorry but no, I am not available here. I will be happy to help you when I return to New York."

"Mister Chen, I am on my way to Boston for another story and not far from New London. I would really appreciate just a few moments of your time. I don't have a camera with me; all I need are some quotes I can use. I mean, if you object to being filmed." Then in a pleading voice, "Please help me, I'm new in this position and if not you, maybe you can suggest some others I might speak with. I want to make a good impression with my boss."

Despite his reservations Chen thought such an interview might work well for Yao. A little publicity might help her journalism career. He would suggest the reporter do an on-camera interview with Yao instead of him. Who knows, maybe *The Times* itself might be interested in a profile of one of its own interns. Besides, he felt mildly duty bound to help Hana, a fellow countryman. Chen acquiesced and suggested they meet for coffee at three that afternoon in a McDonald's on Route 12, just outside the entrance to the Navy base.

"I feel like a real shit," Hana said after ending the call, "leading him on that way."

"What do you mean leading him on? I think what you're proposing would work great on Web TV," Roger said in a weak attempt to justify his duplicity. "You can make your pitch, and I will just happen to be there to piggyback on your interview." Even Roger, anxious as he was to discover Chen's agenda –if indeed Chen had one— felt it was a slimy move, and unfair to ask Hana to participate. But he would go ahead with the ruse, nonetheless. The thrill of the chase blinded him; he had not yet evolved a well-developed capacity for ethical judgement.

But Roger's qualms were unnecessary. Chen never showed. After disconnecting from Hana he called Yao to tell her about his impending meeting.

"Li Hana!" She all but screamed, "She's the reporter's girlfriend. She was at my house during the interviews he conducted. Her story is all bullshit, she's setting you up."

Chen, already skittish, turned furious at the deception. But what could he do? If he skipped the meeting it would seem like he had something to hide (which he did), but he didn't want to go and give Li Hana, or the reporter Barnes, a chance to grill him. He decided to call Hana back, play ignorant and politely cancel the date.

"Hello Li Hana, it's Chen Lin. I'm very sorry but a personal emergency has come up and I am not available to join you today. But I will be happy to speak with you once I return to New York. Thanks for your interest ..."

"Wait," Hana interrupted, "it will only take a few …"

"I'm very sorry, but this is urgent. Call me when I'm back in New York." He hung up.

Hana looked across to Roger driving. "Find a spot to pull over Roger. We have to talk."

Roger's not very well formulated plan had just fizzled. Minutes before they had crossed the bridge over the Connecticut River and were now approaching the town of Old Lyme. They stopped at a diner there to take a break and decide next steps. At this point they were so close to New London it made no sense to turn back. On the other hand, if Chen was going to duck them, why continue on? Sitting in a booth by a window Roger gazed distractedly at the nearby greenery, sipped a diet Coke and tried to come up with a way to salvage their trip.

"It's Saturday," he mumbled.

"Brilliant Sherlock, at least you know what day it is," Hana said sarcastically. She was relieved that the initial plan went bust. Roger had put her in the position of using her professional association at the U.N. to lie to Chen, and she was not at all happy about it. Roger was oblivious, but she had lost a lot of respect for him because of the deception. That added to her disconsolate mood. She was not, in this moment, especially proud of the man she loved.

"No, I mean it is Saturday so I'm not sure who I can reach at the base."

"As in?"

"To see if I can track Chen down and confront him in person."

"Ambush him," Hana said, increasingly unhappy with Roger's actions.

"Hana, I have to resolve these misgivings I have about him. I'm suspicious of his behavior, and his motives, and yet I know that I might be entirely wrong. To be fair to him, and to myself, I want to talk to him."

Roger's ambivalence and his admission of doubt about his own suspicions assuaged some of Hana's irritation. Maybe Roger wasn't being such a selfish bastard after all.

"What are you thinking?" she asked in a more conciliatory mood.

"Patricia Hamilton."

"Who?"

"She's the public relations officer at the Naval base. I have her home number." He fiddled with the food on his plate, a hamburger and fries he ordered only to justify taking up space in the diner. His appetite left him when he heard Chen had finked out.

"Hello Patricia?" Roger reintroduced himself after his long hiatus and apologized for disturbing her on a Saturday.

"No problem, Roger, I'm delighted to hear from a big shot New York reporter. I knew you when." She and Roger had worked on many stories together. Hamilton congratulated him on getting the New York job, a big coup for a young reporter. He thanked her, then asked for her help.

"Pat, I'm following a lead on someone who's been accepted as an intern at the Naval base and I'm trying to locate him, get his whereabouts. Nothing major but I need to hook up with him. Student by the name of Chen Lin. How would I find him?"

She asked him to wait while she checked the staffing directory. Roger's long professional relationship with Hamilton paid off, she came back with Chen's phone number and assignment. "He's working as an assistant to Captain Liam McCarthy in the submarine design division. They have him housed on the base." She gave the location of his apartment. "It's employee housing on Barbel Road right opposite the Commissary. That building has nice views of the river. Not bad digs for a kid." Roger thanked her and said he would give Chen a call.

But a call was really out of the question, it would just tip him off. Better to just show up on his doorstep. Now that he had a destination, Roger's newshound instinct kicked in. He quickly settled his check, and the two continued driving the short distance to New London. At the gate his police press pass and the arranged OK from Patricia

Hamilton allowed the couple access to the grounds. He made his way to Barbel Road and parked in the lot for employee housing.

"What now, Sherlock?" Hana repeated, growing ever more deeply unhappy with their mission.

"Damned if I know," Roger said looking at the multistory apartment house with who knew how many rooms. "I guess we see if there's a directory, or mailboxes which might give a hint as to which apartment is his."

They walked a concrete path around from the back lot to the building's entrance on the side facing the river. An unlocked aluminum-framed glass door admitted them to a small lobby. There was a locked, buzzer-controlled door beyond that. In the lobby was a polished brass plaque, it had a series of buttons with names and apartment numbers listed alongside. Chen Lin was marked on the label for apartment 4A.

"I'm going to ring the bell for apartment 5A," Roger said to Hana. "Whoever answers tell them in Chinese that you are looking for Chen Lin." He rang, and rang again, no answer. Roger then rang 6A, "Hello," a woman's voice with a Spanish accent answered.

"I am visiting Chen Lin," Hana said in Chinese, "Chen Lin please."

"Sorry, no understand."

"Chen Lin please," again in Chinese.

"Sorry, I no understand."

Roger rang the 5A and 6A buzzers again, as if confused about which bell to ring. The woman then did as he hoped and buzzed them in.

Hana thanked the woman in broken English. They entered, took the elevator to the fourth floor and listened at Chen's door. Silence. Roger knocked. No answer. He knocked repeatedly until it was obvious there was either no one home or Chen was refusing to answer. Finally admitting defeat, the two exited the building and made their way back to the car.

It was now close to four o'clock. Since they were stymied, a decision had to be made about whether to remain in the New London area for another day. Roger called his father to say they needed more time, and not to expect them in Old Greenwich for dinner.

"What are you going to do with the car?" his father asked.

"We'll keep it, I'll find a place to stash it in New York until I can bring it back to the house," Roger grumbled. Cars were nothing but a burden in the city.

That settled, the couple returned to the Beamer and waited, hoping to see Chen enter or leave the building. But after the warning from Yao, Chen had decided to make himself scarce until evening. He had taken an Uber to downtown New London where he caught an afternoon movie and followed up with a solo dinner at a riverside restaurant. He didn't return until ten o'clock, well after darkness. By then Roger and Hana had given up, they would find a motel and return the next day. Now knowing where he lived, Roger figured Chen couldn't avoid him two days in a row.

It was less than ten miles from Groton to Mystic, so Roger and Hana decided to spend the night at a hotel in the old whaling port. They found an online ad for the Harbor View motel and got a cottage right on the waterfront. It would have been a perfect honeymoon spot. As it was, this was no honeymoon, and the relations between the two were strained. They hadn't planned an overnight and so didn't have toiletries or a change of clothes. They flopped on the bed to watch the news before dinner, but their feelings of unkempt seediness just added to the dismal mood. Roger, the more oblivious one, tried to address the iciness that had been growing between them. He rolled on his side to face her and asked, "What's the matter Hana? You seem annoyed about something."

Not quite ready to pick a fight, she demurred, "Nothing. Just tired I guess."

"Well, this day didn't quite work out as I'd hoped."

"That's an understatement. At least I wasn't forced to perform an obscene act in your charade."

Her anger finally bubbling up she continued, "You had some nerve springing that role on me. You ambushed me like you were going to ambush Chen."

Roger pulled himself upright and tried to defend his actions, "I'm just trying to follow-up on a big story. To help people being used by a foreign government, and maybe protect this country."

"Bullshit. You were looking for a way to polish your own reputation. You don't care about Chen, about his fiancé Yao, about using me, about your country." Her bitterness getting the better of her, she choked up and tearfully spat out, "You care only about yourself."

Stunned by her anger and obvious pain, Roger slid off the bed and paced the room.

"That's unfair. But you're right. I should not have asked you to fake a story. I was desperate for a way to get at Chen, and I apologize for that."

"Words, words, words. Oh Roger, I love you so much and I can't stand seeing you cheapening yourself. Behaving like a shit. So unethically."

Properly chastised, and deeply in love, Roger slumped back onto the bed. "There's no one whose approval means more to me than you," he said, and mostly meant. He was after all a reporter, and owning a big story remained as much an incentive as anything on earth. But he learned one important lesson that day, he would never again play fast and loose with Hana's own career. "Whatever you think of my actions I promise not to involve you again in this story."

Hana was in no mood to buy into his apology or his promise. Still embittered and embarrassed by his sleazy behavior she aimed a vicious dart at his pride, "You've shown me you deserve to be stuck in that whorehouse you call a *news* station."

The vitriol was spinning out of control. Roger, whipsawed by her expressions of love and hate, knew he was in the wrong. He suppressed the violent retort he was about to make. Instead, he let Hana's own words echo in her mind until, inevitably, he knew she would regret them.

The two sat silently for a full minute until Hana got up and went to the bathroom to wash the tears from her face. Roger, abject and remorseful, moved to the doorway of the bathroom and watched her bury her face in a towel. Both now spent of emotion did what young people do, fell into each other's arms.

"Please forgive me. Never again," he said. Then softly, "Want to go to dinner?"

"Uh huh."

But before they left, the passion ignited in the heat of anger resolved itself in the sweetest, gentlest lovemaking. Their first big fight was over.

The next morning at breakfast Hana said the obvious. "This trip is over. You already know what you need to know, Chen is on the run from you, from anyone asking questions. That can only mean one thing, he's got something to hide. You don't have to force a meeting. You've answered the question you came to ask."

"I was thinking the same thing. What more could I get out of him other than a denial I wouldn't believe. The only question now is where I go from here."

"The government?" she posed.

"Hell no! I get information from the FBI, not vice versa."

"I don't know, this may be a case where a little prod from you could pay dividends."

"Make a deal?"

"You'll tell William Roscoe what you've learned *if* he agrees to tip you first on a raid or anything he finds. So yeah, make a deal."

"Would that make me a government whore?" Roger said with a smirk.

"Let's not go there," Hana said as she kicked him under the table.

They spent the rest of that Sunday visiting the Mystic Seaport Museum where they toured the historic ships, and the recreated 19th Century village. In the evening Roger and Hana drove back to New York, their relationship stronger for having weathered the previous day's storm.

CHAPTER 15
DEADLY MEASURES

Roger's persistence together with the connivance of Li Hana convinced Chen that he was under observation. His position in Liam McCarthy's group, and therefore his mission and his family's fate, not to mention his entire career, was at risk. Once again, he turned to the only person he could trust. On the Sunday Roger and Hana were touring Mystic he called Wu Yao. He was once again in a panic of apprehension, "Yao, I managed to avoid the reporter and his girlfriend yesterday, but I'm sure they'll be back. Maybe with the cops."

This time Yao did not try to hide her fear, "Lin honey, you have to go back to that bastard Zhang and tell him you think you've been discovered. Warn him that he must end any relationship with you, or the entire Chinese espionage program will be uncovered. It would create an embarrassing international incident for his government."

Chen objected, "I don't know if that would make any difference, there is someone over Zhang who is pulling the strings. Zhang is just a terrified quisling trying to keep his own head."

"Maybe so, but do you have any option?"
Despairingly, "I don't see one."

"No! And I think neither do they. If they don't want this whole mess to blow up in their faces, they have to call it off."

"You're right, I really have no choice. I'll tell Zhang I think a reporter is going to expose me and his plan unless he ends it now. Hopefully he'll back off."

"If he does, you can forget this all happened and actually enjoy your internship," she added optimistically.

That was a naïve hope. The moment Zhang Wei finished his disturbing conversation with Chen he contacted Ma Bai in his office at the United Nations. Zhang told his superior what he had just heard about Barnes's snooping, and Chen's panicked reaction.

"So, the only problem at the moment is this reporter, Roger Barnes?" Ma asked.

"It seems so," Zhang responded. He equivocated because he was afraid to mention that there was someone else. That Barnes's girlfriend, someone named Hana something, was also involved.

But Ma was not to be so easily put off. "What do you mean by 'It seems so?'," he asked. "Is the reporter the only problem or not?"

Zhang yielded, "There is some woman involved with Barnes who also tried to contact Chen, but all he remembered was the name Hana. And she spoke Mandarin."

"So you mean she also is suspicious of Chen?" Ma said exasperated.

"I guess, yes." Zhang finally admitted.

When this is over, I'm going to see this guy shot, Ma thought. Aloud he said, "Thank you Zhang Wei. I will take care of everything. Tell Chen Lin to proceed normally. He will have nothing to fear from Mister Barnes."

Ma Bai sat at his desk staring out his window. He was bathed in the soft sunlight reflecting from the glass-walled high rises on the Queens side of the East River. '*It seems*' *I will have to deal with more than one person. Zhang is such an idiot.*

He sighed, picked up his desk phone and dialed an internal number.

"Vladimir Ivanov?"

"It is he," answered his counterpart from the Russian Mission to the UN.

"I should like to schedule a meeting."

A time and place set, Ma contacted his country's commercial attaché and explained his idea. He wanted to enter into an agreement with the Russians and needed permission to make an offer. A very substantial offer which would require approval by the Ministry of Commerce. A call was made to Beijing and given the circumstances; permission was quickly granted.

The following morning, the two wary allies met in the delegate's garden restaurant and chose a quiet spot on the balcony for their coffee and a confidential conversation. This time, as in numerous times past, they were involved in a negotiation. Ma would present a need, Ivanov would counter with a wish of his own, and after protestations of unfairness by both sides, an agreement would be reached. It was a fairly routine bit of business. In this case it involved oil. China needed crude oil, it was already importing nearly two million barrels a day from Russia, and Russia desperately needed a market for its oil. A situation ripe for negotiation.

Ma began by explaining his offer, "Since the western countries have unfairly instituted boycotts of Russian products, particularly oil, because of the war in Ukraine, the Chinese people would like to assist. The People's Republic proposes to increase our purchase of your oil by one hundred million barrels this year."

"That is good news for Russia, and very welcome."

"In addition," continued Ma, "because there is some help you can give to the Peoples' Republic; we are also willing to reduce the five percent discount you normally credit us on such purchases. We propose instead a discount of only two and a half percent of the market price."

"Also good news, and very generous. But what exactly is the assistance you would like from Russia in return?"

This time, unlike in times past Ma's request was not commercial but of a particularly delicate nature. It involved the disappearance, or at least the incapacitation, of two American nationals. On American soil. Ma was proposing that to accomplish such a mission Ivanov would provide the manpower. Employing a tactic that was far from unusual, assassins would be released from a Russian prison as a reward for their service. The Russians had utilized such hit squads multiple times previously. It was a way to eliminate enemies and maintain deniability of the crimes. In the past the victims had mostly been anti-Putin oligarchs or political enemies. But to kill two Americans on American soil was, even for them, an extraordinary request. Ma stopped just short of that.

"We do not need, nor expect, the most radical measures be employed, but rather that these misguided young people be made to understand they are being watched. And of course, dissuaded from the continued pursuit of certain investigative activities." Then with emphasis, "By any means necessary."

"So you would be satisfied if a simple conversation got the required result?"

"That would be our preference. The cessation by these hooligans of anti-Chinese agitation is all we ask."

"But by any means necessary?"

"Exactly."

"I am not sure I can get approval for such a venture. But for discussion's sake do you think we can improve your offer to one hundred twenty million barrels, and at market rate? That is, no discount at all."

Ma was being squeezed but he had no choice. "I think given the special circumstances that can be arranged."

"Good. I will begin the process and we can address the details later."

Within days two Chechen rebels were paroled from prison and given the assignment. That these two men had the capacity to be ruthless to whatever extent necessary the authorities did not doubt. However, the long running hostility between Russia and Chechnya, made their choice potentially very risky.

***

    After the weekend excursion to New London, Roger was back on daily duty in the newsroom, Hana was back at her office in the U.N., and Chen was once again at Liam's side at the submarine base. He was concerned that the reporter might still make trouble but had been reassured by Zhang, who promised there would be further inquiries.
    "How was your weekend, Lin?" Margaret asked when Chen first arrived that morning.
    "Pretty quiet," he said, "I strolled around the base, went to a movie and dinner in New London. That's about all."
    "I heard from the base's PR woman, Patricia Hamilton. She said some reporter contacted her about doing a story on you and your internship. He ever call you?"
    Chen answered as calmly as he could manage, "Yes, he did. But I waved him off, I really don't want or need any distractions now. Told him I'd be happy to talk to him when I return to New York."
    "Probably smart. Besides, if a reporter showed up here Liam would have a fit. He's manic about security and doesn't want any loose talk."
    "My thinking exactly," Chen said with relief. Now he could turn his attention back to his job. One positive of the ever-present external pressures was they encouraged him, almost as a distraction, to focus on his work. He enthusiastically returned to analyzing the possible utilization of carbon fiber instead of stainless steel, for sections of the submarine superstructure. For the moment all he wanted was a few days in which to peacefully enjoy his internship, and mostly to forget Zhang, and that bastard's

demands. Purloining the submarine plans would have to wait until he had settled in, sometime in the next two weeks perhaps. However, what to do about his parents was an ever-present anxiety. It was one worry he couldn't bury for long.

***

While Chen tried to forget the trauma of the past weekend, Roger was debating what to do to reinvigorate his investigation. He was not a cop and didn't want to play the role of government snitch, but Hana had a point, if he wanted the Feds to keep him in the loop, he might have to play ball and give them something. Prime the pump as it were. He had no idea that his visit to New London had inspired a violent reprisal, with himself as the target, or he might not have had reservations about going to law enforcement.

"Bill Roscoe," the FBI bureau chief answered. Then after Roger identified himself, "How you doing Barnes? Anything new on the China front?"

"I was hoping you could tell me."

"We're working it, but nothing interesting for you yet. What's up?"

"I've hit a dead end, but it's an interesting roadblock and I thought maybe you guys could break through where I can't."

"Explain."

Roger told Roscoe about Chen's evasive behavior, the sensitive internship he had, and the suspicions of possible outside pressure being applied.

"He was a longtime activist in the student protests and then suddenly dropped entirely out of sight. Even his friends at Columbia think it's strange."

"Hmmm," Roscoe mulled, "could be nothing. Maybe he just doesn't want to screw up his internship."

"Could be, but maybe not. I'm stymied, I don't want to go to the Navy and bring suspicion on him if he's totally innocent."

"Right."

"But you guys can be more discreet, investigate without making a fuss. Something I can't do. Anyway, I think I've done my duty by bringing this to your attention. All I ask is you alert me if anything comes from this."

"Oh, so you're looking to be tipped off, maybe an exclusive?"

"I leave that to your conscience. Assuming you guys have one," Roger said with a laugh.

"I hear you, and thanks for doing your uh, civic duty," Roscoe said with irony. He was a career agent, nearing sixty. Heavy-set but typically well dressed in a blue suit, white shirt, striped tie and black shoes and socks. Very FBI, or IBM. Roger always thought these guys could be spotted as Federales a mile away. All Roscoe needed was an earbud, a lapel pin, and to whisper into the cuff of his shirt, to complete the picture.

For his part, Roscoe's view of reporters was anything but positive. *Leeches living off the troubles of other people* was the way he put it. And this Chen thing could just be a jaundiced reporter's wishful thinking. On the other hand, his guys on the China case hadn't come up with anything, or anyone, more promising. Might as well sic a couple of agents on Chen Lin and see what they uncover. Probably a good idea to track Barnes as well. Never know what he might turn up.

With just a few calls Roscoe put those inquiries in motion.

***

Devlin McCarthy and Marina were also back in New York. They had returned with the kids to their apartment, located on the first two floors of a brownstone in the West 70's, just a block from Central Park. It was Tuesday evening and they were seated around the kitchen table discussing plans for a two-week journey to Downeast Maine. They had scheduled vacation time together for mid-August. The accomplished sailors were happy with the performance of their boat *Coastie* after its two voyages in and around Long Island Sound. Thinking about the boat, Marina recalled their recent trip to Block Island and the overnight in Essex.

"I'm glad we got a chance to see your father in Essex last week, and even stop in New London," she said, adding, "And I enjoyed meeting that couple, Chen Lin and his fiancé."

"Me too," Devlin said. "That girl Yao is a real sparkplug. But Chen did seem a little reserved didn't he? Sad almost."

"I suppose so, but they certainly seem happy with each other. Perhaps he's just missing his girlfriend. Being away for the whole summer." Then Marina had an idea, "Why don't we invite Yao for dinner? She's probably missing him as well, and a night out might be welcome." "Works for me," said Devlin. "And Chen would probably be happy to know she was being entertained in his absence; and not by some guy," he added with a wink.

The dinner was scheduled for that Thursday, a simple home-cooked Italian meal of baked ziti, roast chicken and salad. Yao arrived with something she thought appropriate, a bottle of Montepulciano. Devlin skipped the wine, preferring a beer. After the kids were shushed off to bed the three adults reignited their warm friendship forged in Essex. They spoke of summer plans, the kids schooling, and Yao's work at *The Times,* which consisted mostly of research for others. She said she was expected to eventually rewrite stories from the Associated Press, and if all went well, to get a chance to report on a story she could pitch herself. Yao was upbeat speaking of her internship, but when the topic switched to Chen she became much more subdued. It did not go unnoticed.

"Do you think Lin is not enjoying his internship?" Marina asked gently, "You seem hesitant to speak of it."

Yao, afraid she was being indiscrete, put on a bright face, turned to Devlin and smiled, "Oh, he loves it. Working with your dad is all he could have wished for." Then, unable to contain herself she added, "But he does worry about his parents. Getting them out of China is always on his mind."

"I don't understand," said Devlin. "Are they in some sort of danger there? Why would he be so worried about them. I mean they've lived there, apparently happily all these years."

Yao started to get agitated, the conversation was getting too close to forbidden territory. "Oh, that's what I tell him. He is worrying for no reason. They're fine, just fine in Guangzhou."

Devlin looked at Marina and shrugged, "Well, okay but if there is anything we might help with, just ask."

Marina, concerned for Yao, was unwilling to let the subject go. "I don't even know where Guangzhou is. Is it far from China's borders?"

"No," Yao answered quietly, "But leaving China for whatever reason is not easy."

"Actually," chimed in Devlin, "Guangzhou is on the Pearl River and not far at all from Hong Kong or Macao. We had to study the area because of all the protests and demonstrations over there." He implied it would be relatively easy for anyone to flee from Guangzhou if determined to do so.

Devlin knew quite a bit more about overseas operations than he was letting on. He was a young graduate of the Coast Guard Academy in 2001, when Islamic terrorists brought down the World Trade Center buildings during the attacks on 9/11. He wanted to participate directly in the hunt for Osama Bin Laden and so resigned his CG commission and trained for the Navy Seals. He eventually served with Seal Team Eight as a Boat Driver, assigned to Djibouti at the mouth of the Red Sea in Africa. He served for a total of seven years, until Marina gave birth to their second child. That's when he retired from active duty with the Navy and returned to serve with the Coast Guard.

"Being near the water, and Hong Kong, I would think Chen's parents could find some way out if they have the resources," he said more specifically.

"Yes, well as I say Lin worries needlessly about his parents. But it's a great wish of his that they can come to this country and live near us. And eventually our children."

Anxious to lighten the mood, Marina brought in dessert and coffee. She had picked-up cookies and pastries to complement the meal, but after biting into one of the cream filled cannoli, Devlin was covered in powdered sugar, leaving him with something of a clown face.

"We can talk more about his parents' situation when Lin returns in the Fall." Devlin said with a full mouth, putting a comic end to the discussion. Much to Yao's relief.

CHAPTER 16
A FEDERAL CASE

Roger Barnes's visit with FBI agent William Roscoe resulted in the eventual mobilization of multiple government agencies. Despite initial skepticism, Chen's access to such a highly sensitive production facility sent ripples of anxiety through most of the country's intelligence establishment, including the DIA, the DNI, the DHS, the NCSC, the DCSA, the ONI, and the NYPD's Counterterrorism Bureau. Within this alphabet soup of government spooks and counter spooks, the operational lead for both the domestic and international aspects was taken by the FBI and the CIA. The Department of Homeland Security, which controls the Coast Guard would also have an operational role to play.

Within days a swirl of background papers was produced and circulated trying to identify who might be doing what, and what if anything was known about the actors. Specifically, their funding, their superiors, their motivation, and their timetable. Ironically, all this activity was built on a single report that a student with an internship at a classified site refused to meet with a reporter. A slim suspicion to say the least; but the job of those many, often rival agencies, is to uncover potential bad actors before they revealed themselves, certainly before they acted.

Since Chen Lin was a Chinese national, he was fair game for the CIA as well as the FBI. Oblivious to the fact he was suddenly under intense scrutiny, Chen did nothing to hide his communications with either Wu Yao, or Zhang Wei, who was still in hiding and holed up in the residence of the Chinese Mission to the United Nations.

The discovery of Zhang's whereabouts was the FBI's first big break in the spy chase which had begun with the discovery of the Chinatown "Police Precinct." The break came when a call Zhang placed to Chen was intercepted by the Bureau. It was Zhang's regular weekly contact to confirm all was going well. The government agents could do nothing about Zhang while he stayed inside the Mission building, but the startling fact that Chen was conspiring with the man who had overseen the Chinatown "Precinct," turned what had been a speculative investigation into an urgent matter.

Roscoe realized Chen had to be neutralized, and fast. The trick would be to do that without scaring off Chen's handlers. The government wanted to identify whomever else, beyond Zhang, might be implicated. Roscoe's first move was to alert Chen's supervisor, Liam McCarthy. It was not a welcome communication at eight o'clock on a Monday morning.

"You want to see me? What about?" was McCarthy's immediate response to an FBI inquiry.

"It has to do with your new intern; I'd rather not discuss it over the phone. I will be arriving in New London by noon. Can you meet me then in your office?"

McCarthy alerted Margaret to clear his calendar, and to tell Chen to take the day off, don't bother to come in. "Tell him I have a confidential meeting in the office, and I'll see him tomorrow first thing."

"What about me? You want me to disappear too?"

"No, you're cleared. I'd rather you be around, unless this guy objects."

Not two hours later the helicopter carrying Bill Roscoe from New York's Wall Street Heliport landed at the base in Groton. He was immediately taken to McCarthy's office where after brief pleasantries, and confirmation of Margaret's top security clearance, they got down to business.

Seated facing Liam's desk Roscoe laid out his concerns, "We have every reason to suspect that your intern Chen Lin is under the control of China's Ministry of State Security and that he has taken this internship to gather classified information. We don't have hard evidence yet, but want to be sure he is absolutely restricted in his access to any such information."

Liam and Margaret were stunned, rendered almost speechless, "But he is such a quiet, friendly ..." Liam began, but then cut himself short. *Of course, he would be.*

"Just so you are aware," Margaret said, "as of now Chen Lin has not had access to any of our latest classified material, all of it is kept in a secure facility." She meant the office safe.

"What we have been working on with him is the design of a diving plane, but that is run of the mill stuff, nothing extraordinarily sensitive there," Liam added.

"Can you tell me what you are working on which might be of special interest?" Roscoe asked Liam, not totally familiar with what was being done there.

"Sure, it's no great secret that we are in the late stages of designing the Columbia, first of a new class of submarines. It is meant to be a substantial improvement over current models. But everything inside its skin is top secret. Chen has not had access to any of that."

"So, if a foreign actor were interested in work being done here it is most likely about the Columbia?"

"Yes."

Assured that, to date at least, Chen had not been able to steal anything important, Roscoe relaxed. He said nothing definitive had been decided about what to do about Chen; if he had already stolen designs, or even had access to them, they would have to pick him up. As it was, he might be better used as a conduit to provide false information to China, either knowingly or not. It depended on whether Roscoe thought Chen could be flipped. Turned into a double agent.

"What do we do while you decide?" Margaret asked, still shaken by the news.

"I suppose what you have been doing until now, that is give him work that won't compromise anything important."

At this Liam bristled, "No way. I don't want him in this facility at all. If you are convinced he's up to no good, then this is no place for him to be roaming around."

This put Roscoe in a spot. He didn't want to leave Chen where he might do damage, but on the other hand he also would like to have the chance to flip him. Chen could be extremely valuable both for what he was working on now, and for what he might know about China's broader efforts at industrial espionage.

"Tell you what," he had a proposal for Liam. "Don't do or say anything to him today. But when he arrives for work tomorrow, we will have a greeting party. As much as it pains me to do this," he was referring to their interagency rivalry, "I am going to ask the CIA's New England station chief to join us. Chen doesn't know it yet, but his days working for the Ministry of State Security are over."

With Chen now safely on ice, the meeting adjourned. Bill Roscoe left saying he would confer with his brass, invite the CIA chief, and prepare for the next day's confrontation.

"Liam, I can't believe that young man is a spy." Margaret said sadly after the FBI agent left, "I think I'm a good judge of people and I really like him. So much for woman's intuition."

"And I had my son and daughter-in-law meet and sail with Chen! They too were charmed by him and his fiancée. Do you think maybe she too is caught up in this?"

"Well, if not it would be an awful way to start a marriage, concealing a secret life like that."

"So, it's likely she too is involved," Liam said shaking his head. "What a shame."

"Let's not get ahead of ourselves. We don't know for sure about any of this," Margaret said, "we'll know more tomorrow."

***

Chen Lin was not overly concerned when asked to stay away for the day. It was natural for Liam to have secure meetings to which he would not be invited. He decided to spend the day visiting Mystic and the historic sailing ships there. He was always fascinated with ship construction and would enjoy touring the old hulls and examining them with an engineer's eyes. Mystic was only eight miles away, a quick Uber ride, but he decided to check in with Yao before leaving. She was already at work at the Times and was surprised to get his call. He explained about his day off and his travel plans.

"Good, I'm glad you have some free time. Enjoy the day."

Chen was always cautious about what he said on the phone, but now free of the office and the smothering umbra of his assignment, he let his guard down. "I'm especially happy not to have to speak to my "friend" at the Mission. My next report isn't due until next week."

Yao, who had been editing a piece of copy was distracted and anxious to get off the phone, but his unguarded words brought her to attention. "Enough said," she said as a warning, "be discreet."

Brought up short, Chen quickly started talking about what he hoped to see in Mystic, then clicked off. But he was not concerned. All was going very well, and he had a free day all to himself.

He would have been horrified to learn that his call to Yao had been listened to and recorded. And it would be one of the things he was going to be asked about, come tomorrow.

When Chen Lin opened the door and strode from the hallway and into Liam's office the next morning, it was as if he were going through a transforming portal, exiting one life and entering another. It would be far from a painless rebirth. Facing him in a semi-circle we're the familiar faces of Liam and Margaret, both looking uncomfortable, and two strangers, Bill Roscoe and Nicholas Ferrante of the CIA. An armed Navy seaman closed the door behind him. He heard the lock click as it shut.

"G..G.. Good morning," he stammered, at once confused and comprehending, as if he always knew this moment would come.

"Am I interrupting something? Should I leave?" he said, trying as much as possible to sound nonchalant, and keep the terror he felt from distorting the smile on his face. It was at moments like this, when taken by surprise, that he felt most immature, as if a child caught in a grown-up world he was not prepared to navigate. He was after all a scholar, a scientist, not a James Bond action hero.

Liam spoke first, "Lin, these people are agents of the United States government, they believe you have not been entirely honest with us and want to speak to you." He pointed to a chair placed so Chen would sit facing the group. All were seated except Margaret who stood leaning against the wall behind Liam. Her eyes were downcast, as if she couldn't bear to watch what she knew would be unpleasant; distressed at what someone she liked was about to endure. Chen glanced at her, understood what her attitude implied, and refocused to face his inquisitors.

"I don't understand," he said weakly.

Bill Roscoe identified himself, introduced Ferrante and then laid out their concerns. "Mister Chen you have accepted a position in a naval facility of great importance to the security of this country, and we believe you may have taken this position for the benefit of a foreign power. Namely China."

Chen knew he had been found out, but still he stammered, "Wh..wh..why would you accuse me of such a thing?"

Roscoe told him of the phone intercepts, specifically his contact with Zhang, a known Chinese intelligence agent. Chen calmed slightly; he had a ready answer.

"Mister Zhang is well known to the students at Columbia. He does not like the protests in which we have criticized the government of Xi Jinping. Sometimes he calls to complain directly to me. I ignore him."

"Yes, we are familiar with his activities. But tell me, what exactly is the report about, the report you are expected to provide him next week?"

That caught Chen by surprise. How did they know about his reporting to Zhang?

Roscoe was fishing here. He had no direct information that Chen's "report" was for Zhang. Chen hadn't given a name when speaking on the phone yesterday to Yao. But Chen only remembered that he had been careless, he very well could have said Zhang's name.

Roscoe didn't want Chen to have time to think. He pushed harder. "You are aware that Mr Zhang is a fugitive? Hiding out in the Chinese Mission?"

"No, I...I...really..."

"And you are directly communicating with this fugitive, without notifying the authorities who have been looking for him?"

Chen's head was beginning to swim. He couldn't remember what he had said to whom, or when.

"And instead of revealing his whereabouts you told

your girlfriend Wu Yao yesterday that you were going to report to him."

"No... no... well yes."

"Is Ms Wu also reporting to Zhang? Is she working with you?"

"No!" Chen said with heat. "She is totally innocent."

"But she knows you're in touch with a Chinese spy master. And what you're doing here. Doesn't she? Isn't that right?"

Chen felt like he was being pummeled, repeatedly jabbed with punches he couldn't parry. The news that his calls to Yao were being monitored both terrified and infuriated him. He had no idea what these people might have learned. Now he regretted having told Yao anything. He started to sweat.

"No. She is a victim as well." He almost sobbed.

At this point Ferrante of the CIA broke in. He was to play the good cop. "Listen Chen, we know how these people work, and the pressure they can apply to completely innocent people. We know why you were asked to take this internship, and why you couldn't say no. And we want to help you."

He lied. He had no idea what particular pressure Chen faced, but he was well aware of the enticements, or threats usually employed to get an asset to cooperate.

Before his promotion Ferrante had been the chief technology officer of the CIA's Boston Station. An MIT trained chemist he was originally hired by the agency's Directorate of Science and Technology. His remit was to monitor the movement of materials needed to fabricate weapons of mass destruction, chemical or nuclear. During Syria's civil war he tracked the use of sarin gas in 2013 by President Bashar Al-Assad. The experience developed in him a healthy disgust for despots. Now as head of the agency's Boston bureau he was betting that Chen, a young student just beginning his career, was not an ideology-driven spy but was being coerced by the Chinese intelligence service.

"We have little to gain by arresting you now," he continued calmly, "but exoneration is possible, and certainly preferable for you."

"You have a lot to lose here," Roscoe added, baring his threat, "your career, your girlfriend, your freedom. So, think carefully about what we are going to propose."

Roscoe and Ferrante had no way of knowing, but their proposal had a good chance of being accepted since Chen was already full of hatred for Zhang, and whoever from the Ministry was pulling his strings. He was also angry with himself for caving under their pressure. He was ready to get out from under all this heavy manipulation but, and it was a big but, the safety of his parents remained paramount.

"Here's the deal," Roscoe said, "you will now work for us. We…"

"Wait!" Chen interrupted, "You threaten me with arrest. But if you do that, those who sent me would know why I could not help them. Arresting me would accomplish what I most desire, that I become free of them, and my parents would no longer be threatened. For that freedom, arrest is a penalty I would be willing to pay."

Chen's emotional outburst may have been injudicious, but it cleared the air. He had admitted he was supposed to spy, and most importantly why. Now the Feds could refine their offer for him to flip, to become a double agent.

Nick Ferrante spelled out the deal, "Most importantly for you, by agreeing to work for us you will not be arrested, your future life no longer imperiled.

"In return we will demand that you forward to Zhang any disinformation we provide about the Columbia program. Or anything else we want to feed them. You will also reveal whatever you learn about Zhang's superiors."

Ferrante then added that the CIA would try to help his parents ... if it could.

"No guarantees, but what exactly do you want for your parents?" Ferrante asked.

"I want them exfiltrated from China and brought to join me in this country."

"We have a global reach, but extracting Chinese civilians from the mainland would not be easy. All I can promise is that we will try."

Sensing victory Roscoe brought the negotiation to an end, "Are you with us? Will you do what we ask?"

Did he really have a choice? Chen knew he did not. The days of anxiety ridden duplicity were not yet over, but there was now the possibility of a positive, rapid, and final resolution. With resignation and some measure of relief he said, "Yes."

"You realize you will be under constant surveillance. Any wrong move, any attempt to deceive us and you will be arrested, and jailed and probably never see your parents or your fiancée again. You understand?"

"Yes."

Roscoe bullied him, he wanted the young man totally cowed. And he was. But paradoxically it was also a moment of victory for Chen. Even though he would now be leading three lives: student, spy and counterspy, at least he felt he could soon be free of the reprehensible Zhang.

"Does that mean he gets to remain here, on this base?" Liam asked with incredulity. "That's insane!"

Ferrante answered him, "Captain McCarthy, you will now have two jobs to perform: foremost your Columbia responsibilities but also assisting Chen to draw up fake blueprints to pass on to China."

One important thread had yet to be tied and it was Margaret who pointed it out, "What is Chen Lin's fiancée supposed to know about all this?"

The thought of lying to Yao caused Chen a gut-wrenching spasm. He grimaced.

Ferrante saw his pained reaction and said, "For her protection, and your own, it would be best if she believes nothing has changed in your relationship with the PRC. What she doesn't know she can't compromise."

Roscoe, turning good cop now that they had bagged their prey, added in a solicitous tone, "Once this is over and your parents are safe you can explain everything. She will understand."

But even as those words were spoken all present understood human nature enough to know it was most likely not true. If he lied to her now about his secret life, Yao would probably never fully trust him again. Such fundamental deception could ruin all their future happiness. Aware of that, Chen decided he would lie to these people, not to Yao. He would agree here to keep the truth from Yao, but have not the slightest intention of keeping to that agreement. With that decided he relaxed. Roscoe and Ferrante would do what they had to, and he would do what he had to. It was only fair.

Chen nodded to Ferrante, "Yes, you are right. She should not know anything has changed. I understand."

Chen's passage into this new reality had required a painful rebirth, but it was accomplished. That final issue settled; the meeting broke up. Now all that remained was for the new double agent to be put to work.

After Roscoe and Ferrante left, Liam looked at Margaret, "Ever have to babysit a spy before?"

She shrugged, but happy with Chen's decision to cooperate, and to survive, she had a smile on her face.

CHAPTER 17
GABE GETS A TIP

Every year Gabe Breslin would send out Christmas cards to a select number of friends with one-hundred-dollar bills enclosed. These "friends" were cops who worked in some of New York City's most active police precincts; the annual gifts were a token of appreciation for keeping WNOW's police reporter informed of potentially interesting cases.

Gabe would call in a couple of those favors early that sleepy August morning. The big town was unusually quiet. Sultry summer weather had inspired some overnight bar brawls and minor domestic violence, but nothing worthy of making the nightly news. Gabe sat at his desk at home and sipped his morning coffee. He grimaced at its sour taste and grumbled; it must have been sitting too long on the hot plate. He flipped through the *Times* and the *News,* no inspiration there, and so began working the phones. He called the 43d Precinct in the South Bronx, and the 108 in Queens, nothing shaking. His third call was to another of his Christmas "friends" working in the 60th Precinct, which covered the Brighton Beach area of Brooklyn. The Six-Oh was in a largely Russian speaking neighborhood, and home to many members of the Russian Mafia. Worth a shot.

"Hey Gabe, how's it going?" Sergeant Wilkes, the desk officer on duty greeted him.

"Quiet Wilkey. Very quiet. You hearing anything interesting?"

"Actually yes. Nothing confirmed, but there's been chatter about some out-of-town muscle coming in to do a job. Local bad asses are grumbling about being passed over."

"Any idea of the who and the what?"

"No, but in this neighborhood if someone is being flown in from outside, rather than employing one of our own goofballs, they're probably coming direct from Moscow."

"And you got no idea what the job might be?"

"Nah. So far it's just low-level whining. But if the static reaches us, it's at least interesting enough to get these local fuckoffs pissed at missing out."

It's not much, thought Gabe, but worth following up. He thanked Wilkes, clicked off and called a mobbed-up guy he knew, a minor player with hopes of making the big time. He was a Russian émigré, a bartender in one of the Little Odessa restaurants located in the shadow of the elevated train tracks on Brighton Beach Avenue. Gabe had done a favor for his sister, a high-end call girl who worked out of a hotel on the Upper East Side. Kept her name out of a story he did when she was swept up in one of the hotel's periodic raids.

"Sergei, you up?"

"Fuck you Gabe. I am now. Anyone tell you I work at night?"

"I have a C-note for your time. What are you hearing about some out-of-towners flying in to do a job?"

"Could be."

"From the motherland?"

"Yeah."

"More?"

"What's it worth?"

"Another C."

"It's a contract job. Couple of Chechens. Don't know the target but Putin's SVR is just the middleman. I hear the paymaster is Chinese."

"Strange. What could bring those two snakes together?"

"You're the reporter. Do your job."

"Nothing else? For the money, it's thin borscht what you're feeding me."

"It's about some nasty publicity the gooks want stopped."

"No idea what sort of publicity? Maybe industrial espionage?"

"You're talking above my pay grade."

"Hmm. OK, the check is in the mail."

"Fuck off. Pay me next time you visit."

"My love to your sister."

Could be all bullshit, but it also could be he was on to something. If it was a job engineered by the Chinese, using Moscow agents, his best bet was to go to the Feds. That meant a call to Bill Roscoe.

"Roscoe," the FBI chief answered.

"Hiya doing Bill, this is Gabe Breslin from WNOW."

"Good to hear you Gabe, I've been talking to that new guy from the station, Roger what's his name."

"Barnes?" Breslin said with an edge. "What about?"

"That Chinese Precinct story," Roscoe said with a laugh. "Seems he stole your story," then twisted the knife, "big-footed you Gabe."

"Yeah, thanks chief. Appreciate the sympathy. But speaking of the Chinese..."

Breslin then went on to explain what he was hearing and asked what the FBI knew about any collaboration between the Russians and Chinese. Because it might concern the sort of recent publicity that had embarrassed the Chinese, Roscoe hemmed and hawed. He didn't want another reporter nosing around and, like Roger, getting a bead on Chen. "Well, I don't know, but it could be that series of reports by Barnes got under somebody's skin."

This was all very close to home, very close to what Roscoe didn't want to talk about. To Chen. But Breslin's news that there might be a plan to stifle news coverage of Chinese spying meant Barnes, who was spearheading such reporting, was the likely target. And if, as Breslin was hearing, imported goons were part of the stifling, it could mean Barnes was in real jeopardy.

It was common knowledge, and Roscoe certainly knew, that the Russians had repeatedly in recent years killed, or attempted to kill, troublemakers both inside and outside Russia. They had no qualms about assassinating opponents, and there was no doubt they would do so again if needed. But the connection to the Chinese was mystifying. Why would the Russians help the Chinese stifle news coverage? What could be the nexus? That was a question Roscoe would pose to the CIA. The answer might lie with Nicholas Ferrante.

But for now, Roscoe wanted to keep Breslin at arms length. "Thanks Gabe. At this point I think you know more about what the Russians might be up to than I do. If there is a connection with the Chinese, it probably has to do with the coverage of that phony Chinatown precinct. How it might tie into what you're hearing, the possibility of foreign operatives, I'll investigate. It certainly is troubling. I promise to bring you in first if I find out anything more."

"I'm going to hold you to that Bill. Thanks."

After the call Breslin started to add up what he knew, or thought he knew: Russian agents of some sort were being brought into the U.S. or were already here; they were being asked to silence press coverage embarrassing to the Chinese government; that could mean the stories Roger Barnes had produced (he could think of no others recently reported).

What he didn't know: Why the Russians want to help the Chinese; who would be directing the operation, and what they mean by silencing the coverage. Could they actually be thinking of threatening or even killing an American reporter? Inconceivable! He had to go to Brighton Beach to nose around in person, but first he'd better talk to WNOW's station manager to give him a heads up about his concerns.

After he hung up with Breslin, Bill Roscoe's subsequent call to Ferrante was equally disturbing. He told the CIA chief what Breslin was hearing, "Gabe's informant thinks negative publicity is what incited a reaction. Whatever form that reaction might take."

"We should let Breslin keep thinking that. But for my money, I don't believe it's likely those TV reports of Barnes would anger the Chinese enough to precipitate calling in heavy muscle. It's not the first time the media has told the story of industrial espionage." Ferrante thought for a moment then speculated further, "It's more likely they want to keep Barnes from outing Chen. He's the key person here. The goal would be to protect Chen, keep him in place at the Electric Boat Works and allow him to complete his mission."

Roscoe quickly concurred, "Using Russian operatives to silence Barnes keeps the Chinese out of the picture, giving them deniability. And if the shit hits the fan and Barnes is hurt, the Russians can say, "Don't look at us, we have no dog in this fight."

The motive was uncertain, but apparently the likelihood was real that some imminent action was planned. Roscoe said they must immediately warn Barnes of the potential danger he was in, and that he'd better end all contact with Chen. By getting Barnes to back off, their newly minted double agent would get shielded from both the press, and the suspicious Chinese. It was a win, win. Meanwhile, the FBI, together with NYPD Counterterrorism, would start to track down whoever the Russians were planning to send, or had already sent, into New York.

The situation domestically was convoluted but looked to be coming together. For his part, Ferrante had to deal with a more delicate issue; a long-distance operation to assist Chen's parents' exodus from Guangzhou. It would be complicated in the extreme since according to Chen the couple was under constant observation, almost house arrest. He had promised Chen his parents would be extricated if possible, but fulfilling that promise would require the cooperation of multiple security services, the participation of rebel groups in hostile lands, perhaps hired contractors, or agents currently in place in foreign territory.

There was much to do on many fronts, but first he would join Bill Roscoe in New York. The two of them had to visit the offices of WNOW-TV News and ask for the cooperation of Dan Porter, the Station General Manager and Steve Wills, the News Director.

***

The office of WNOW's General Manager was on the fifth floor, one flight up from the newsroom. When Roger Barnes walked out of the stairwell and knocked to enter, he could see through the half-open blinds on the office's glass walls some others were already there, apparently waiting for him. Roger was keyed up, apprehensive, wondering why the boss wanted to see him. No reason had been given. He was told simply to come on up. Now! The presence of others added to his unease. He was scheduled to leave with a crew for Brooklyn in half an hour, another stabbing in the subway. The third this week.

Roger opened the door and was greeted by a phalanx of somber faces. The GM of course, with the News Director seated next to him, and Gabe Breslin; three WNOW-TV ducks in a row. Then there was Bill Roscoe from the FBI, *what the hell is he doing here?* seated on the office couch next to someone Roger had never met.

"Hi Gabe," Roger said in a confused mumble. He looked toward the fifth, unidentified person in the room.

Roscoe stood up and was the first to speak, "Roger,

good to see you. This is Nick Ferrante of the CIA, Boston Station."

Ferrante stood to shake hands, nodded briefly then sat down without saying anything.

Roger sat in a chair facing the others. Dan Porter, the General Manager got right to the point, "Roger, we are going to put you on a leave of absence for three weeks effective immediately. According to these gentlemen it is necessary for your own safety."

Bewildered Roger said, "I have a crew waiting …"

"Don't worry about that," interrupted Steve Wills, the News Director, "it's taken care of."

Roscoe then took the lead in explaining the reasons for the meeting and why they wanted Roger to disappear for a while. "Apparently, your series of reports on Chinese attempts at intellectual theft has angered some powerful people. According to what your colleague here found," he indicated Breslin, "there is a good chance you might be in some danger from hired thugs."

Roger turned to Breslin, his mouth open but silent in non-comprehension.

"It's just rumor at this point," said Breslin, "but in calling around to sources in Brighton Beach I found there is good reason to believe you're being targeted in reprisal for those reports you did."

"As in physically targeted?"

Breslin just nodded.

"You can't be serious," Roger all but stuttered, "those reports were not flattering to China, but neither were they totally new. Certainly nothing that should generate a reprisal."

"It's what some reliable sources are telling me."

"But Gabe, those are Russians out in Brighton, why would they give a damn about something embarrassing to the Chinese? Makes no sense."

Afraid this speculation might lead to Chen, Roscoe stepped in again, "We're thinking the same thing, so we have to dig deeper."

Roger then exploded the government's hopes of keeping Chen out of it, "It must be about Chen Lin!" Roger said emphatically.

"Chen who?" the WNOW trio said in unison.

Ferrante almost groaned aloud, and Roscoe put his hands over his eyes, barely repressing a smile. He liked Roger, for a reporter he really wasn't such a bad sort, and since he was the one to finger Chen, probably deserved to know what was really going on.

To his bosses, Roger explained Chen's role, how he had tracked him to New London, was given the brush-off, and how he had told Roscoe about his suspicions.

Wills, the News Director went apoplectic. "You told the Feds but didn't tell us what you found? Are you crazy?"

Roscoe stepped in again, "Take it easy Mister Wills, Roger really didn't have anything but a gut feel. We decided it was worth checking out, and without telling Roger we eventually confronted Chen."

Dan Porter the General Manager asked, "So all this talk about Roger's on-air reports inciting the threat of violence is bullshit?"

Ferrante finally spoke up, "The quick answer is ... maybe yes. It is important to the U.S. government that

Chen's involvement be kept out of all discussions of this matter. I am warning everyone in this room not to say a word about Chen to anyone. Very delicate negotiations involving him are ongoing and any mention of our interest in him threatens to undo our efforts."

Roger, sensing he was being sidelined rebelled, "So, what happens to me? If I go on a leave of absence does that mean Gabe gets to pick up my story just when it's likely to break into something big. I'm left out in the cold? Sitting on a beach somewhere? That's bullshit!"

The meeting, which had begun as a simple request that Roger take a leave of absence to protect himself, had degenerated into a squabble over newsroom politics. But Ferrante had a solution which, even as he said it, was as much a surprise to himself as anyone.

"Mister Wills how you use your news gathering resources is your call, but I suggest Mister Breslin pursue the unusual Russian involvement in this. Their threats, if real, are bound to lead to something undoubtedly newsworthy, and exclusive to you." He then turned to Roger, "And as for you Roger Barnes, if you can accept it, I'm offering to embed you in a mission which will take you out of harm's way here, and provide you with unique access to a story that you will not only report, but also have the opportunity in which to participate."

Roscoe, the FBI chief, stared at Ferrante dumbfounded, *What the hell does he have in mind?* Their interagency rivalry meant the FBI and the CIA were always jealous of any positive publicity going to the other.

Something that always had an impact on Congressional funding. Was he suggesting some PR stunt for the press? *Fucking CIA and its cloak and dagger bullshit.* But Roscoe had to agree, whatever the pretense, getting Barnes far from New York and away from Chen was necessary.

Even Steve Wills, the News Director, lost his scowl at Ferrante's proposal. Thinking of one of his reporters embedded in a high-profile spying operation he couldn't resist smiling and saying aloud, "Sleeper Spies: A WNOW-TV Exclusive Series of Reports."

CHAPTER 18
COLLATERAL DAMAGE

Roger was still suspicious that he was being shunted aside with this promise of exclusive access to… to what? He had no idea. Ferrante had not elaborated on what he had in mind. Hana listened to Roger gripe that he didn't trust either his bosses or the Feds. Or Breslin for that matter. Gabe could have invented all this crap about the Russian mob just to get him bumped from a story he broke.

"I can't see any reason why the Russians would come after me or give a damn about a Chinese operation going bust. It makes no sense."

"Unless they want a piece of it."

"A piece of what?"

"Of whatever Chen is offering of course."

Roger, who with his leave of absence had begun sleeping at Hana's, was pacing her living room. He stopped, thought about what she said, and slowly took a seat on her couch.

Yes, of course. Assuming Gabe was being honest, Chen's access to the Columbia submarine project had to be what the Russians wanted to be in on.

"What do you think Hana, who among the Russians and the Chinese could be running the Chen operation? Who was the deal maker here, behind it all?"

"Could it be the fugitive from the Chinatown 'precinct?'"

"Maybe." He began to ruminate likely scenarios: Where could such a conspiracy have been planned? It had to be where the principal actors were known to each other, and knew the students involved. Where did both countries have such knowledgeable, high-ranking personnel in proximity? *Why the UN of course, it was so obvious,* he thought, prompting a grin.

Roger's calculating mind immediately latched onto who could most help ferret out these likely officials, but it meant he must once again turn to Hana for help. He had already abused her friendship once, when he got her to lie to Chen about doing a story about him. This was going to be a delicate ask. He tried a little circumspection.

"Hana, who among Chinese diplomats at the United Nations would likely be aware of the plan to insinuate Chen into a U.S. submarine contractor?"

"Most likely whoever at the Mission was responsible for overseeing that Chinatown 'precinct,' or the 'Thousand Talents Program' as the Chinese like to call it."

"And that would be?"

"Beats me. But I would guess the chief cultural attaché. Or maybe the public relations or communications officer. They have the most contact with U.S. nationals, or with those Chinese students attending American universities."

"Any way you could get me a couple of names?"

Hana, burned by Roger once, gave him a withering look. "Why don't you just check the U.N. staff directory. They'd be listed there. You don't need me."

"Yeah, I guess you're right. But if it turns out one of them is involved with manipulating Chen it could turn into a major scandal. A story you might break exclusively." Roger was seducing her by stoking her own ambition. It worked. Despite her initial reluctance she bit the apple. Reporting on it from the UN might make her own career, allow her to move to a more mainstream news service. She agreed to get names and look for possible links to the Chinese 'precinct.' The apparent source of the covert threats.

Roger had one other inducement for Hana's help. He was quick to point out that both he and she were known to be working together to confront Chen, "The Chinese know you were with me. If I'm in any danger, physical or otherwise, you might be also." In other words, her self-interest, not only his selfish needs, should convince her to work with him.

The unfortunate possibility that Hana could also be a target of reprisal was understood by Ferrante of the CIA. And like Roger, he thought such a threat to the woman might somehow be made to work to his benefit. And he had an idea of exactly how that might happen.

***

Chen Lin and Roger Barnes were now under the control, and protection, of both the CIA and FBI. But also sharing intimate knowledge about the plans to steal the Columbia blueprints were their girlfriends, Wu Yao and Li Hana. Each woman had shared her boyfriend's confidences and either one could expose the planned espionage.

The tap on Yao's phone meant the Feds knew of her conspiring with Chen to keep his mission alive. That knowledge meant Yao posed a particular problem for

Ferrante; *Was she just innocently standing by her man, or was she herself working for the Ministry of State Security? Or conversely, did the Chinese think her intimacy with Chen a security risk which threatened their plans? Putting her in danger as well?* These were questions Ferrante had to get answers to quickly. He decided to cast his intelligence net a bit farther, to go beyond the Agency's assets in Russia to non-state actors in this country. Specifically, to the Russian criminal underworld in Brooklyn. He called Gabe Breslin.

"Gabe, I think there may be some collateral damage linked to Barnes's reporting and his trip to New London you should be aware of."

He then explained about the women, and his fears of their exposure to potential violence. "Perhaps when talking to some of your friends in Brighton Beach you can ask about them and shed some light on their vulnerability."

Breslin thought it unlikely, so far no one had said anything about women, but agreed to report whatever he heard.

Ferrante also shared his concerns about Wu Yao with Roscoe at the FBI, "Bill, what do we know of Chen's girlfriend Wu Yao. How witty is she?" Agency jargon meaning, how much does she know and whose side is she on. "Can you get me a dossier on her?"

"Sure, but why the concern, you think she's in danger?"

"Either that or she could be a plant and a risk to us. Whichever it is, we might have to move her away from the action."

All aspects of Ferrante's jury-rigged plans were coming to a head, seemingly simultaneously. A convoluted scheme to extricate Chen's family was taking shape and he was already considering staffing decisions. He needed to know if the women, as well as Roger, had to be removed for safekeeping, provided protection, or in the case of Yao, placed in custody.

     But before finalizing those local decisions he had to bring his bosses up to speed. Then he'd mobilize the assets needed in the Far East by reaching out to the CIA Chief of Station in Taipei, Taiwan.

CHAPTER 19
GOING ON OFFENSE

Nicholas Ferrante went to the Moynihan Train Station in New York where he boarded the Amtrak to Boston. He had reserved a seat in the quiet car to avoid distraction and took the opportunity to draft a memo to his superiors in Washington.

To: Director
From: Boston
Subject: Operation Neptune

To update you on the status of our response to the current concerns viz a viz the Columbia project.

We have initiated multiple actions in this country and overseas.

1. To protect the asset in place we have isolated him from any further contact with unauthorized personnel. (Specifically including reporters.)
2. We are attempting to identify the person(s) in overall control of the other side's efforts.
3. I am assembling a team to extricate the asset's family using contract personnel.
4. NYPD Counterterrorism, with our assistance and that of the FBI, is investigating rumors of foreign operatives smuggled into this country purportedly to silence criticism of their Eastern ally.
5. Navy Intelligence is overseeing the creation of an appropriate dummy device to submit to the

other side. It must be ready to be delivered by the end of the month.

The form of that counterstroke by the Navy was to be an elaborate disinformation campaign. Liam McCarthy and Chen Lin were ordered by Navy Intelligence to fabricate fake submarine plans for eventual dissemination to the Chinese. The goal would be to provide the Chinese design sketches of a fictitious boat, a distraction designed to protect the new Columbia Class submarines from effective countermeasures.

In his office at the Navy base Liam McCarthy pointed to a sheaf of blueprints on his drawing table. "Lin, the layout of our Ohio Class subs are well known to the Chinese government. There is nothing in these documents that would be new to them. What I want you to do is alter these in a way that will look real, as if they pertain to the Columbia class with substantive looking changes, but which will have no relation to reality."

"You want me to come up with designs which look innovative but are not?"

"Right. Use your imagination. I will check to be sure you don't accidentally put something in there which might be useful to their engineers."

Chen looked uncertain, unsure he was competent to do what was asked, "I can fool with the externals of the sub, the hull structure and so forth, but I don't know anything about the internal systems."

"Start with the hull, and we'll take it from there."

Chen began to devise what purported to be a new technology which, if copied, would create misdirection for China's own submarine research and development programs. It was both parry and thrust.

While Chen went to work reinventing an old submarine to look radically different, Liam took a break from his analysis of the last Columbia sea-trial. He called Margaret aside.

"Nicholas Ferrante wants my help finding crew for the Asian extraction."

"To get Chen's parents out of Guangzhou? What sort of crew?"

"Sailors. His plan calls for a small boat with a crew of 'tourists' to cruise innocently up the Pearl River and carry the old folks out."

"Whew! Talk about sticking your head in the tiger's mouth. It's pretty daring."

"Yes, but really it should not be especially dangerous. And it might be just outrageous enough to work."

"Well, you have a whole Navy yard full of sailors to choose from."

"Yeah, but I mean sailboat sailors, not submariners. The crew must look the part of civilian tourists, be competent, and on top of that, also speak Chinese."

"I don't want to cause you domestic anxiety but we both know who would fit the bill." Margaret was referring to Devlin McCarthy's Navy Seal history. This sort of extraction was precisely what he had been trained to do. And Marina had the skills as both sailor and linguist.

Liam anxiously rubbed his eyes and whispered, "What do you think?"

"He's your son. Together with Marina they have the necessary expertise, but there is at least some risk involved. And they do have two kids."

Liam looked relieved, "Yeah, I guess it's crazy. Forget I mentioned it."

"But don't you think it's their decision to make?"

"No!"

Liam's definitive rejection did not last long. After mulling it over he decided that, after all, it would be best to allow his son and daughter-in-law to decide for themselves.

That evening the couple were in their New York City apartment planning for their cruise to Maine. They had a three weeks' August vacation and were to shove off the next weekend. The two children would go with them.

"Hi dad, what's up?"

"Something I'm reluctant to mention but think you have a right to know about."

Liam briefly explained what the CIA was planning, that it had to do with protecting Chen and the Columbia project, that it would begin very soon and, if he and Marina were interested in leading the expedition they would likely be approved.

"What? You've got to be kidding! Just days before we leave for Maine? Wait dad, I'm putting you on speaker." Devlin wanted Marina to hear what his dad was proposing.

Her first reaction was predictable. She was not pleased. "You mean we cancel all our summer plans, send the kids back to my mother and travel half a world away? I think not."

Liam immediately backpedaled, "Okay, enough said. I'm not suggesting you do it, I just thought you had a right to know what was afoot."

Devlin asked, "Why us? The CIA has an army of operatives they can call on."

"Two quick reasons, your particular skills, and the timing. This operation must get underway in days. There's almost no time to assemble a team with the same qualifications."

"How long do you anticipate the mission will take?"

"I'm not privy to all the details but probably a week, maybe two tops."

"What's the risk assessment?"

"I don't really know; you'd have to talk to the CIA to find out more. But I gather the team would be composed mostly of amateurs who, if discovered, could claim ignorance, or just stupidity."

"You mean no physical danger?"

"I expect just what you face on a normal sail in unfamiliar waters."

"Could we be arrested?"

"If discovered I'd suppose you'd just be tourists who wandered to someplace you shouldn't be. Unlike the Russians, the Chinese are not arresting Americans on trumped-up charges."

"Yeah, I guess you're right about that."

The questions by Devlin meant the issue was not really settled yet. Not definitively rejected. "Let us talk about it and we'll get back to you."

Devlin and Marina had always been flexible and able quickly to shift priorities and goals. They were very unlike Liam, who found it difficult to change direction once he'd set a course for himself. It was something he envied in the youngsters. But even for these two, for whom a sailing adventure was irresistible, this was stretching their resilience. Their kids would be devastated, sure they loved their grandmother but ... they would have to be rewarded big time. Disneyworld?

"And all the research I've done!" complained Marina, "The stopovers on Cape Cod and the islands of Downeast Maine, all would have to be scrapped." Her head was telling her that saying a quick no to this particular adventure would be the right thing to do. Her heart was more ambivalent.

Devlin played advocate. "On the other hand, Maine isn't going anywhere, delaying until next year won't be such a sacrifice. The Far East for the North Atlantic. Not a bad trade."

After the first disruptive shock subsided Marina's wanderlust kicked in, "Sailing the Pacific is tempting, something we've always said we wanted to do."

"And there's not much risk involved. We're just visiting sailors on an exotic adventure."

"That's a role I know how to play."

And then there was Chen and Yao, for whom Devlin and Marina had developed a real affection. If successful, saving his parents would be an immense gift to those soon-to-be-wed young people.

Marina reminded Devlin of what he had said during their recent dinner with Yao. "Well big mouth, you told her if there was any way we could help get Chen's parents out of China we would."

"I didn't say exactly that, but sure I would like to help."

"What do we tell the kids?" Just posing this question meant Marina's decision had already been made.

"They are only five and three, they'll get over it and we'll make it up to them."

"I don't know," Marina demurred, "you think they will hate us forever?"

"Dad says it should be only a week, two weeks max. When we get back, Disneyworld, and they won't even remember we were gone."

***

With Devlin and Marina on board, Ferrante had assembled the most critically important part of his crew. Since Roger was already promised a berth, he needed just one more person to complete his staffing. Another Mandarin speaker was essential for backup and so if Hana was also being threatened, it would serve to have her join alongside Roger; both to protect her and for her language skills. There were other benefits to including the couple: Roger would provide additional muscle on the boat, if not sailing expertise, and Hana would add language redundancy, and an always welcome additional hand aboard the vessel. That decided, it was time to pull all the pieces together.

***

"Roger, it's Nick Ferrante. I want you ready to join my crew in three days. By this Saturday. You will be flying to Asia."

"Asia? What exactly is this project you've drafted me for?"

"All will be explained when we meet. Oh, and before you go, I will want to speak to your girlfriend Li Hana."

"Hana? What do you want with her?"

"This might disappoint you, but I'm going to request that she join you."

"You've got to be kidding!"

"We have reason to believe whoever is unhappy with you has designs against her as well."

Roger had already come to that conclusion, so he readily agreed it made sense for Hana to also disappear from New York for awhile. But he explained to Ferrante how and why she was already looking into some possible connection between China's United Nations' personnel and the manipulation of Chen.

Intrigued, Ferrante said, "Very good idea indeed. But let us take over that angle of inquiry. I am afraid she may already be in some danger," he then added, "I want the two of you to come to a meeting in our New York office, nine a.m. on Wednesday. I'll introduce you to the other team members and finalize plans for your departure this weekend."

"Wait, what about Hana's boss? She can't just up and leave her post."

"Don't worry about that, the government will notify her boss that Hana's translation skills are urgently needed for an upcoming conference in Taiwan. Convenient don't you think?"

"You guys are pretty imperious, aren't you?"

"What can I say, national security and all that. Your tax dollars at work."

Roger snorted derisively, "Right. We'll see you Wednesday."

"Explain to her why we want her to desist from snooping around the Chinese Mission. No sense poking the tiger sooner than we need to."

The meeting of the Guangzhou team took place in the Federal Building in Lower Manhattan. After depositing their personal electronics in small lockers, the participants were ushered into the "SCIF" room, a space designed to be secure from listening devices. In the way of mind-numbing government nomenclature, it was labeled the Sensitive Compartmented Information Facility. Anyone in a SCIF was said to be, "working on the high side." The SCIF did have windows, but they were layered with a special material to block electronic eavesdropping. The claustrophobic room was furnished with desks and secure computers and phones but was otherwise plain, without art on the walls or decoration of any kind.

Coffee and donuts were on a desk, allowing an informal moment for the strangers to shake hands and introduce themselves. They then settled around an oblong conference table, Roger and Hana seated next to each other, Devlin and Marina across from them, and Nicholas Ferrante at one end between the couples.

"Thank you all for agreeing to participate in this project," Ferrante began. He was relaxed, as if they were meeting to consider the creation of a new neighborhood playground. But the mood changed quickly when he opened by saying, "This mission is not especially dangerous, but it is also not risk free. Be assured however, we will take every precaution to ensure its success and your quick and safe return."

Roger, impetuous as ever jumped in, "Why don't you start by telling us exactly what we are being asked to do, and why each of us is here."

"Sure. Excuse me, I didn't mean to get ahead of myself; and I must pause now to tell you that everything we discuss in here is privileged information. If you agree to stay you will be bound by our government's secrecy laws. You will never, without permission, divulge what you are told here or you will face prosecution. If you cannot agree to that please leave." Eyes glanced left and right but no one moved.

Ferrante continued, "Okay then, you all know Chen Lin and his fiancée Wu Yao. And as you four are also already aware, Chen has been forced by the Chinese government to spy on this country's Columbia nuclear submarine program." The four nodded, affirming their previous knowledge of Chen's forced acquiescence.

"We, that is the security services of the United States, have reached an agreement with Chen Lin by which he will cooperate with us, do our bidding. As you can imagine, this is an extremely important arrangement." More silent nods of assent. "For our part, we have promised to try to extricate his parents from China. You all will be part of that initiative. As a matter of fact, the principal part."

Looks of concern and doubt were exchanged by the foursome. China? What had they got themselves into?

"And how exactly are we supposed to accomplish that? Sneak into China and kidnap them? It sounds insane. And why the four of us?" Roger pressed.

"Let me explain first what it is we want you to do. Hopefully, that will help you understand why each of you is here."

Ferrante then laid out the plan as it had been negotiated with the Chief of Station in Taiwan. The four of them would fly to Hong Kong ostensibly as tourists. There they would be introduced to participants in Hong Kong's so-called *Water Revolution*.

"The name refers to the movement's shapelessness. Flexible, able to dissolve and reassemble in any form. The militants you'll meet are students who took part in the city's long simmering, often violent anti-China protests. They consider us allies in their struggle."

He explained the students would take the four of them to a local marina where they would be provided with a chartered sailboat. Those arrangements will have been already made by the CIA. The Americans would then begin a weeklong cruise in the South China Sea, pretending to be tourists on a sailing adventure.

"Hong Kong is located near the mouth of the Pearl River. The area is a popular cruising ground. Just ninety miles up the Pearl is Guangzhou, where Chen's parents live. You will meet his parents there, take them onboard, and sail downriver to the gambling mecca of Macau where we will be waiting to extract them."

Devlin, skeptical like Roger before him, huffed loudly at that. Even with his experience, he objected to Ferrante's overly rosy presentation. "You certainly make it sound easy. Get a yacht, sail a hundred miles into an alien country, pick up people we have never seen before, who don't know us, and then spirit them away. Really? And with a crew composed mostly of amateurs? I see potential trouble at every stage. Even something as uncontrollable as the weather could sabotage us."

Ferrante didn't flinch or try to sugar coat it. "You're right. At every stage something could go wrong. For example, at this moment I don't know how reliable the students in Hong Kong are, or the exact boat they'll provide, or the security on the river, or precisely how we will get Chen's parents to meet you. Everything at every juncture will be fluid and require you to be flexible. These plans are more a general outline than a precise directive. Hopefully, by the time you arrive there this weekend we will have more concrete information."

"And how will you get that information to us?" Devlin asked.

"By the folks who will meet you in Hong Kong, and an encrypted satellite phone with direct link to me."

"And what happens once we drop the parents in Macau," said Marina, speaking for the first time, and as usual focusing on specificities.

"Macau is directly across the Pearl River delta from Hong Kong. We'll fly Chen's parents out from there. And you all as well, if that becomes necessary."

Hana turned the discussion back to their recruitment, "Why me? What am I doing here, or Roger, or any of us? Why have you chosen us, mainly civilians, to do this?"

"Two reasons, because you have the specific skills we need, and because you are here and available right now."

Ferrante pushed his chair back and addressed each couple separately, "Devlin, as a former Navy Seal and current officer has all the expertise required and will lead this effort. Marina because you are an experienced sailor and speak Mandarin, and Cantonese, especially valuable in Guangzhou. Also, you both have a personal relationship with Chen, and his fiancée, that should prove helpful dealing with his parents."

Roger, hearing that he would be teamed with a Navy Seal got enthusiastic. It meant he had a character who was sure to add interest and drama to his reports. Besides, he was a little star-struck at the thought of working with one of the country's legendary warriors.

Roger looked at Devlin with renewed interest. "A Navy Seal?"

"Actually, I was called a Special Warfare Combat Crewman. A boat driver. We're the guys who deliver the Seal operation teams to where they have to go, and then get them out again."

What exactly did you do?" Roger asked.

"I was stationed at a U.S. base in Djibouti, Africa. The Chinese had constructed a base of their own right next to ours, so it became an intelligence war zone. Nonstop snooping on each other."

"So, you were a spy?"

"I was a Seal Boat Operator, but we had other duties."

"Such as?"

"To gather information my team would pretend to be sailors on a charter boat. Just touring the Red Sea. We travelled in company of other boats, real cruisers, we visited local ports and gathered whatever intelligence we could."

"You pretended to be civilian sailors?"

"Right."

"Just like we will be doing?"

"Uh, huh."

Now it was clear to everyone why Devlin was picked for the current operation.

"Tell him your team's motto," said Ferrante.

Devlin smiled, "On time, On target, Never quit."

"Ooooohkay," Roger said.

Ferrante stood and paced, as if the momentum of the operation was already beginning to accelerate, and he with it.

"Now, I have to lay down the law here. Because you will be operating on a boat there can only be one person giving orders and that person, given what you just heard, is going to be Devlin. It won't be a democracy. He will be your captain and when on the boat you will do what he asks, when he asks it. No questions. And if for any reason he is incapacitated Marina takes charge. I think you all will agree that makes sense." The four, suddenly sober, nodded their approval.

As if he had burned his nervous energy, Ferrante sat again and faced Roger.

"Roger knows why he is here, he will be given permission to document this extraction as an embedded reporter," then he added pointedly, "though not until we say he is free to make what he sees public. Unprecedented access for a CIA operation. When the time comes you truly will have a scoop, an exclusive."

Lastly, he turned to answer Hana, "And you Hana for your knowledge of Mandarin of course, but also because we want you out of New York for as long as it takes to wrap this up. For your own safety."

"My safety?" Hana questioned, "why might I be in any danger."

Roger answered, "Hana, it's like we talked about. Whoever knows I was tracking Chen knows you have the same knowledge. Until they think Chen's work is done, they might do anything to protect him."

Ferrante nodded to confirm Roger's words, but then added, "Hana please know that there are many people working right now to identify, and neutralize, any potential threat against you, or Roger, or anyone else involved. But we have to assume, if the rumors we hear are true, that these are dangerous people, and we are anxious for your welfare. It may be ironic but despite the uncertainties of this little adventure, you could be safer in the South China Sea than hunkered down here at home."

"Little adventure!" Hana said with a high-pitched squeak, then smiled as she grabbed Roger's hand, poked him in the stomach and said, "Here's another nice mess you've got me into."

Everyone laughed.

CHAPTER 20
OPERATION NEPTUNE

The drop-dead date for the completion of all aspects of Operation Neptune was set for Monday, the second of September, Labor Day. Two weeks away. That holiday marked the end of the summer break, students had to be back because classes for the next semester at Columbia would begin that week. Most importantly for Chen Lin and those involved in the submarine deception, it marked the end of his internship. As far as the Chinese knew he would no longer have access to the Electric Boat Works, so everything he had accumulated, or fabricated, must be ready for delivery to Zhang by that time.

The same deadline was faced by the other two elements of what had by now been given the code name "Operation Neptune," for the three prongs of the god's Trident. The tripartite nature of the investigation meant the clock was ticking for all of them: for Chen, for the team going to Guangzhou, and for those dealing with the Chechens.

The division of labor for these three initiatives was straightforward. Nicholas Ferrante and the Boston branch of the CIA would lead the Guangzhou raid. William Roscoe and the FBI working together with Naval Intelligence, would oversee the creation of the bogus blueprints to be drawn by Chen Lin and Liam McCarthy. Finally, the NYPD Antiterrorism Bureau tapping into the resources of both the FBI and CIA would lead the hunt for the Chechens, or whomever it was the Russians were believed to have brought into the country. Of course, Gabe Breslin was also a source, and a beneficiary, of information found about the assumed assassins. A chance for yet another exclusive report for WNOW-TV. The station was now enmeshed in the investigation.

Ferrante rushed the departure of the foursome to Hong Kong because of the press of time. He explained his current thinking to Roscoe at the FBI.

"I fully expect the exfiltration operation to take less than a week, but I want a second week available as slopover, a cushion in case things did not go as well as hoped."

"How will they be equipped?" Roscoe asked.

"Nothing special. While traveling they will pack like tourists. No weapons, radios, or extra hardware. Just clothing appropriate for the weather, personal toiletries, and standard mobile phones and iPads."

"Passports, visas and ID's?"

"All provided by us. If questioned, none of them will be traceable back to Chen in any way. Especially Roger and Hana."

"What about comms?"

"A satphone will be provided in Hong Kong."

Roscoe sat silent for a moment then shook his head, "I don't know. Even with Devlin in command ..." He let his skepticism hang unspoken, like a black cloud of obdurate reality to dim Ferrante's apparent optimism.

"Look Bill, I've got no illusions. The chances of getting Chen's family out of there are probably no better than fifty-fifty; it's a calculated gamble but we made a deal ..."

"Yeah, and those poor shmucks are the chips."

"Patriots."

Roscoe was glum, pessimistic. "If you say so Nick, if you say so."

Ferrante countered that the risk for the foursome was minimal, "Honestly, I don't think Devlin and the civilians are in any danger. They can always claim they were tourists who wandered where they shouldn't. If anything, a stern warning and they'd be let go. It's not like it's Russia."

Roscoe still demurred, "Unless they're stopped with Chinese citizens aboard."

Ferrante threw his hands up at that, signaling there was always some danger involved. "All we can do is minimize the risk, not eliminate it."

"The trip downriver with their human cargo will be a nailbiter."

For the CIA officer the calculus was hard-nosed, if also hard hearted, "If Chen's parents make it out, great, we can celebrate. But even if they don't, we will have done what was promised. That's what I care about."

***

Ferrante was happily relieved when that Saturday afternoon, Roger, Hana, Devlin and Marina were finally aboard their flight over the north pole and across the Pacific. Their sixteen-hour flight landed at seven in the evening the next day. They went through passport control and customs without incident. After collecting their luggage, the four were met outside the international airport by a waiting van.

The driver was a member of one of Hong Kong's rebel groups.

"My instructions are to take you directly to the hotel. It is located on a marina in the Gold Coast area. Near Pearl Island."

"I think you know more about our plans than we do at this point," ventured Devlin. "We've been given precious little in the way of preparation."

The driver smiled, "Don't worry, we are all on a 'what you need to know, when you need to know it' basis."

"Isn't that something like the blind leading the blind," Roger quipped.

"A briefing is scheduled for tomorrow morning, after which you will check out of the hotel and go aboard your boat."

"I just want a shower and a bed as soon as possible," Marina said in Mandarin, "I feel scuzzy all over."

"Me too," echoed Hana.

The driver looked at the women and nodded to himself; he figured the agents must be multi-lingual. He was not aware that only the women understood Chinese and apart from Devlin, all were civilians.

The drive took them past the Hong Kong Disneyland, a little bit of transplanted California, around Tung Wan Bay towards Butterfly Beach.

Using their fake passports the two couples checked into a luxurious high-rise hotel and without so much as a late day snack, showered and went to bed.

The next morning they received a message on their in-room phones to please meet at eleven on the twentieth floor, Room 2015. Late enough for them to have a good sleep and a bit of breakfast.

At the appointed time and place they met a young man and woman who said they would be their contacts in Hong Kong, and available for any unforeseen issues which might arise.

"We do not know who you are and neither do you know us," said the woman, a slim but very intense looking college student. "But we will help as we can."

Her partner said, "We have a boat provisioned for your use now. It is a fifty-foot catamaran and can easily sleep six. We were assured you can you handle such a vessel."

Devlin answered, "I'd like a walk through and some instruction on the electronics and navigation aboard, but other than that if we have charts, fuel, food and water we should be okay."

"What do we do with the boat once we have completed our project?" Marina said.

The woman smiled. "Unfortunately, we are inventing this as we go along. Ideally, you would return the boat here at the marina. However, there is a good chance that won't happen. And to be truthful, I don't think anyone really cares what happens to the boat."

"You mean we could just ditch the boat. Anywhere?" Roger said nonplussed.

"As I understand it, what happens to the boat is not a major concern to anyone involved."

"Ooooohkay," said Hana, "I hope those people 'involved' don't feel the same way about the folks on board that boat. I would like to make it back home."

"That is not for us to say," the woman said with a smile, "but I am under the impression your welfare is *not* of minor importance."

"Well, that's good to hear!" Hana said with a snort.

CHAPTER 21
THE RUSSIAN CONNECTION

Of the three lines of attack simultaneously underway, two were totally manipulated by Federal security agencies: the fabrication of fake submarine plans, and the extrication of Chen's family. The third initiative, the hunt for the Russian hit squad, required outside, that is local New York City involvement. That was going to come from the NYPD and Gabe Breslin who had already started his deep dive into the Russian connection.

Breslin figured he'd gotten all he could from his local contacts, his next approach would be to Joseph Mitchell of the NYPD Counterterrorism Bureau. Mitchell's sources in Brighton Beach might not be any better than Gabe's, but he was privy to more confidential information emanating directly from Russia.

"Joe, it's Gabe Breslin. I'm tracking down some rumors floating around Brighton Beach."

"Hi Gabe, rumors about what?"

"Scuttlebutt tied to the Chinatown Precinct story. From what I'm hearing the Russians are looking to put a gag on that reporting. Helping their Far East cousins."

"Interesting," Mitchell said evasively, not knowing what Breslin was privy to, "what are you hearing?"

"Mother Russia putting a bear hug on anyone pushing anti-China stories. I heard muscle has been brought in from Moscow. A couple Chechen guys."

"And who are you hearing this from?"

"Among others, your friend Bill Roscoe, and some spook from the CIA based in Boston."

"Nick Ferrante?"

"That's him. They are concerned about the safety of our hot young reporter Roger Barnes, your recent buddy. So they briefed the brass at WNOW. Which is I how I got involved."

"Don't remind me of Barnes, his story about Zhang Wei got me in a hell of a lot of trouble."

"See, that's what you get for talking to newbies."

Mitchell gave a rueful laugh but then relaxed. The fact Breslin had been brought into the investigation by the Feds made it easier for him to open up and share what he knew. A case of one hand washing the other. But first, thinking of the grief he got for talking to Barnes he added, "Now this is on deep background, agreed?"

"Agreed." That meant what he would be told could not be publicly reported.

"Well, you're hearing right. There's a full court press on for information about what at this point is only conjecture about a possible Russian hit job in the works. You said you heard this from the Feds ... and others. Who are the others."

"Couple of sources in Brooklyn."

"Brighton?"

"Yes."

"Figures. As of now we don't have much."

Mitchell said inquiries were already being made in Moscow and among New York CI's, Confidential Informants. He also said they were actively trying to locate recent arrivals from Chechnya and had a couple of leads. The most promising involved two brothers recently released from

Moscow's infamous Butyrka prison where they had been serving a life term. Mitchell said the brothers had been sentenced as terrorists who fought for Chechen independence from Russia back in the 90's. According to the CIA they were freed by Russia's Federal Security Service, the principal successor to the old KGB.

"What the Feds are telling us is that the two released men, Aslam and Shamilov Borz, were then seconded to a brother agency, the Foreign Security Service or the SVR, which handles foreign intelligence. The two disappeared after their release from prison."

This was Breslin's first big break. Up until then all he had to go on was that the men he was looking for were thought to be Chechens. And the only archival news he could find involving anyone from Chechnya was of the Boston Marathon Bombers: Dzhokhar and Tamerlan Tsarnaev, who were also brothers. But their arrest in 2013 brought nothing but fear and shame to the Chechen community, most of which was centered in Paterson, New Jersey.

"Joe, you know the biggest Chechen community hereabouts is in New Jersey?"

"Sure," said Mitchell, "we're already working that area."

"Right, but I think that could be a dead end."

"Why so?"

Breslin explained his reasoning.

"Anyone working for Vladimir Putin would be persona non grata in New Jersey. I think these guys would rather try to disappear into the Russian underground in Brighton Beach."

Breslin told Mitchell, instead of Paterson he would return to Brooklyn and concentrate his efforts there. Now he had something he didn't have before, a couple of names.

That afternoon Breslin drove his own car to Brooklyn. It was a long way from his place on King Street just south of Greenwich Village to the area called Little Odessa. He drove down the West Side Highway through the Brooklyn Battery Tunnel to the Belt Parkway, exited on Ocean Parkway and parked under the elevated train tracks on Brighton Beach Avenue. It was five-thirty on a Friday afternoon and in the shadow of the El local bars and restaurants were preparing for the usual weekend invasion of tourists and celebrating locals. It didn't take much of an excuse for the Russian expats to party with a big dinner punctuated by ice-encased bottles of vodka planted on each table. Breslin locked his car and ambled over to Third Street and into the darkened expanse of the Restaurant Georgia. Sergei was behind the bar polishing wine glasses.

"Wine glasses? Does anyone drink wine in this joint?" Breslin said sitting on a stool.

"The women. Got to have wine for the women. Now what the fuck do you want, or are you here just to give me my money?"

No one else was around, so Breslin opened his wallet and slid two one-hundred-dollar bills across to Sergei.

"A man of my word," he said. "There could be more of those. I got names."

Sergei stopped wiping long enough to stare at Breslin and mumble, "What, you want to get me killed?"

"Nobody cares about them Sergei. Their own people hate them for working for Putin, and the Russians hate them for being Chechen. You'd be doing everyone a favor."

"You're wrong. But what's it worth?"

"Depends on what you got. Tell you what, I mention names and you nod yes, or shake no. You don't have to say anything, and you get another two of those notes."

"Five."

Breslin winced but this could be the whole ball game, he nodded okay. Then he said, "Aslam and Shamilov Borz."

Sergei looked around, confirmed that the restaurant was still empty, then nodded in the affirmative.

Bingo. Breslin grinned, congratulating himself.

"Where? Here?"

This time Sergei shook his head. "No."

That took Breslin by surprise. Not in Brighton? Then where? And why?

Sergei visibly relaxed now that he knew the people Breslin was looking for were of no interest to the Russian Mafia. "Those guys are nowhere around here. Their whole family are heroes in Chechnya. The Russians in this neighborhood would love to see them dead."

Breslin was now totally confused. Everything he assumed about the brothers was apparently wrong. Maybe Mitchell was right after all, he should be looking among the Chechens in Paterson, New Jersey. Dejected, he slumped and exhaled.

"Pour me a Belluga Gold, double, on the rocks."

Sergei poured the vodka and Breslin passed him his money.

With the money in hand Sergei became more loquacious.

"You'll never find them. The Chechens keep their lips tight as a virgin's snatch. Only the Ukrainians could hate Putin more. They're like Islamic warriors and will protect these guys."

Heroes? Hating Putin but working for him? Nothing made sense. He'd already laid out nearly a grand only to find he was sniffing around the wrong neighborhood. But it wasn't all wasted, at least now he knew he had the right two men. Finding and stopping them however, that apparently was going to be a bitch.

Driving back to Manhattan Breslin used the car's Bluetooth connection to call Mitchell again.

"Joe, ain't it time for you to be home with the kiddies?"

"What, and miss a call from a TV star? For what do I deserve two calls in one day?"

"News. Good news. Considering the source, it might not hold up in court, but I got confirmation on those names you gave me."

"Who's the source?"

"You know I can't tell you. But he's always batted a thousand with me."

Breslin told Mitchell the missing brothers were said not to be in Brooklyn. Moreover, they were hated by the Russians there, so had to be someplace else.

"And get this, according to my very expensive source, they are considered to be heroes back home. So maybe you can use your worldwide gossip service to find out why."

Mitchell hid his excitement. Sounding almost bored he said, "Alright, I'll ask around."

"And let me know what you hear?"

"That would only be right."

CHAPTER 22
A LOOSE THREAD

Operation Neptune was well underway, but before the extraction of Chen Lin's parents could be accomplished there was one very important loose thread that still had to be tied. The couple had to be notified that help was coming, and they had to be able to assist in their own escape. Communicating with them was not going to be easy, they were under constant observation and telephone, or internet communication was impossible without interception. The solution would eventually require the assistance of Wu Yao.

      Ferrante, who had alternated between suspicion of Yao, and concern for her safety, ordered Chen not to tell her that he was now cooperating with the Americans. Ferrante said it was for her own good, but it was an order Chen never had any intention of obeying. The very weekend after his encounter with the Federal authorities Yao visited Chen in his dorm room at the base. It was there while lying together on his bed, in the hushed dark of evening, that he stared sadly at the ceiling and whispered his secret to her. His mission had been discovered, and he must now become a double agent. To his surprise Yao was not upset but delighted. She leaned over him, reached both her hands behind his head and pulled his face close to hers.
"My darling Lin," she said with tears of relief in her eyes, "this is the most wonderful news. You no longer need fear that scoundrel Zhang Wei."

"They told me not to say anything about this to you for your own safety."

"Don't worry about me, I will say nothing."

"Lying to you was not an option for me."

"I would never forgive you if you kept this from me. I am your partner in all things. Please never forget that." She stroked his face softly, kissed him and added with intensity, "If there is any way I can help, I will." The lovemaking which followed was fueled by an overwhelming confluence of relief and desperation.

***

The opportunity for Yao to be of assistance came much sooner than either could anticipate. It was the same day the China Sea voyage began that Ferrante approached Chen with his problem. "Chen, the operation to exfiltrate your parents has begun, but we urgently need a way to communicate. The entire plan depends on our ability to coordinate with them. To tell them who's coming, when and where."

"But I can't reach my parents without the Chinese authorities monitoring everything I say.

"Is there anyone in China who could act as a go-between. Talk to them privately or get a message past whoever is watching them?"

"No one I could trust, no."

"There must be someone who would be willing to help, any relatives?"

He answered quickly, "No."

But Chen then had an idea. There were some people who were not relatives, *yet*, but hopefully soon. Their involvement would bring Yao out of the shadows, and perhaps solve the problem.

"There is a couple who might help. They are travel agents in China who arrange shopping tours to western cities. They make a lot of money, and so the government allows them to enjoy freedom of movement, and communication."

Ferrante was intrigued. "You think they might be able to get your parents out of the country?" He said with optimistic surprise.

Chen quickly dashed that hope, "Nothing so simple. I couldn't ask them to take such a risk. But they could get a message to my parents."

"How so?"

Chen thought for a moment, "Maybe send a brochure to my parents advertising one of their trips; and include a note from me."

"And security wouldn't see it?"

Chen grew pensive, then smiled.

"Sure they would, but they wouldn't understand."

He explained his idea. "As a child my parents called me by a favorite animal of mine. A nickname. They called me 'Squirrel,' song-shu in Mandarin. If I can get a message to them and indicate it is from song-shu they would immediately understand."

"But no one else?"

"Exactly."

"Sounds possible. Who are these travel agent people?"

"The parents of my fiancée Wu Yao."

Ferrante caught his breath. He was still not entirely certain Yao wasn't a Chinese plant. "Chen, are you sure you can trust her? Many lives would be imperiled if you opened up to her and she exposed this operation."

"Mister Ferrante if she is not trustworthy, she would have already exposed me."

Ferrante's voice went up an octave, "She knows about us?"

It was time to come clean, "Yes. And I have trusted her with my life, and the wellbeing of my parents. Do you need more guarantee than that?"

Ferrante grimaced, then smiled, "I guess not." He asked, "How can you be sure Yao's parents would agree to help. It sounds like they have a good life there; why get involved in something like this?"

"Could you deny such a request from your child?" Chen answered his own question. "Neither could they."

***

Chen Lin's parents almost discarded the travel brochure the moment it arrived. It promised a two-week tour of Paris with plenty of opportunities to shop for Western clothing and jewelry, normally impossibly expensive in China. For a modest couple such a trip was extravagant under normal circumstances, now that they were under virtual house arrest it was a fantasy. They were confused as to why they would receive such a mailing, but the cover letter was interesting because it said in gushy terms, that this was 'not only the Year of the Rat, but also of the Squirrel! For our clients the perfect year to find and collect little treasures and squirrel them away.'

The description of the trip promised 'an exciting opportunity to meet westerners, make new friends, and be transported to a welcoming destination full of new possibilities.' Finally, it admonished the couple to 'Grasp this once in a lifetime opportunity, you will never regret the decision to follow The Squirrel's example. Contact us if interested.'

Chen's parents didn't understand exactly what was being communicated, but they thought the repetition of "squirrel" odd. The couple decided to phone the travel agency to see if the communication meant what they suspected it might, that their son was trying to reach them privately. The conversation that ensued was oblique almost to the point of opacity, but clear enough.

"My wife and I are interested in your upcoming 'Squirrel Tour,'" said Chen Lin's father into the telephone. "We are not at liberty to take advantage of it at the moment, but it sounds interesting. Who is organizing it?"

"We have contacts throughout the world and get many exclusive offers," Yao's father responded. "This one comes from someone in the West who calls himself, 'The Squirrel;' simply meaning someone who likes to collect desirable objects. The trip promises to be a true treasure hunt."

"Yes, from your brochure it seems tempting, but as I say we are presently unable to participate."

"We understand that at the moment you are not free to travel," Yao's father said. "But we are hopeful that will not be the case soon; that any unfortunate misunderstanding with the authorities will be resolved. And we want to offer our services for when that time comes."

Chen's father said he hoped he was right, but they really did not have the resources needed for such an excursion.

"Circumstances do change, who knows you might get a pleasant surprise. I've seen it many times before," responded the travel agent. "So, if you don't object, and since you are interested, I would like to remain in touch." They exchanged mobile phone numbers. "Please feel free to text or call if your situation allows. Meanwhile, you will hear from me promptly if I think there is an opportunity you should be aware of."

"Thank you so much."

"Not at all. We are at your service." He repeated, "I'll be sure to notify you if we have an opportunity we think you should be prepared to accept."

Chen's perplexed parents discussed the strange communication. They had no idea who these travel agents were, and so were immediately suspicious. Given the government's apparent animosity, an animosity that was somehow linked to their son, they could only assume the authorities were trying to entrap them in some illegal venture. And use that against him. On the other hand, it might be Lin who was trying to reach out to them. But if so, for what purpose? They had already spoken to Lin about joining him in America after he graduated. It was a wrenching decision to leave their ancestral homeland, but they decided they would do it to spend their remaining days with him. Could this "Squirrel" message be his way of telling them to prepare to leave? On reflection, that did seem the more likely explanation, but they would wait to hear again from the travel agents. If indeed they would call again.

By Monday morning in Hong Kong, Devlin received an assuring email from the States saying that *Arrangements have been made for a welcoming reception; all here send best wishes for a successful voyage.*

It was time to take possession of the boat and shove off.

***

Even as the team in Hong Kong was preparing to embark, Chen Lin and Liam McCarthy were deciding how to doctor the submarine blueprints they would give the Chinese. Chen wanted to fall back on his expertise in materials science.

"Look Liam," they were now on a first name basis, "I don't know, and don't want to know, anything about the inner workings of the Columbia sub, even in a bastardized way. What I'm suggesting is we feed the Chinese only changes to the external configuration of the submarine, a configuration which can be as fanciful as we like."

"Right," said Liam, "but changes to the profile of the boat wouldn't convince anyone the design changes are radical enough to warrant being called a new class of sub."

"That would be true," Chen countered, "*if* the skin of the boat remained number 80 steel, like all your other subs. But what if we propose making the superstructure of the boat out of a completely different material?"

"How would that help?"

"We could sell it as making the submarine almost undetectable to current systems."

Liam saw where Chen was going, "You mean akin to what the Air Force did to the B-2 Bombers?"

"Exactly," said Chen. "And it is the sort of radical innovation that would intrigue a naval architect. Something to be explored and repeatedly tested. It would keep Chinese engineers busy for a long time. Of course, they would still want to know what changes were planned for the power plant and payload, but I couldn't be blamed for not getting everything they wish for. This would be enough to satisfy them and get me off the hook."

"And screw up any counter measures China might contemplate."

"Yup, send them on a wild goose chase."

The question then was what sort of material could be used instead of the steel that was long the standard in submarine construction. It had to be something at least as strong, and infinitely malleable. Something able to be molded into fanciful shapes designed to confuse sophisticated sonar systems.

Chen had the answer, "Instead of steel I am going to build critical sections of our fake submarine out of carbon fiber."

"Would that actually work?"

"Absolutely not," Chen said with a big grin.

CHAPTER 23
THE TRIPLE OFFENSIVE

When Devlin, Marina, and their crew of two amateur sailors arrived at the Gold Coast harbor on Tuesday morning, they found a fifty-foot sailing catamaran waiting at the dock. The name "*North Star*" was stenciled on its sides. Devlin remarked that the boat wasn't new. "She's probably about ten years old, but even at that has to be worth north of a quarter million dollars." He couldn't believe she might have to be scuttled. *I'll do my best to keep that from happening.* He loved boats and purposely destroying one was anathema to him. He grabbed a stanchion, pulled himself aboard and did a quick exploration. The boat had four cabins down below in the pontoons, one located fore and one aft on each side, and two heads, or bathrooms. There would be plenty of space for their needs, even after picking up their two passengers.

Marina noted that tied alongside the catamaran was an 'RIB,' a rigid inflatable boat ten feet long. "There's our dinghy," she said. It had a stiff fiberglass floor supported by inflatable rubber pontoons and was equipped with an outboard motor. "It will carry six people easily, if we need."

Roger and Hana, less sure of their footing, climbed cautiously aboard *North Star* stepping from the dock to the swim platform on the stern. They found their way below and claimed a cabin in the big pontoon on the left, or port side. "This space is a lot bigger than I thought," Hana said, "the bunk mattress is almost queen sized." They dropped their meager baggage and returned upstairs to the main cabin.

Unlike the cramped cockpit of a monohull, the cabin

of this catamaran was a broad flat space enclosed by wrap-around glass windows and doors; almost all of which could open for air or permit access to the outside deck in the back. With its cushioned couches it looked almost as comfortable as her living room at home. Hana approved, "This boat has more floor space than my New York apartment."

Roger nodded, looking around. "And it's a lot neater too." A quip which earned him a poke to the ribs.

Devlin mused that a big advantage of the catamaran was that it always sailed upright, did not heel. The two spacious pontoons on either side would keep the boat level, riding flat over the water: a big benefit when there'd be four non-sailors aboard.

The main helm station with its broad, and confusing, array of instruments faced forward. Devlin and Marina were there getting acquainted with all *North Star*'s systems. Assisting them was a yacht-yard mechanic, a trusted friend of the students.

He and Marina chatted amiably in Mandarin as they went over the instruments: the engine controls, GPS, electronic chart plotter, auto pilot, radios and other innards vital to the safe operation of the vessel. Devlin, with Marina's translation, switched the switches, punched the buttons, tapped the computer screen and twirled the dials, getting familiar with the boat's controls.

Devlin picked up a pair of headsets hanging on a hook near the wheel. "Are these for onboard communications?" he asked.

"Yes." They were wireless walkie-talkie radios

which allowed the crew to speak to each other while working away from the helm. A great help, especially in bad weather. "We won't be able to use them though," said Marina. "The radio signals, weak as they are, might be picked up by Chinese security." Devlin disappointed, grunted his agreement.

The boat also had a fully battened mainsail, the battens were there to keep the sail shaped properly, similar to the battened sails of a Chinese junk. The jib, the sail on the bow was wound around a roller-furler on the forestay. Best of all, since everything was controlled from inside the main cabin, the sails could be adjusted without the need to scramble forward, or up onto the cabin roof where the mast was stepped. "She should be very easy to sail," Devlin said quietly, "no drama."

"Famous last words," Marina offered, knowing at sea there was always the possibility of unwanted drama.

Finally, they started the engines. There was one in each of the two wide pontoons which supported the deck. Two engines meant the boat could spin on its axis, if one were in forward gear and the other reverse. It was a very maneuverable craft. While still tied to the dock Devlin put the engines in gear, first one then the other, to test the transmissions. Again, no problem.

Once Devlin confirmed that the fuel and water tanks had been topped-up, and *North Star* could easily make the two-hundred-mile round trip with plenty of both to spare, it was time to go.

"Thank you so much," Marina said to the mechanic, and turned to the two students who had accompanied them. "And of course our thanks to you as well. Wish us luck!"

"Before we go," said the woman student, "a parting

gift. It arrived by courier from the States last night." The clandestine shipment contained an encrypted satellite phone disguised as a late model iPhone. It would be their link to the support team back home and was received with relief and gratitude. Now they needn't feel entirely isolated and unattached.

"And one other thing for you." She handed Devlin a thin envelope. "Some paperwork."

Devlin took the envelope and stepped aside to open it. "Very good," he said and pocketed the contents. It was a counterfeit registration showing the boat was registered to a charter company in Guangzhow. Just in case.

There were thanks and handshakes all around. The visitors left, and the group gathered around the table on the open-air back deck to review their plans. It was two o'clock in the afternoon.

Devlin, in command, spoke first, "I think we should agree on some ground rules about how we manage ourselves for as long as this project takes. I am captain of this boat and expect everyone will do what I say about sailing her. But that's only as regards the boat. I'm not the only one with a brain here and expect everyone will pitch-in as they're able."

"Well, that's good to hear," Roger said with pique in his voice. Never one to enjoy being second banana, he was having a tough time dialing down his need for the spotlight. But what Devlin said made sense, and so he had to accept it.

"I think…" Devlin caught Roger's intonation but continued firmly, "I think all other major decisions, where our personal safety is involved, should be made by consensus. But since there are four of us, and so the possibility of deadlock, I'd like to propose that if we're ever stuck over some course of action, Marina gets two votes."

Roger and Hana were visibly taken aback. Noticing, Devlin said, "Sorry guys, but my thinking is simply that she and I are quite a bit older and more experienced than you two, and unless you really object, it gives us an agreed way to settle differences amicably."

Again, neither Roger nor Hana could find a strong reason to complain, so the leadership roles were established: Devlin for boat management and Marina the deciding vote on the level of risk they could accept.

Devlin said they would take four-hour shifts manning the boat. "Hana and I on one watch, Marina and Roger the other." That way there would always be a seasoned sailor, and a Chinese speaker, on deck while the other two rested. There were a few other details to iron out. "We will try to keep radio silence, but if other boats hail us we'd have to answer. I think any radio communication should be handled by Hana. Her accent is better than Marina's and her voice shouldn't arouse the interest any of us would."

Finally, turning to Roger he asked about the video recordings the reporter was supposed to make.

"I brought three cell phones and a number of sim cards," said Roger, "I intend to do all my shooting using the phones. The phones are high definition so the video will be perfect."

"What about the audio?" Hana asked.

"Just whatever the phone picks up. No microphone. I'll record narration back in the studio." He added, "Hana, I hope you'll be second camera." He was referring to her expertise as a video producer for the United Nations.

"Don't worry I'll only shoot your good side," she teased.

"Whattaya mean good side? I don't have a bad side."

"And they say women are vain!"

"Good, we're settled then," said Devlin. "Now our first decision, when should we shove off?"

There was no immediate urgency, if all went well the hundred-mile trip upriver to Guangzhou should take about twenty-four hours. They all agreed the more time they spent sailing at night the better. But they also wanted to arrive in Guangzhou after sunset, which might require splitting the journey, sailing through the first night, then holing up somewhere until dusk the following day. Maybe even laying low for a second day, it all depended on the speed they could make.

"I am going to set a minimum speed of five knots," said Devlin. "If the wind doesn't cooperate, we'll use the engine."

"Why don't we just motor all the way?" Roger asked.

Marina answered, "Because we are tourists on a leisurely sail, taking the wind as it comes. If it looks like we are making a bee-line upriver it could arouse suspicion."

"Yes," added Devlin, "I think it would be wise to assume all vessels in these waters are being tracked. The Chinese Coast Guard is very efficient."

"That's not very comforting," Hana said grumpily.

"Any nosy inquiries and Hana it'll be your job to charm them into leaving us alone." Devlin said with a smile.

"You are too kind, my captain!"

Devlin went on to explain that since it was summer the winds would most likely blow from the northwest, more or less right on the nose. That meant they would have to do a lot of tacking, working their way to windward. And since it was August, the sun wouldn't set until seven at night, and rise again at six in the morning. They'd have fewer than eleven hours of darkness.

"If we leave at five this afternoon we'd go about sixty miles by dawn tomorrow. Not bad," said Marina. "Let's get underway at five."

The others concurred and all decided to try to nap until then. It would be a long night.

***

The time difference between Hong King and New York was thirteen hours. Five in the afternoon for the crew of *North Star*, was four in the morning for Gabe Breslin; and he was having a lousy night. He had thought he had a good bead on the whereabouts of the Borz brothers, but now knew he was wrong. True, they could be anywhere, but it seemed most likely they would go to where a warm welcome awaited. From what Sergei said, that meant a Chechen community, and in this area that most likely meant Paterson, New Jersey.

By six that morning Gabe, unable to sleep, decided he couldn't stand tossing and turning any longer. Besides, his restlessness was annoying his wife. He threw back the sheets and stiff-walked his way to the bathroom; why did his bones seem so reluctant to start the day? Getting old wasn't for the faint of heart, he mumbled to himself.

Now past sixty his hair was thinning, and while in the shower he noticed with dismay even the hair on his legs was disappearing. His whole body was going the way of his testosterone, fading away. *But I ain't dead yet*, he thought as he poured dry cereal and milk into a bowl, and with the help of a double shot of espresso rallied for the day ahead. He pecked his wife on the back of her still sleeping head, found his car where he left it on King Street and drove up the West Side Highway to the Lincoln Tunnel. Once in Jersey and driving against the early rush hour traffic headed to New York, Paterson was just a half hour away.

Gabe had called a friend at the Star Ledger, a local paper, who suggested he start by talking to people in the area near Paterson Falls. So that was his destination. First stop was to a police precinct there.

He showed his NYC Press Pass to the desk sergeant and invented a reason for his visit. "We want to do a story profiling the Chechen community, and why they are so supportive of Ukraine in its war against Russia." Russia had invaded Ukraine earlier in the year and the Ukrainians received vocal support from many European immigrants. Especially those from former Soviet states.

"Yeah, they are that for sure," said the cop. "They hate the Russians. Lots of anger in that community. They march, shout slogans, down with Putin signs, all that bullshit."

"You got the names of any leaders? People who might be willing to talk to a reporter?"

The cop dug around his desk and pulled out a flyer

that had been posted around the city. It advertised a pro-Ukrainian demonstration for the week previous. "Like we don't have enough problems of our own in this town. We don't need this shit."

"I thought Chechnya was once part of the Soviet Union, why do they hate the Russians so much?" Gabe was playing more ignorant than he was but wanted the cop to offer up whatever information he had.

"It's like a religious war. These Chechens are Muslim, persecuted by Russia forever. They want to be independent, not Russian. So, they think by supporting Ukraine in its fight, they increase the chances of Chechnya getting free. The enemy of my enemy, and all that."

The sergeant made a copy of the flyer. Gabe thanked the officer, left, and walked to a nearby diner. He read the flyer over another coffee, this one 'regular,' with milk and enough sugar to inject jet fuel into his metabolism. He sat at the counter. When the waitress came to refresh his joe she glanced at the paper.

"You're a little late mister. That street party ended last week." She was a trim redhead who looked to be in her late fifties, not that much younger than him. But her red hair still looked like the real thing.

"So I gather," Gabe said, giving her an ingratiating, 'let's chat' smile. "I'm a TV reporter working on a story about the Chechens in Paterson and want to speak to some community representatives. Maybe you can help?"

"Hang around here long enough and most of them will stop in. What kind of story you doing? About those demonstrations?"

"Yeah. Why this community cares so much about what's going on in Europe."

"You won't have trouble finding people to talk to about those things." She pointed to one of the faces on the flyer, one of the protest organizers. "That guy, Opti Aliev is probably your best bet. He is like the mayor of our people."

Our people. So, she was Chechen herself. "You related to him? He's a redhead, like you."

"Nah, for some reason a lot of us have red hair. It's common here."

He was surprised. Never having met someone from Chechnya he'd assumed they all had dark complexions, long black hair; the men with black scraggly beards. Like he'd seen in war footage from Afghanistan or the Mid-East.

"Well, it's more attractive on you."

She smiled, happy for the complement even if she knew he was putting her on.

"How might I go about contacting him?"

She tensed slightly, perhaps not wanting to get involved, he thought. Then she relaxed.

"Well, everybody knows him around here, so I guess it's no secret. He can usually be found in the community center right down the block."

It was just after nine when Gabe went looking for the man. As he walked his cell phone buzzed in his pocket. It was Joseph Mitchell from the NYPD. "Where are you Gabe?"

"Paterson, going to interview someone, what's up?"

"Paterson? Good luck. We've been hoping to get someone there to open up. No way. It's like trying to pry open an oyster with your fingernails."

Mitchell wanted Gabe to go somewhere they could talk freely, so Gabe backtracked to his car, got in the passenger side and shut the door.

"I promised I'd let you know, so here it is. We did some digging into the Chechnya wars and now know why the Borz brothers are considered heroes. It goes back twenty years but turns out the whole family is like royalty there."

Mitchell explained that in 2002 Alois Borz, the father, was a leader of the Chechen rebels who invaded the Dubrovka Theater in Moscow. They held the entire audience hostage.

"The raid was part of the Chechen terror campaign for independence from Russia. Vladimir Putin, responded by pumping knockout gas into the building. Unfortunately, the gas created a panic and more than a hundred people died: Chechens, Russians, everybody; many were executed by the Russian troops, including Alois."

"Nice guy, Putin."

"An angel. Anyway, passions and savagery were pretty high on both sides. In retaliation for the attack on the theater, Russian soldiers stationed in Chechnya raided the Borz home. Some of the troops gang-raped the mother. While the two boys were in the house! The boys were twelve and fourteen at the time."

"That radicalized them?"

"One might assume. The two were caught five years ago after participating in a botched bombing against a Russian hotel. They were sentenced to the Butyrka prison in Moscow, where everyone expected the Russians would throw away the key."

"Father killed, mother raped, the two boys…"

"Yeah," said Mitchell, "they're like a Gold Star

family in Chechnya."

"So why let them out now?"

"Best thinking is they made a deal; the men could go free if they do this hit. Releasing the Borz men was an attempt by the Russians to make nice, to reduce tensions with the Chechens while also doing a favor for the Chinese. It's like a win-win."

"But why help the Chinese? And who is behind it all?"

"That," said Mitchell, "remains a big question. Or questions."

"And why are the boys reneging on the deal? If indeed they are?"

Even Gabe could answer that one himself. Two boys watched as their mother was raped, their father killed because of Putin. Not likely they would work for him; more likely they'd want to slit his throat.

"Go talk to whoever you got there, but I'd be very surprised if you get anything worthwhile."

"Ok, it's my turn to return the favor," Gabe promised, "I'll let you know what I hear."

***

Operation Neptune's three initiatives were in their critical final stages; action was underway in the China Sea, New Jersey, and Connecticut. With the deadline for Chen's return to Columbia imminent, the pressure was on for completion of his counterfeit blueprints. They had to be radical, believable, and replicable. The last so the Chinese would be induced into spending time, money and expertise into devising countermeasures for what was in essence a phantom boat. If lucky, the blueprints might even convince the Chinese to try to build such a craft themselves. The more disruption the fake plans could cause the better.

"This profile looks like something out of a comic book," Liam McCarthy said, looking at Chen Lin's latest effort.

"Yes, it does look a little grotesque, like a water snake with all those undulations in the boat's skin." Chen offered proudly.

"Not only the curves along the hull, but also the projecting wings at the bow and stern. What's their alleged purpose?"

"I'm describing them as variable pitch battens to confuse sonar waves."

"All made of carbon fiber?"

"Yes. The entire skin will absorb both sound and light waves, making the boat virtually invisible."

"Sounds like science fiction," objected Liam.

"It is," Chen said laughing, "but you shouldn't criticize too much since the designs will have your name on them."

"Obviously a work of art then," Margaret interrupted.

"What about how the boat's skin is attached to the inner frame. Since you can't weld the carbon fiber how are the two sections held together?"

"Chewing gum and gaffer's tape," Chen joked. "That's the real trouble with this whole thing. There's no way the boat will survive a dive of more than five hundred feet.

The bolts holding her carbon exoskeleton and steel frame together will just pop out, and the boat will implode on itself."

"Wouldn't the Chinese engineers also know this?"

"Sure, they would if they were working with carbon fiber. Which they're not. Remember, my doctorate is in alternative materials for shipbuilding, and so far, the only people considering carbon are some operators of deep-sea submersibles in this country."

"And…"

"And all tests so far have shown the use of dissimilar materials leads to disaster."

"Then why would the Chinese believe these plans?" Chen grew serious, "Because they think I have a solution stolen from the U.S. Navy. Your solution. It's exactly what they want from me."

"They'd be building a death trap."

"Yes. But it will never get that far."

Both men assumed if the Chinese did decide to replicate the design it would first be tested on a model, then a prototype. There was no conceivable way it would actually be produced. The design had to be convincing, but inevitably self-destruct.

Liam and Chen congratulated each other. They had built a believable Trojan Horse; now they had to pick the right time to deliver it. A decision that largely depended on the successful completion of the other two aims of Operation Neptune. And of those two, Chen was most anxious to hear from Liam's son Devlin, eight thousand miles away and, hopefully, on his way to Guangzhou.

***

It was now the third week of August and the pressure on Zhang Wei, still holed up in the Chinese Mission, was unrelenting. Ma Bai kept demanding updates and confirmation that Chen was doing what he was committed to do. Zhang in turn tightened the screws on Chen, each call slightly more desperate.

"Time is getting short Chen Lin, are you making progress? Can you guarantee you will have what has been requested of you?"

"I will have something good for you, I can promise that. Whether it is all you desire I cannot know. But I will keep my word and you must keep yours."

"Don't tell me what I must or must not do! You are in no position to make demands," Zhang Wei said in an agitated huff, then moderated his tone, "All is well in Guangzhou and will remain so as long as you do as instructed."

Chen didn't respond, simply grunted then clicked off.

All conversations between Zhang and Chen Lin were being recorded by the FBI, but the Bureau still did not have a handle on who was masterminding the plot. Ma Bai's name was never mentioned. But Zhang wasn't the only one feeling tense over the approaching deadline; the spy boss himself was also getting nervous. *It seemed always to be so. The closer you get to the end of an operation the higher the level of anxiety.* To be so close to a major victory made any possibility of its failure so much more unbearable. Once the submarine plans were in hand so many potential catastrophes would be avoided, including the possibility that he himself might be unmasked. Ma Bai had already stopped worrying about Chen being discovered. There had been no further investigation of him by anyone, including that reporter Roger Barnes. Barnes had just disappeared. *Probably assigned to some frivolous feature story by his news station. These reporters were like pesky bees, buzz around you for a while then fly off to find nectar in another flower.* To attack the American reporter now was pointless. It was just as well the Russians had lost track of their own hit men.

Ma decided to tell his UN colleague Vladimir Ivanov to call off the dogs. China would honor its oil purchase agreement even without using Russia's iron fist. The two men met as usual in the UN's patio restaurant.

"Any word yet, Vladimir?"

"No." Ivanov pretended to be unconcerned, "But don't worry the men who were sent here are dependable ..."

Ma cut him off, "Forget it. Too late. Time has worked in our favor. The need for extraordinary means has passed. I relieve you of our agreement with all thanks for your willingness to help. As a sign of goodwill our purchase agreement stands as we negotiated. So, no hard feelings."

Ivanov was taken aback but grateful for being let off the hook. He had no idea where the Borz brothers were and, thankfully finding them was not his responsibility. He was convinced that releasing them was a giant blunder on the part of someone in Moscow, but he, insulated from the Kremlin by a distance of thousands of miles could pretend to embarrassed outrage. Someone would have to pay for the incompetence, but it wouldn't be him.

The two diplomats shook hands on the conclusion of their arrangement and returned to their offices. It was too early to celebrate, but back at his desk Ma Bai was already congratulating himself for what, so far, was a job well done.

Zhang Wei was also projecting a quick rehabilitation from his recent bumbling debacle. With Chen's design submission just days away he will have saved face. He expected to be extricated from the Chinese Mission and sent back to China as quickly as could be arranged. Zhang was supposed to be in New York for a three-year tour of duty but was "forced to return sooner," as he explained in a letter to his wife in Beijing. "This latest project of ours is on the verge of being successfully completed. Because my identity has been compromised, through no fault of my own, I expect to be home soon, most likely before October. I am sorry I can't continue here, but I am excited and delighted to be returning to you and Jie. It's hard to believe he will soon be seven years old!" Zhang, concealing his blunders, had every reason to celebrate. Just getting out alive and returning home free was the best outcome he could possibly expect.

CHAPTER 24
MISSION TO GUANGZHOU

The catamaran *North Star* left her berth in Hong Kong's Pearl Island Marina shortly after five in the afternoon and towing the dinghy astern, headed west into the setting sun. The Marina was located within a man-made harbor; its floating docks and finger piers protected by a semicircular groin of riprap —massive stone blocks. A small opening permitted egress. Once *North Star* was free of the protective jetty and the sails raised, Devlin changed direction slightly to a more southerly course to take advantage of the northwest breeze. This would make it appear to anyone who might be paying attention that they were headed to Macau, about thirty miles away. If that were truly their destination, an observer could conclude, they'd easily make it in time to get some gambling in before retiring for the night. As they moved closer to Macau the foursome could see the garish lights of the casinos lining the shorefront. *Las Vegas by the sea*, thought Roger. However, enjoying the casinos was not in the cards for this night.

They were about halfway across the estuary at seven o'clock when the sun touched the horizon. The wind held steady, blowing about ten knots and backing slightly to the west. It was a fortuitous shift which gave them a good sailing angle as Devlin tacked the boat to the right and headed northeast. The deepening dusk meant *North Star* could more safely end the pretense of heading for Macau. With the wind on their beam they were sailing in the direction of Shenzhen Airport located at the mouth of the Pearl River.

"Roger, why don't you take the helm for a while," said Devlin. "You might as well get a feel for it. Just stay on this course, forty-five degrees on the compass."

Roger took the wheel and enjoyed a rush of excitement. He'd never sailed before, and the sense of power transmitted by the sails to the boat's hull thrilled him. The swish of water passing beneath his feet added an audio accompaniment that magnified the sense of speed. The view of the big genoa sail in the bow, almost pink in the long rays of the sinking sun, and the gurgling sounds of the passing seas made him think of the need to get video of the passage.

"Hana, could you take my phone and spray the boat?" By 'spray' he meant for her to shoot as much of the moving boat's operation as she could. Without showing faces. They were under strict orders never to visually identify anyone except Roger. Hana did as she was asked and went below, using one of his phones to gather video of the living quarters. She shot video of their bunks, storage spaces, and the views out the portholes. Back up in the main salon she took close-ups of the various instruments and their readings, she sprayed the galley, the table and banquets. Then she captured Roger at the wheel in wide, medium and close-up, with tight shots of his hands, his eyes, even his feet. She went out to the stern and shot the wake of the boat as it disappeared aft, as well as the pontoons cutting through the water and various views of the sails. After that, she lay on the deck looking up, and from the bow looking back. In short, she took pictures of almost every aspect of the boat, except the other people, and not the boat's name. If possible, the boat was to remain anonymous. The "B-roll" video Hana was collecting was meant to cover Roger's narration as needed. She knew that when editing, you could never have too much B-roll.

She returned to Roger at the wheel. "Do you want to record anything now, anything on-camera?"

"Sure, good idea," he said. After a moment's thought he looked directly into the camera, signaled Hana to record, took a beat, counted down three, two, one and began. "We are underway in the South China Sea. If all goes well, we're about a day away from our destination. We expect to sail through the night, and hopefully avoid interception, if not detection. There is no possibility of any vessel getting through these waters without being detected by the Chinese Coast Guard. But it would also be impossible for them to stop every boat. Fingers crossed they'll assume we're just another tourist boat out to enjoy a sunset cruise."

Hana had to stand very close to him to be sure she got his audio recorded clearly. When he stopped talking, she leaned in, kissed his cheek and hugged him. The shared danger had a sobering effect on both of them. Roger's usual swagger was now tempered with anxiety and concern, especially for Hana. With his free arm he pulled her tightly to him, feeling very much they were a team.

While Hana had been recording Roger's stand-up, Devlin had taken the encrypted Sat Phone, stepped out onto the open back deck with Marina by his side and called Nicholas Ferrante's number. It was six o'clock in the morning in Boston, Ferrante jumped awake to answer the call.

"Go ahead," he said without preamble.

"We are underway and probably just one full day from our objective."

"Excellent. Any unwanted interest so far?"

"Negative."

"I'll pass on the information to those concerned. Please get back to me when you are within two hours of arriving, and also if anything unexpected arises."

"10-4." They clicked off.

Devlin looked at Marina, "Well, the wheels are in motion. No going back now."

She gave a weak smile, "Let's hope it will all be happily finished in a day or so."

***

As soon as he disconnected from Devlin, Ferrante got on the phone to Chen Lin. He awakened him from a sound sleep in his dorm room at the base.

"Lin." He too had begun using Chen's given name, "I've heard from our friends at sea who are closing in on their destination. Please pass on the news."

Chen had been prepared and waiting for this call. It meant he had to get word to his parents to prepare to leave their home. Most likely forever. Even though they'd planned a future move to America this abrupt departure was a difficult but necessary precaution. Who knew how his bogus submarine plans might be greeted by the government? If they suspected he was now working for the Americans, it could be very bad for his parents.

Chen called Yao. The most critical link in the

communications chain; her parents, had to be mobilized.

"Hello," a sleepy woman's voice answered. "Good morning Lin. What's up?"

"Good morning sweetheart, I need that favor we talked about. It seems we're about a day away from the planned meeting."

"OK, I understand. Will there be more news coming?"

"Yes. A firm time for the meeting."

"Good. Very exciting."

"Yes. To put it mildly. I love you, let me know when you've spread the word."

"Love you too."

The next communication was to Yao's parents. She texted them: *Very happy to hear that squirrel voyage you're sponsoring is going to happen within days. You should let anyone interested know. It promises to be a very rewarding trip. But time is short. Only a day or so to go! Good luck with arranging it! Love, Yao.*

After having traveled half a world away and back again, the message was delivered. Chen's parents once again heard from Yao's father.

"Mister Chen I am happy to tell you the trip we have organized through the "Squirrel" is soon to depart. We are anticipating a departure within days." Of course, Chen's parents once again said they had to refuse. They were still not free to travel. At least not officially. But they gathered their valuables and keepsakes and began to pack. All they needed was a time and place. If it was a trap, it was a risk they were willing to take.

***

Once he clicked off with Ferrante, Devlin decided it was time to begin the crew's watch routine of four hours on, four off. They'd all been awake since early morning, so he decided to let the first watch have a short three-hour shift.

"Marina, will you and Roger please take over until midnight? Hana and I will take the overnight. You two return at four a.m. for the early morning hours."

"Sounds good," she said. "At least we'll get to see the rising sun."

"Whoopee," said Roger laughing. "Up with the sun! Not my idea of a good night's rest."

"I'm sure the beauty of it will make it all worthwhile." Hana teased.

Before going below to nap Devlin consulted with Marina on the course for the next couple hours. At their current speed they should be in the vicinity of the Pearl River mouth by eleven that night. That would be just about at the latitude of Shenzhen Airport. They would then shift from a northeast to a northwest heading which, if the wind held as it was, or backed further south, would allow them to sail all the way to Guangzhou. But if the wind veered to the north, it would mean they'd have to tack, and substantially slow their progress. Typical sailing uncertainties. They would not be able to give Ferrante a better ETA until they were much closer to the city.

That settled and everything moving as well as could be hoped, Devlin and Hana went to their respective cabins to get some shuteye. Roger and Marina were left to keep watch.

CHAPTER 25
A VERY DEAD END

After concluding his call with Joe Mitchell, Gabe Breslin pocketed his phone. He exited his beat-up Ford Escape, a victim of dings and scratches inflicted on the streets of New York, and retraced his steps toward the Patterson Community Center where the waitress directed him. It was still early on a Tuesday morning which meant the Center had opened but not yet come fully alive. From just inside the entrance, he could see a large open gymnasium with a basketball court in the center. Around the perimeter were pool tables, old fashioned pinball machines, and a shuffleboard court. All deserted. He took a few steps around the side of the court and saw along the left wall were meeting rooms, and a cafeteria. Also quiet. However, there was a swimming pool in the basement which catered to early morning fitness fanatics, at least as Breslin labeled them. He could hear locker room chatter echoing up from the showers. No one seemed to be in charge, since the welcome desk was vacant.

"Can I help you?" A voice from behind startled the reporter. It was a man who'd entered the building immediately behind him.

"Hi, I'm Gabe Breslin from WNOW-TV News and I'm looking for Opti Aliev. I was told I could find him here."

"News? You doing a story about our demonstrations? All very legal I have to say."

"Well yes, that's partly why I'd like to speak to Mister Aliev."

"Partly?"

Ignoring the question Breslin asked, "Is he around?"

The man, who appeared to be in his forties was short, stocky and dressed casually in tan corduroy slacks with a flannel shirt. His rolled-up sleeves revealed bare muscular forearms. Tough. Made Breslin think of a lumberjack.

"That's me. What's a reporter want with me?"

"Can we sit?"

Aliev was the director of the Center. He took Breslin to his office, a small room just off the entrance. The walls were decorated with a Chechnya flag, pictures of Aliev with various people, none of whom meant anything to Breslin, and framed news clippings describing various events of the many continuing Chechen uprisings.

"I hope you're here to report on our neighborhood's steadfast support of the gallant Ukrainian people in their struggle against the Russian barbarians."

"Yes, and maybe some other things the Russians are up to."

"OK. How can I help."

Breslin decided this guy looked like he wouldn't appreciate pretense or bullshit, so he'd best forget the protests and get right to the point.

"Do you know the Broz family?"

Aliev stiffened, surprised as if suddenly jabbed. After a moment's flare of anger, he broke into a wry smile.

"I see," he said, "you have other interests."

"Yes. I understand two members of the Broz family are here. In this neighborhood. I'd like to speak to them."

"I don't know where you get your information ..."

"Very good sources."

"But there are no Broz family members in this country. If there were I would know about it."

To emphasize he knew what he was talking about Breslin said, "My understanding is these two young men, heroes in your country, were sent here on a mission for Vladimir Putin."

The mention of Putin's name caused a visceral reaction. Aliev's face contorted.

"That beast! No Chechen would ever do anything for him."

"So I understand. But nevertheless," Breslin decided to go out on a limb. "It's known that Aslam and Shamilov are here to carry out a mission for Putin."

"No such thing will ever happen. I can assure you of that."

"How can you be so sure. Have you spoken to them?"

"I am saying the Borz brothers are not here and will never be found here. There is no possible execution of any Putin initiative."

"Well, that would be very good news if true. But I know," again Breslin took a gamble, "I know the Russians asked the brothers to carry out a deadly mission for the ultimate benefit of the Chinese."

"Another good reason no Chechen would be involved. The Chinese also delight to persecute Muslims."

Fishing for more, Breslin in a conspiratorial voice pressed "Assuming such a scheme was in the works, from your knowledge of Russian methods, and speaking only theoretically, how do you think such a Russian, Chinese agreement might be arranged? Who would be involved?"

Aliev, seeing there could be some profit for Chechnya in this exchange, agreed to play along. "Names? No idea. But speaking only from my past knowledge of how the bastard Russians operate, I would assume such devilry might be hatched in an unsuspicious place of mutual interest."

"For example?"

"For example, where the scoundrels innocently meet and dine together. You know someplace like ... someplace like at the United Nations." Aliev said with a broad smile. "Not a bad place to start."

"I see," Breslin smiled in return. "As you say, unsuspicious. But about the Broz brothers?"

"As I said they are not in this country, or I would know about it. And if they were somehow to be here, and escaped my knowledge, you can be assured they'll disappear into this great and vast country and never be found."

That seemed definitive. Try as Joseph Mitchell and the NYPD, or Bill Roscoe and the FBI might, those two men were to be permanently protected by the Chechen community and would likely never be found. For all he knew they might even have returned to Chechnya

Breslin stood up. "Thanks for speaking with me. I think we're done."

The two men stood, shook hands, and Breslin returned to his car. He owed Mitchell a call.

"Joe, I think you're right. There's no way these people are going to finger the brothers." He explained about his conversation with Opti Aliev. "But an interesting thing,

Aliev all but admitted the whole scheme was cooked up by Russian and Chinese diplomats at the United Nations. Just as Roger Barnes said he suspected."

    Mitchell let that sink in for a moment, considered where it might lead then said, "Thanks Gabe. Now we're even."

    Breslin clicked off and headed back to New York.

CHAPTER 26
ON THE PEARL RIVER

The *North Star* sailed without incident for the next two hours while Devlin and Hana were below trying to nap. They'd approached to within five miles of Shenzhen Airport, the point at which they were to change course to the northwest. Roger and Marina were relaxing on a cushioned banquette with the auto pilot in control when the VHF radio crackled. A young but official sounding female voice broke the evening silence.

"Good evening, this is Shenzhen Airport Security. The sailboat approaching from the southwest, please identify yourself." Both Roger and Marina jolted upright, not expecting to be so quickly spotted. Since Hana was below, Marina had to answer the call. Making an effort to control her nerves she said, "This is the vessel *North Star* out of Hong Kong. Go ahead." She had no alternative but to give the true name of the boat.

Roger quickly grabbed his phone and started recording the conversation.

"Good evening *North Star*, please be aware you are approaching the restricted perimeter zone around the airport." The impersonal voice sternly explained that no unauthorized shipping was allowed within four miles of the runways which ran along the shoreline. She then asked if *North Star* needed to enter the forbidden zone and was asking for permission.

"That's a negative Shenzhen Security. We will change course to the northwest. We are bound for Guangzhou and will not approach any closer to the restricted zone."

"Thank you *North Star*. Have a good evening. This is Shenzhen Airport Security out."

"Thank you, *North Star* out."

Roger and Marina stared silently at one another until Roger said, "What was that all about?"

Marina explained, translating what had been said. Then added, "Well, so much for leaving the communications to Hana. Someone forgot to tell the Chinese to wait until she was on watch before calling."

They laughed, a little unnerved but happy that they seemed to pass their first test with Chinese officialdom. Roger was impressed. Marina's accent had apparently not set off any alarms or created undue curiosity. She handled a communication with coolness, which otherwise could have instigated an interrogation or worse a physical search. Despite her discernible accent she spoke with a calm matter-of-factness which the listener accepted. Roger applauded her performance.

"Very nice voice control on that transmission. You could be an actress."

"Thanks. Lots of butterflies, but I guess I controlled them well enough not to sound panicky."

"Very nice indeed," he said with real appreciation. An impressive woman. And apparently when Devlin said all boat traffic in that area was being monitored, he wasn't kidding.

Marina punched the new course numbers into the autopilot and the boat swung easily to the left. With the wind now well behind the beam on the port side, Marina showed Roger how to ease the mainsheet and the genoa to a more downwind setting. The chart plotter showed their exact location as they left the wide bay and entered the narrowing Pearl River Estuary. They were doing a steady six knots, a suitable speed, so there was no need to start the engines. They had doused all the cabin and exterior lights except for the instruments and running lights; a red light on port, and green on starboard. The cockpit was dark, quiet, and almost cozy. The city lights on both sides of the river provided a colorful backdrop, a kaleidoscopic curtain surrounding the blackness of their watery highway. Lights of every color, including garish blinking neon, in all directions as far as they could see. It gave a good hint of the immensity, and density, of China and its population.

"You know," Roger mused, "back in the States we're happy if we get a million viewers for any broadcast. Here, they talk in the hundreds of millions watching any particular program. Just unbelievable numbers."

"Yeah, and every one of those millions are just like us. Wanting to live in peace with their loved ones."

Roger stared at her, slightly taken aback. "Here I was talking about a potential TV marketplace, raw numbers, but you're right. When you talk hundreds of millions, you forget the humanity they represent. Each a life no better, no worse than mine or yours." He grew pensive. "And now we're working to create a weapon that could annihilate many of them. I hope we know what we're doing."

"Yes. This whole balance of power thing, Mutually Assured Destruction, depends on leaders acting rationally. Doesn't give you too much confidence, does it?"

"Terrible to think avoiding Armageddon depends on

the wisdom of our politicians. Or theirs! And of course there is always the potential for a misunderstanding, or an accident. Scary."

Marina, who had a jaundiced view of Roger, thinking he was a little too self-obsessed, looked at him more kindly. Perhaps she was wrong. He *was* a little immature, but probably a decent guy for all his youthful braggadocio. Marriage, and the responsibilities it required, would probably help, and Hana seemed tough enough to straighten him out. She wondered though, do people in their mid-twenties marry these days? Building careers, not families seemed to be more desirable paths for young people now.

Sharing the close quarters of a boat easily engendered such introspection. Marina knew, either someone's idiosyncrasies and biases drove you crazy, or conversely you could develop an understanding and fondness for a shipmate. A fondness you never suspected possible. Marina's few extra years of life, and her experiences as a mother, made her a little more sympathetic to the growing pains of these young people, and their extended adolescence. *They just need time.*

Looking at Roger's cellphone she turned to the business at hand. She asked, "How do you anticipate using the video you're shooting?"

"We made a deal with the government that when the time is right, meaning when they say it won't harm any ongoing operation, I will have a first ever exclusive of a CIA mission. Sort of like what you see when reporters are embedded with frontline troops. In this case a frontline exfiltration operation. But it's embargoed until then."

"Can they prevent you from breaking the embargo?"

"The deal is, I shoot the footage but the government owns it. If it's used without permission the station could lose its license. Believe me, we'll abide by the agreement."

Just then, since it was approaching midnight, Devlin came topside. "Hi you two. You're both awake I hope."

"We only dozed for an hour or so," Roger teased.

"Yes, we were disturbed in our sleep by a radio call," Marina added.

"What! Who called?" Devlin said alarmed.

Marina explained the airport security check and that all seemed to go well.

"You really have to congratulate your wife," Roger said. "Totally cool under fire. They know we're here but seem okay with it."

"Well, we never expected to go undetected. Just so long as they don't stop us."

"Stop us from getting where?" asked Roger. "Have you been given any specific destination in Guangzhou for our rendezvous?"

"I was told we would get instructions once the family was notified. Unless that is, we can find a place first which we think might work."

"We are running out of time for that decision to be made," Marina interjected.

"I do have an idea," Devlin said. "I'll check its location on the charts tonight. Why don't you two hit the sack; and Roger please wake Hana to join me."

Marina briefed her husband on their new course. Then, like Roger she went below.

When Hana arrived topside, she was disheveled and

irritable. She'd flopped onto her bunk fully dressed, and though anxious to get sleep found herself repeatedly checking the clock, frustrated at being still awake as the minutes ticked by.

"Hello Devlin," she said grumpily, "I hope you slept better than I did." She sleepily dragged herself to the coffee pot only to find it empty. "Thanks Roger," she grumbled, "I'm sure he drank the last of the coffee and didn't think to brew more."

Devlin was surprised at her accusatory reaction. What did it say about her relationship with Roger? But he responded sympathetically, "Don't worry Hana, we'll only have a day or so of short shifts. Then you can get back to a normal night's sleep."

Hana looked sheepish, embarrassed by her own bad humor, "Sorry Dev, I'm a real bear if I don't get my eight hours."

She made a new pot of coffee. As they drank Devlin showed Hana how to keep an eye on the electronic chart and plot their progress. The combination of caffeine and something new to learn, quickly dispelled her ill temper.

"We're headed here," he said, pointing to an area off a large island labeled 'Longxue.' "There's a big commercial port on the left side of the river where cargo ships are loaded. We don't want to get too close to it. Be sure the autopilot keeps us well away, in the middle of the river. From there we head almost due north to a heavily wooded island called Dahu. Here." He indicated another large island. This one in the middle of the Pearl River. Unlike almost everywhere else nearby, they could see that this island was without housing of any kind. At least according to Google Earth. "What I'm thinking is, in the morning we duck-in behind Dahu to this quiet area behind it. We can anchor and spend the daylight hours there before pushing on tomorrow night."

"Pushing on to where exactly? Where are we going to make the pickup?"

"I'm thinking here." He pointed to a spot about twenty miles upriver from Dahu. "If we leave at sunset, we can make that easily by eight tomorrow night. Then pick up our friends, and head back while it's still dark."

"Why there?"

"It's the Whampoa Military Academy."

"Military Academy?" Hana blurted in surprise. "That sounds a little dangerous to me."

Devlin explained it had once been a school but was currently a military museum and a very popular tourist destination. "From what I've read, many local tourists arrive by boat so there has to be docking space available." It would not be unusual for a boatload of tourists like them to stop there. It was also a logical site for Chen's parents to visit.

"What makes it even more perfect, the Academy can be reached by the Metro. Chen's parents can take a subway almost to the door."

Hana saw on the chart that the Academy was located on Changzhou Island. An easy destination if the wind and weather stayed benign.

***

It was just noon on the east coast of the United States when Devlin again called Ferrante on the secure phone. He told him what he was considering, and where they might arrange to pick up Chen's parents. Would that location work for them? The CIA man would find out and get back to him as quickly as possible.

"I'm assuming we'll spend from sunup to sundown today, anchored off the island of Dahu and wait there for word from you." Devlin ended the call and turned to Hana. "Well, let's see what they say. It's almost crunch time."

"How are the American authorities contacting the parents?"

"I don't know, and it's best we don't. Safer that way for whoever is the go-between. Besides," he added, "it's best we just concentrate on our end of the business." Something which was fine with Hana.

The two then settled in for the run to Dahu. So far the weather was cooperating, as were the Chinese authorities. They would keep a lookout, and if not disturbed again they could relax until dawn or at least until four a.m. when Roger and Marina would take over.

These evening hours were the perfect time for shipmate chatter, to get to know one another a little better. Devlin's curiosity over Hana's relationship with Roger, which seemed to be somewhat tentative, got the better of him.

"How long have you and Roger been dating?"

"Almost two years already."

"Plans?"

"Nothing definite. We take it one day at a time. He has a lovely family and is kind and loving himself. And ambitious. But so am I and so ..."

"And still very young," Devin interrupted.

"Well, you know women, once past twenty-five thirty looms and the clock is ticking."

"Pressure from parents?"

"Nah. Well, not from my side. His mom and dad keep making noises."

They sat quietly watching the shoreside lights glimmer across the water, shards of color flickered on the wavelets towards them. Almost mesmerized, Hana spoke first in a hushed voice, "Roger and I are both an only child. Small families."

"And?"

She sighed, "Sometimes, I think we are both too self-absorbed to think of sharing a life. We like what we have now."

"Nothing wrong with that."

"I suppose."

Quiet again. The familiarity of sharing the helm, the close quarters, the calm of the night, was working to loosen their tongues.

"Kids?" Devlin asked.

"Yeah," Hana laughed, "and his name is Roger. Can you imagine my big baby a father?"

"Is that a problem for you?"

"Among others."

That put a period to further conversation along that line. Devlin altered tack. After a few moments' pause he asked, "What do think about Chen Lin and Wu Yao? Since we are going all this way, to all this trouble for them."

"I never met Chen Lin. Have no idea what he even looks like."

"Really? My father said the reason the Feds caught him was because you and Roger tracked him down."

"We did, but he refused to see us. It was only on Roger's hunch the FBI got involved."

Hana went on to tell of Roger's plan to lure Chen to a meeting by having her pretend to be working on a story about him. "But it didn't work. He blew us off anyway." She added she was still upset that Roger put her in that position. Asking her to lie. She frowned at the thought. Devlin could see the resentment in her tightened lips.

"But his being found out has actually worked for the best. For Chen I mean," he said.

"Yes. I suppose so. I did get to meet Wu Yao on the night Roger interviewed her for one of his reports. I liked her very much."

"So did we. Marina and I met both of them one night after work in Connecticut."

He went on to explain about their dinner in Essex, the night the four spent aboard their boat and sailing together to Groton.

Hana gave a rueful laugh, "Funny, those two are in all this trouble, a half a world away from home, their very lives and families threatened, and yet they seem more settled than Roger and I."

Devlin considered her disquiet and tried to reassure her, "At your age both of you are still working out who you are as individuals. I wouldn't worry too much about the rough patches. Whoever said, 'a happy marriage is the union of two forgivers' was right on the money."

"As long as one person doesn't have to do all the forgiving."

"Exactly. The trick is to acknowledge we're all individuals and must endure our partner's inevitable foibles. Occasional stupidity is the human condition. Like neglecting to refill a coffee pot!"

"Yeah!" Hana gave a chuckle. So, he had noticed her annoyance. What a perceptive man Devlin seemed to be. His equanimity was contagious, her previous pique evaporated. She felt suddenly brighter and was willing to share more with Devlin, but it was about time for their watch to end so they had to get back to business.

"I'm sure you two will survive," he said, "Now, why don't you go down and wake that man of yours. It's time for him to come topside. We need to hold a strategy session."

When all were gathered around the helm station Devlin explained his plan. Whampoa made sense to all, and the vote to propose it as the pickup site was unanimous. Devlin was relieved Marina did not have to use her extra vote. Better to avoid any divisiveness at this critical juncture. He called Ferrante again and gave him their suggestion.

North Star was working her magic, turning a crew of disparate individuals into a team.

CHAPTER 27
September
THE FINAL PHASE

For those aboard *North Star* it was four a.m. Wednesday. In Boston it was a day earlier, three p.m. Tuesday, only days before the start of the long Labor Day weekend and the end of Chen's internship. For Operation Neptune there was much that had to happen and happen quickly, almost simultaneously: Chen had to deliver his allegedly purloined plans to Zhang; the guard watching the parents' house had to be dismissed; and word of the where and when of their impending rescue had to reach the parents. Once those tasks had been accomplished, *North Star* would be given the go-ahead to make the pickup. Nicholas Ferrante only had little more than twelve hours to get it all done.

His first call was to the FBI. Ferrante explained to Bill Roscoe what needed to happen Stateside. And when.

"Bill, those plans are ready for delivery, right?"

"Yes. All set. We just need the go-ahead to deliver them. Chen can do it this evening if necessary."

"Perfect. Let's do it. But he must make the handover somewhere outside the Chinese Mission. We don't want to risk he might be snatched by those inside. Equally important, he must make clear to Zhang that he won't pass along the information unless the guards overseeing his parents are removed."

"Understood."

"Please have Chen accompanied to be sure there's no mischief in the handover."

"Of course!" Roscoe replied with some irritation, resenting any inference he'd do otherwise.

Ferrante then called Yao and outlined the plan for Chen's parents to go to the Whampoa Academy at eight o'clock that evening. It would be up to Yao's parents to get the message delivered. They'd become the final link in the chain of communication.

Yao carefully composed a text to her parents which they would get on waking. *"Mom, Dad, I was excited to hear you're ready for a shopping trip with that "Squirrel" person. Sounds great. If as you make it to New York I'll be so excited to see you. Meanwhile, enjoy your visit to the Whampoa Museum this evening. Should be interesting. Also, you should know my internship ends tonight. We anticipate a big sendoff beginning at eight p.m. So much happening! Talk soon. Love you both, Yao."*

Her parents were shrewd enough to decode that. They understood Chen's parents would be expected at Whampoa at eight that evening. How would they get there? Yao had no idea. But at least Chen's mom and dad would get the message and know where they were expected to be, and at what time.

Once Ferrante knew the message had been delivered, he called the *North Star* crew.

Dawn was breaking on the Pearl River when Devlin answered, "Go ahead."

"Your suggestion is accepted. Spend an enjoyable day swimming near your island paradise, then in the evening meet your friends where and when you suggested."

"Perfect. Thanks. You know all we have are some photos of them taken years ago."

"Yes. The but the parents will confirm identity. I have asked that they arrive at the exhibit entrance by eight. Be there to greet them."

"Sounds perfect."

"One more thing. Tell your shipmates we've confirmed there is absolutely no reason for concern about their safety here in the U.S. I'll explain fully when they return, but it turns out our fears were premature."

Devlin looked over to Roger and Hana standing nearby and gave them a thumbs up, "Excellent news, I'll pass it on."

"OK. Any problems let me know. Good luck!"

They clicked off.

For Roger and Hana, the reason there might be concern for their safety was always unclear. Roger had even suspected talk of his being a target was all just a ruse to get him off the story and give it to Gabe Breslin. So, news that the worry was ill-founded, while certainly a relief, was received with little overt emotion.

"I guess it's their job to worry, but the idea that anyone would really come after us seemed pretty far-fetched," said Roger.

Hana agreed, with a smidge of doubt. "Right. I mean we didn't know anything about Chen that others didn't know." But despite Roger's blithe dismissal of the threat, she was astute enough to know the Feds must have uncovered some information that warranted getting the two of them out of town. The explanation could wait until they returned to New York.

Neither she nor Roger were aware of the details involving the Chechen hit squad, nor that the person who did the most to defuse that threat was Gabe Breslin. Something which would have rankled Roger no end. Breslin's successful investigation in New Jersey meant it was "Mission Accomplished" for at least one prong of Neptune's Trident.

***

While Ferrante was mobilizing the crew in the China Sea, it was up to Roscoe of the FBI to get the ball rolling in the U.S. He called Liam in his office at the Navy base. Liam was standing beside Chen when the call came in. They had the newly drawn set of plans laid out on the architect's table and had been photographing them using Chen's phone. It was decided that Chen would not send copies to Zhang electronically, but rather print them out. That way there would have to be a physical handoff which could be watched and recorded.

"Liam, it's Bill Roscoe. Everything is in place. You've got the go-ahead to get the kid moving."

Both men smiled with relief. Their carefully fabricated fake was ready to be delivered.

As soon as photos of the plans were printed, Chen made the call to Zhang in the Chinese Mission.

"I have what you want and will be able to deliver them tonight."

"Excellent," a relieved voice replied, "I'll meet you here in the lobby. What time will you arrive?"

"Sorry, I can't do that. I will take the train in and meet you by the clock in Grand Central Station. I will be there at eight tonight. Sharp."

"That can't be. I must remain in the Mission."

"Where you must be is your problem. I have what you want and will give it to you, or someone you send, where and when I said. That's it. This is very dangerous for all of us, especially me." Then with a vehemence unusual for him, "Don't fuck it up."

Zhang was at once enraged, fearful, and helpless. The handover was too important to let anyone else handle. He would have to take the chance, leave the Mission, and meet Chen in person.

"And something else," Chen said, "I want confirmation the intimidation of my parents has ended. I will destroy what I have for you and surrender both of us to the authorities, unless you do as I say and agree to let me speak with them. You have two hours to make that happen."

"But it's five o'clock in the morning there!"

"I'm sure it is news they will be happy to be awakened for. I am going to be on the train to New York shortly. I'll be awaiting their call."

"Wait..."

Before Zhang could protest, Chen hung up.

It was almost five in the afternoon.

"Come on Lin," Liam said, "I'll take you to the heliport."

There was never any intention of Chen taking a train. A Navy helicopter would fly him from New London to the

Wall Street Heliport in lower Manhattan. There they would be met by Roscoe's agents and shuttled to Grand Central. Chen and the agents would wait in a string of black SUV's on Vanderbilt Avenue, at the west side of the Terminal, until the planned meeting time.

Shortly after seven o'clock Chen was sitting in the passenger seat of the SUV a jumble of nerves. He could feel dampness in his armpits and jumped when his phone buzzed. A huge relief, it was his father in Guangzhou.

"Hello son, what is happening? We have been told all is now resolved, that our 'protective' detail has been removed, and to call you. Are you all right?"

The sound of his father's voice did much to calm him. "I'm fine dad. I have done a small favor for the government, and they have graciously responded. You should now consider yourselves free to go about your normal activities. How is mom?"

"Much better since the guards outside are gone. So, you are saying we are once again free to go as we please?"

Chen assumed his parent's phone was tapped so spoke carefully.

"Absolutely, please do as you wish today. But listen, I am in the middle of something important here and must cut this short. Please give my love to mom and tell her we will talk again tomorrow morning, your time, when I am less busy."

They said their goodbyes and hung up.

Chen smiled at the agent next to him, "Looks like I will be able to deliver the goods. Is everyone in place?"

"We're all set. You want to continue to wait here in the car?"

"No. I'd prefer to head for the Food Court downstairs

and sit there before going to meet him."

The officer had two of his men exit their SUVs, follow Chen and stay with him. A photography detail would remain in place in the main concourse. The document handoff was just minutes away.

Chen slipped into the building through the side door on Vanderbilt Avenue, walked down the broad marble steps to the main concourse and still farther down to the Food Court level. He picked up a coffee at one of the shops, sat in its reserved seating area, and waited. In his left hand he clutched a wide manila envelope. It never left his hand. At five minutes to eight he walked to Platform 119 where a train from Stamford, Connecticut had just arrived. He joined the exiting crowd and walked in the midst of them back up the stairs. On the Concourse floor he stopped, confirmed the presence of his two shadows nearby, and with purposeful strides moved to the middle of the vast and busy space.

All around him commuters were buying tickets, scurrying to and from trains, and tourists stood agog, heads tilted back staring at the star constellations painted on the ceiling. And of course, taking pictures. So many were taking pictures no one would notice the young couple standing by the clock doing the same. It was toward them Chen walked because standing next to them was Zhang Wei. At Chen's approach Zhang gave a start, his nerves taut, emotions strung out. Improbably, almost ludicrously, he was wearing a Yankees baseball cap pulled low on his forehead. Chen almost laughed when he saw it. But Zhang suspected there would likely be face recognition cameras situated in the

Terminal and wasn't taking chances. He didn't pay attention to the young couple taking selfies nearby; pictures in which he was the primary focus.

The two men did not waste words.

"Mister Zhang I brought what you asked for."

"Thank you, Mister Chen. You received the confirmation you requested I assume."

"Yes."

"That is good."

"My internship ends in two days, so this is goodbye. I expect we will never have the opportunity to renew this relationship."

"One never knows," Zhang said ominously. Then with a weak smile, "But probably not."

"I'm afraid in this instance, never means never. Goodbye."

Chen turned and walked back toward the train platforms while Zhang exited toward the 42nd Street doors. He never noticed those 'tourists' taking movies of the handoff, and of his departure.

As he made his way out, Zhang did not realize how lucky he was to perform this errand. The envelope he was carrying was the only reason he had not been instantly arrested. Getting the phony plans to his superiors was more important to Operation Neptune than picking up a low-level Chinese agent. As a matter of fact, his delivery was so important he was followed back to the Mission, just to be sure he returned safely. It would be very inconvenient for everyone if he were mugged by a local miscreant walking home.

CHAPTER 28
RIVER RUN

The crew of *North Star* was much too excited to sleep. At their pre-dawn strategy session they approved making Whampoa the pickup site for Chen's parents. They also debated and settled on how they would try to accomplish it. Much of the debate revolved around who would land on Whampoa and who would stay with the boat. It was a sensitive issue. Roger felt one of the men should go ashore with one of the women, for muscle if needed. Devlin agreed, but for a different reason. He said if both women went ashore the boat would be essentially mute, unable to converse with anyone either in English or Chinese.

"We can't use English on the radio without being instantly discovered. And of course, neither Roger nor I speak Mandarin or Cantonese. If the two of us are alone on the boat and anyone hails us, we would be unable to respond."

Marina thought otherwise; given traditional Chinese courtesy she felt two women together were likely to be given deference ashore, less likely to be accosted by strangers. She was insistent; there would not be any need of 'muscle.' "Plus," she said, "we can take a handheld VHF radio along. If anyone calls the boat, Hana or I will answer using the handheld. You guys just stay silent."

Her argument made sense. Even though both Roger and Devlin were not happy with letting the women go it alone, they came to see the logic in it. *North Star* would anchor offshore. The men would stay aboard out of sight, and the women would take the RIB dinghy to the Museum's dock.

    That settled, with Marina at the wheel they continued to their interim stop, the island of Dahu. So far, the timing was working out as hoped; *North Star* arrived at the island of Dahu just as dawn was breaking. Now to find a safe place to lay to, out of sight.

    On the catamaran all the lines controlling the sails were led back inside the cockpit. That meant Marina was able to reduce sail without stepping outside and making herself visible. With Devlin's help she rolled the headsail, the jib, around its roller-furler, then dropped the mainsail into a boom bag —its canvas container. With the sails down they motored around to a cove on the northwest side of the island. The water, sheltered from the river's current was calm as a pond. The cove was remote from any houses, the perimeter shrouded in trees and still in the shadow of the rising sun. Since the catamaran didn't have a keel it only drew about three feet. It could motor close to the forested shore where it almost disappeared from view. At least from three sides. The narrow entrance to the cove looked out on the main river and within sight of whatever boat traffic sailed by.

    Devlin asked Roger to join him on the foredeck so he could instruct him on the anchoring procedure. Roger would be asked to handle the task alone when they arrived at Whampoa and so he needed to know the drill. Roger then gave Hana his phone and requested she videotape whatever she could of the operation. Getting the footage he needed, given the confined space of the boat and the restrictions on what could be shown, was going to be difficult. Hana's perceptive eye would be critical.

Marina checked the depth of the water and the wind direction. Satisfied, she picked a place to drop anchor. Devlin took Roger to the foredeck and showed him how to use the electric windlass. They were in about ten feet of water. Since the wind was light and expected to stay that way Devlin said they'd only need to drop about thirty feet of chain for a secure hold. The windlass would let out six feet of chain every five seconds, so Roger should count out thirty seconds and that would be more than enough chain to anchor safely. Once the anchor hit bottom Marina put the boat into reverse to string out the chain and set it firmly in the bottom.

"Nicely done. Simple," Devlin said. "Of course, depending on the weather, it could be a lot trickier."

"Now the hard part," Marina said once they were all in the cabin, "waiting out the daylight."

"Let's hope we're left alone," Hana added. "I don't relish the idea of having to explain ourselves to anyone."

"Tourists enjoying a day on the water," said Roger. "Maybe we should play the part and go swimming." Hana gave him a look that seemed to say ... "Please grow up."

But Devlin agreed. "Sure, why not? After breakfast we should do our best to keep as busy and relaxed as possible." He and Hana would take the opportunity to get some sleep since they'd been up all night. Roger and Marina would keep watch until noon. Shifts would change again at four in the afternoon. Devlin wanted them all to be rested before they moved to Whampoa. There would certainly be no sleeping after that. At least not until their guests were safely deposited in Macau.

Once everyone was settled, Marina set *North Star's* VHF radio to Channel 13, the international channel for commercial marine operations. That way she could keep an ear on the chatter between nearby boats.

The morning radio traffic was light until about ten o'clock when the nearby fuel oil tank farm began receiving deliveries. Large self-propelled barges made their way to and from the docks along the water's edge, the captains signaling their intentions over the radio. They passed a fair distance north of where Marina had anchored, but occasionally a crewman seeing Roger on deck in the distance would wave a hello. The simple act of man-to-man recognition made him pensive again.

Back in the cabin he took a seat next to Marina. "Just another working stiff trying to pay the bills," he said. "Little does he know he is waving to a minor player in the game of international power politics."

"Very minor players." Marina said, lumping herself and all of them in the same game.

"Small fry trying to save the world from the machinations of the masters of the universe."

Marina laughed, "Small fry trying not to get fried themselves." Then, "You really want to go for a swim?"

Seeing a sheen of spilled oil on the water, and remembering Hana's sour expression, he demurred. "In daylight the river doesn't look too inviting. I'll skip that idea."

"I noticed Hana thought you were a little crazy to contemplate a dip."

"Just another instance of her playing stern mama to her naughty little boy. I'm afraid she thinks of me as not quite ready for prime time."

"Meaning?"

"In need of more seasoning, fermentation, time in the bottle. In other words, I need to grow up."

Trying to lighten the mood Marina joked, "Yeah well, you men are just slow to mature. Devlin is ten years older than you and I still tie his laces."

"I just hope she's willing to hang around while I develop whatever gravitas she's looking for."

That prompted a touch on the arm from Marina, now truly fond of this young man. "She's lucky to have you. Hang in there."

Their moment together was interrupted by a ring tone from the satellite phone. Marina answered, "Marina here."

It was Ferrante. "Hello, just checking to see if you are in position, and all is well."

"Yes, and yes. We're anchored where we said we'd be. Anticipate leaving at dusk to arrive at the location by eight."

"Excellent. If you don't hear from me, it means all is good. Call when you're on your way home."

After they disconnected Marina relayed what was said to Roger, "Home. Has a nice ring to it."

Just moments later a staticky squawk came from the VHF radio, "Sailboat at anchor off Dahu, this is the Harbor Master at Port Yanwei. Come back please."

Marina groaned, not again. Couldn't he wait until Hana was available? Just then as if in answer to prayers, Hana, who'd been preparing for the next watch, ran up the steps from below. She snatched the microphone from Marina. The Harbor Master repeated his call, "Sailboat off Dahu, please come back."

"This is the boat *North Star* go ahead please," Hana said, doing all she could to keep panic from her voice. The three sailors stared at one another, fearful of what might come next.

"*North Star* this is the Harbor Master. I see you have anchored off Dahu. This is a warning ..." the three almost groaned aloud, "A barge towed by a tugboat is due to arrive in one hour. We use that cove as a staging area. The barge will be anchored there. I am sorry to disturb you, but you must depart that area. And soon. Over."

Flooded with relief that they weren't going to be boarded Hana replied, "Understood. We will depart shortly. Thank you, Harbor Master. *North Star* out."

"Thank you *North Star*. Yanwei Harbor Master out."

"So much for our day of rest," said Marina. "Time for another strategy session."

Marina went below and entered the stateroom where Devlin, with a concerned look on his face, was just pulling on his pants. "What's up hon, I thought I heard somebody on the radio."

Marina explained, prompting a sigh of exasperation from her husband. "Well, that's an unwanted wrinkle. I guess things have been going too smoothly to last."

The four met in the cockpit and hashed over the possibilities: They could sail straight for Whampoa and spend the day at anchor there. They could sail back out into the river and loaf along all afternoon. Or, they could sail part way and try for another secluded spot to anchor. There was no strong consensus until Roger suggested, "I think the most dangerous thing for us is to be floating directionless up and down the river. So that option is out. As for anchoring someplace new, what is the advantage of that? We could just invite another expulsion. I would opt for heading to our destination and anchor offshore there. After all, if it is a heavily trafficked tourist spot, we could get lost in the crowd."

No better option presenting itself, they all agreed and prepared to up-anchor and sail away. Under the table, Hana squeezed Roger's hand approvingly.

Reversing the arrival procedure, Roger went forward to raise and stow the anchor, while Devlin took the wheel and motored forward and then out of the cove. They raised sail and by one p.m. were again heading upriver. The wind had started to swing to the north again. Instead of coming from behind them it was now on their left, on the port beam. It was a good angle of sail for *North Star* allowing them to maneuver easily around the many barges and other watercraft on the river. The Pearl was a busy commercial waterway. Too busy to use the autopilot, they had to keep a constant watch on the traffic.

"We're doing a little better than five knots," Devlin said. "Let's slow down a little so we don't arrive at Whampoa too early." He ordered the sails eased and headed more to the center of the river. The current there was flowing more strongly against them, the combination of the less efficient sails and opposing current dropped their speed to just a little more than two knots, not much better than standing still. "Good that should do it." he said. Then, "How about some lunch? Anyone hungry?"

The boat's refrigerator was small but supplied with enough food for a couple of days at sea. There were containers of soup, vegetables and a variety of pork, beef and chicken slices. And of course rice, indispensable here. Roger offered to act as sous chef, with Hana providing the culinary expertise. It was a common arrangement for them at her house. The day was sunny and the water calm. Perfect for a picnic lunch aboard. Once the food was heated in the microwave, the three not actively working sat around the table on the port side of the boat. Devlin stayed at the wheel.

"On a slow boat to China," Roger said laughing.

Hana agreed, "A very slow boat." After the short scare back on Dahu the mood once again turned upbeat. They were a few short miles from their destination. If all went well, shortly after nightfall they would be sailing back over these very waters on their way home. Every foot passing under the hull was a foot closer to the end of this journey.

Marina began clearing the dishes and food containers saying her cleaning up was only fair since Roger and Hana did the cooking. She looked out the window and saw that the jib was beginning to flap, and a belly began to form in its forward edge. "The wind must be heading us," she said. Devlin looked at the wind gauge and confirmed the breeze was not only moving forward but dying altogether. "I think we might have to start the engines. No wind, and against the flow of the river won't work for us."

Roger gave Marina a hand reducing sail as Devlin started the two engines, one in each pontoon. Hana went topside to arrange the mainsail in its boom bag. Part of her job was to be a visible Asian presence on the boat for anyone looking with binoculars. The others tried to stay inside as much as possible. Certainly if close to a passing ship.

They hadn't motored for more than fifteen minutes when Devlin saw a red light on one of the starboard engine gauges. "Uh, oh," he said, "Houston we have a problem." The instrument indicated the engine was beginning to overheat. "Marina, can you take the helm please? You will have to run on just one engine. Take it slow."

"What's up?" Roger asked. Devlin told him, "Engine running hot," as he stopped the faulty engine.

"I know a lot about diesels," Roger offered, "I can help."

"Thanks," said Devlin, "my boat's engine is also a diesel; let's both take a look."

A box of tools and another of spare parts were in a clearly marked locker in the cabin. The two men hauled the boxes to the hatch above the starboard engine. They swung the hatch open. Looking in Roger groaned at the cramped space. There was hardly room for one man's arms, much less their two bodies.

"It's most likely the impeller," Devlin said, meaning the propeller like device which brought seawater into the cooling system.

"Definitely not something found in a car," Roger said.

"No. And a part on a boat that always seems to die at the worst time."

"Murphy's Law!"

The two men got to work. "Why the hell do they build the entire boat around the water pump!" Their chatter and occasional laughs and curses could be heard as Devlin struggled to unscrew the pump's cover.

While the men were buried headfirst in the bowels of the boat, Hana joined Marina at the wheel. Despite the circumstances —there did remain one good engine— they could smile at the sounds coming from the back of the boat.

"I think the real reason Devlin has a boat is so he can spend time working on it," Marina said.

"Roger is the same with his ancient car. I think puttering with it is when he is most relaxed. When he has his head under the hood."

"Just boys! I guess they never change."

"Oh, don't say that. I keep waiting for Roger to grow up," Hana said with a laugh.

"Probably a long wait," Marina said commiserating, "I remember when I married Devlin, I swore I would get him to dress like a grownup. You know, more fashionably. Well, I'm lucky he wears a uniform every day. Otherwise, he'd always be in shorts and flip flops."

"You mean it's hopeless?"

"Changing a man? Pretty much." Marina said, "You ever hear the expression, 'Marry the man today, change him tomorrow.' Forget it. Change him? Won't happen."

Hana took mild comfort in that. Then asked, "Tell me Marina, how have you managed having your career at the UN with two kids. I know that hidebound place. It can't have been easy."

Marina was pleased to play mentor to a woman who appeared to have the same questions she had herself not many years before. "It really wasn't bad when Richard, my first child was born. We managed very well. My mother was a great help. Still is. The real challenge came with the birth of

Cynthia. Two children make for a whole different workload."

"But you thought having a second child worth it?"

"Oh, Hana I can't begin to answer that question. To say 'worth it' when speaking of your own children isn't possible."

"Priceless?"

"Exactly. But not painless!" With a small smile Marina added, "And more pain might be on the way."

"You mean …?

Marina had no intention of saying anything more until she told Devlin. She gave a woman-to-woman shrug and left it there.

"Oh wow! Big decisions. I'm not anywhere near ready for them yet."

"Understandable. You'll know what you want when the time comes."

Hana was not so sure that would be true. Besides, how do you know when the time has come?

While Devlin was working, Roger took out his phone to capture more video of their travails. It was necessary to show some of the nuts and bolts of making the journey. Again, he avoided any faces, showing only Devlin's hands at work as he grumbled and gasped. Finally, grunting and flushed, Devlin pulled his head out of the hatchway and handed two screwdrivers to Roger. "Here young man, you're skinnier than me. You reach down and use these to pull the old impeller out of the pump."

Roger did as requested. With guidance from above he replaced the broken part and screwed the cover back into place. The two returned to the cabin. Marina restarted the engine which ran smoothly, and cool once again.

CHAPTER 29
WHAMPOA

North Star arrived in the waters off Whampoa shortly after six with the sun low in the west. Motoring slowly Marina picked her way along the shorefront until she found the slips used by the three tourist ferries that serviced the island. Just beyond them to the south was a bend in the river that was well out of the way of the river traffic, which was still busy at that hour. Once again Roger went forward to the bow and took control of the anchor, he and Marina in sync as she backed down and snugged-up the chain rode. Hana was standing at his side, trying her best to hide his features from any prying eyes.

Once again 'Team Neptune,' as they'd begun to call themselves, settled in for a snack before getting on with the night's work. Marina took the lead in this last-minute strategy session while they grazed a platter of cheese, crackers and edamame.

"I think Hana and I will need at least fifteen minutes to get the lay of the land and orient ourselves before we are supposed to meet the parents at eight. Backtiming from eight, we should arrive ashore at seven-forty-five. If we allow fifteen minutes to ride and stash the dinghy, that means we shove off from *North Star* at seven-thirty.

"The less time ashore the better as far as I'm concerned," said Hana. Everyone agreed. After all, they had no right to be on Chinese soil. If caught, the two women could easily end up in a prison, at least temporarily. And not incidentally have created an international incident.

"If all goes well you should be back by eight-thirty, right?" Roger asked, looking at Hana with concern.

"Let's hope," she said quietly. Now that departure was imminent, the seriousness of the situation had them in a somber mood. Until then the ride up the Pearl River had been almost a lark, only slightly spiced with fears of discovery. While on the river they could always claim they were tourists gone astray in the waters off Hong Kong. But once ashore, who knew what might happen if stopped and questioned.

No one wanted to mention it aloud for fear they would jinx themselves, break their charmed run. All were aware of their exceptional good fortune. They had come to the attention of the authorities twice, were twice hailed on the radio and twice asked to move. Both times they managed to avoid closer inspection. Could this luck really last? Still ahead were the most dangerous parts of the mission, stepping onto Chinese soil, and the final run down the Pearl with two escaping Chinese citizens aboard. So far all had gone their way, but to remark on it was tempting fate. Superstitious? Sure, but still … So, each of them kept their fears to themselves.

It was in that state of mind Devlin asked himself, *why was the last leg of any operation always the trickiest?* With a catch in his voice he said to Marina, "If at all possible, speak to no one until the couple approaches you." He was having second thoughts about the two women going alone onto the mainland without backup of any kind. But really, even if Roger and he were with them, what could they do if the women were discovered? They would not be able to fight their way out, a ridiculous thought one hundred miles up a Chinese river. So, everything depended on Marina's and Hana's wits, courage and resourcefulness.

At seven o'clock the women changed out of their sailing clothes and into dresses and shoes more appropriate for touring a museum. Even though it was dusk, they added sunglasses and short caps. By seven-thirty all was ready. The men hauled the dinghy to the starboard side of *North Star* and tied it tight. The two women climbed down onto the pontoon and clambered aboard the small boat. Marina started the engine. Happily, the four-stroke Yamaha made very little noise or smoke. The lines were released, and they motored toward the shore about fifty yards away.

In a small cove to the south of the ferry-slips was a spacious dock set aside specifically for the use of visitors arriving by boat. Three other dinghies and a small launch were already tied there. *North Star's* dinghy would not be out of place. There was no appreciable tidal change this far up the river, so it was an easy climb out of the boat and onto the dock. The sun was close to the horizon meaning there was still plenty of light. Even so the dock's spotlights had been turned on in anticipation of the coming darkness. A quick glance to the top of a light pole showed Marina there was a camera focused on the area. With luck it wouldn't be continually watched, just making a recording which could be viewed if a theft or other problem was reported.

Marina kept her head down and away from the camera as much as possible, Hana was free to walk as she pleased. Having learned how to tie a line to a cleat, Hana made a quick job of it, and the two women strolled from the water's edge onto the museum grounds. They arrived at the rear of a series of buildings beyond which they could see what looked to be a main street, with cars, buses and pedestrians strolling by.

"The main entrance must be off that big street," Hana said to Marina in Mandarin. They would speak only in Chinese for as long as they were ashore. The two women walked slowly toward the busy thoroughfare sure that their timing so far was as planned. Marina checked her watch and saw there was still a good ten minutes before they were supposed to arrive at the main gate to the museum complex. They took a few steps to the left and saw only residential apartments. Reversing direction, they quickly spotted what they were looking for. The museum entrance was marked by two large white stone pillars flanking an elaborate metal gate. Beyond the gate was a small grass courtyard with neatly trimmed hedges bordering a concrete walkway that led directly to the museum's main doorway. Rather than walk into the courtyard the women strolled some twenty yards past the entrance and stopped to reconnoiter.

"Well, we're here," said Hana. "Now let's see if they show up. It will be a nasty surprise if we did all this for nothing."

Despite Ferrante's assurance that all was on track, who knew what might possibly happen at the last minute. There were so many variables.

"I don't know how Chen's parents were supposed to get the word, or even if they ever agreed to leave," Marina said as her eyes searched the darkening street. "For all we know, they might never have heard we were coming, or they could have decided to forget leaving, and stay in China!"

Hana also looked up and down the avenue, there were plenty of passersby but no one obviously looking for them, "I hope they do show, but show or not, I'm ready to get home to my boring life back in New York."

"My kids are going to be near squeezed to death when I see them."

"The Feds said Roger and I would be safer coming here; but I still don't understand why you and Devlin got roped into this ... wait, look at that couple."

A distinguished looking mustachioed man in a black fedora and black rain slicker, accompanied by an elegantly dressed woman walked out of the museum gate. They hesitated for a second, turned and stared in the direction of Hana and Marina. It was three minutes after eight o'clock. The two women walked quickly back toward the gate and approached the couple.

"Excuse us," said Hana, "we are supposed to meet someone here this evening and I was wondering ..."

"No, so sorry," the man interrupted, "it would not be us. We are just looking for a taxi. On our way to dinner."

"Oh, forgive me. Thank you and have a lovely evening."

The women watched as the couple strolled back in the direction of a nearby street corner where traffic was heavier, and the availability of a taxi likely greater.

Just then the VHF radio Marina had tucked in the inside pocket of her jacket clicked twice. It was Devlin signaling from the boat. No voice, just click, click. Marina answered by doing the same, pressing the transmit button twice indicating that all was well. Which it was … sort of. They were unmolested by any security but beginning to worry. It was getting to be ten minutes past eight and still no sign of anyone coming toward them.

Hana turned when the door to the museum opened and a shaft of yellow light brightened the entryway. A young family exited and was silhouetted in the doorway, two children chattering excitedly next to their parents. Disappointed, Hana exhaled deeply. Then, just as she was turning back to search the street again, she noticed someone briefly illuminated by the inside light. Someone standing in the shadows on the right side of the courtyard. Stepping aside the gate she let the family pass and whispered to Marina, "Someone is waiting there." They entered the courtyard and found a slim, medium height man standing next to a woman both ostensibly trying to read a brochure from the museum in the dim light. The man was wearing a warm jacket against the night chill, and the woman a short wool coat. He had a backpack at his feet, and she carried a large purse. Large enough to be stuffed with a variety of personal effects. If it was them, they must have been able to take only their most treasured possessions. When the two women approached, the man looked up expectantly and appeared relieved when Hana introduced herself. "Hello, we are supposed to meet some friends here at eight o'clock."

"Yes, as are we," the man said. "Friends of our son."

"What is his name?" Marina asked.

The woman smiled at the face of the westerner. "His name is Lin. Chen Lin."

"He has a favorite animal?"

"Squirrels," said the father.

"So we have heard," Marina said bowing in greeting.

The foursome exited the courtyard and strolled together in the direction of the docked dinghy. Marina whispered the outline of their plans as they walked. The couple was putting their fate in the hands of these strangers. It would ease their anxiety if they knew what to expect from here on out.

CHAPTER 30
A ROOKIE ERROR

The dinghy ride back to *North Star* was short and without incident. Chen's parents were welcomed aboard in hushed tones and asked to secrete themselves below. No one spoke above a whisper. From here on they would try to stay as invisible as possible.

When all gear was safely stowed, and the dinghy tied off, the anchor and its chain were taken up as quietly as the crew could manage. They drifted away from the anchorage and when out of earshot of any nearby boats, started the engines. Motoring as slowly as possible to avoid creating a wake, the boat slid surreptitiously back into the main river. The sails remained furled to keep the boat's profile as dark and low as possible, its silhouette scarcely discernible against the glittery distraction of shoreside lights. In the sky the new moon was completely dark. Without its light the stars stippled the heavens but gave little illumination. The river flowed velvet through the night's blackness. Marina at the helm welcoming the darkness muttered to herself, *No moon. Lucky for us*.

Devlin was anxious to put distance between *North Star* and the Whampoa rendezvous point. Once beyond the museum's anchorage and back in the southward flow of the river he gently increased the engine rpms. The added power, combined with the thrust from the ebbing current accelerated their speed.

Devlin passed the helm to Roger with instructions to

follow a course he'd laid out. On the chart plotter's screen, located directly in front of the steering wheel, was a little icon in the shape of a ship. "It shows our position," said Devlin. "Just keep that icon moving along the line marking the course. It will take us home." Once Roger settled in at the controls Devlin asked, "What's our speed?"

Roger checked the gauges, "Twelve knots."

Devlin considered that a little faster than might be prudent, but not excessive. At that speed they should reach Macau shortly after daylight. Devlin was as fixated on his goal as a marathon runner in sight of the finish line. He congratulated himself, *Our timing is going to be ideal.*

He was mistaken. The boat's speed was actually much faster than twelve knots. Roger had checked the wrong knot meter ---a rookie error. There were two speedos on *North Star*: one of them used GPS to measure the boat's speed over the ground, which is the speed between any two points on earth. What is usually thought of as a speedometer.

The other knot meter measures the speed at which water is flowing past the hull. It gives the boat's speed through the water, a speed which changes with the direction of the current. If a boat is traveling in the same direction as the water in which it floats, the speed shown on the meter will be reduced by the speed of the current. That's the instrument Roger had checked.

The moon phase added to the confusion. Because a new moon increases the tidal pull, the Pearl's southward current was running much faster than usual, better than four knots. So *North Star* was actually traveling downriver at more than sixteen knots, not twelve.

The speeding boat did not go unnoticed by local radar. It was ten-fifteen, only an hour after they left Whampoa when a flashing blue light started moving along the coast on their left. Devlin, sitting by the port side windows, watched the light gradually begin to gain speed, angle toward them, and rapidly close the distance.

Devlin ran to the helm and checked their speed, "Oh shit!" Too late he noticed Roger's mistake. "Police!" Devlin shouted, pointing out the blue light and taking responsibility for the mistake, cursed his own carelessness. He retook the helm. It was unintentional but he'd violated his own dictum about avoiding any suspicious maneuvering. Speeding downriver in the direction of Hong Kong was sure to catch someone's attention.

"Hana, come to the helm quickly!" he called as he slowly brought the throttle back. "See this course on the compass? 125 degrees. Just keep steering that course. If they ask you to stop, bring the throttle lever up and let the engine idle."

He turned to Marina. "Go down and waken Chen's parents. Get them up here right now."

"What?"

"Be sure they bring their passports."

"Roger, go down with Marina and the two of you stay out of sight. I'll join you in a minute. We're about to be boarded."

Just then a gravelly voice came from the radio, not overtly threatening but firm and commanding, "This is Coast

Guard patrol boat 254 to the sailboat traveling downriver off Dashatou. Come back please."

Devlin gave the microphone to Hana, "Whatever he's asking ... just answer him calmly and cooperate. Try to stall them until Chen's parents get here."

Hana pressed the transmit button, "Hello Coast Guard, this is the sailboat *North Star*. Go ahead please." Her hand was shaking but her voice held steady.

"Good evening *North Star*. Please switch to Channel 21."

"Roger that, switching to 21."

Devlin whispered urgently to Hana. "It will be just you and Chen's parents aboard, got it? Going to Macau."

He handed her the boat's fake registration. "Here. Show this if asked. We will be hiding below. Just keep them from searching the boat."

Those brief snatches were all the instruction Hana got. Everything she did and said from then on would have to be improvised.

The team's charmed cruise up the Pearl River had come to an abrupt end. They were sure to be boarded and searched. *There's no way that guy is racing toward us just to wave hello,* Hana grumbled under her breath. Sure enough, no sooner had Hana switched to Channel 21 as requested, than the patrol boat radioed, "*North Star*, we will be approaching you from your port side and ask you to please heave-to for inspection."

"Certainly, sir I will stop and stand by. But may I ask why you are stopping us?" Hana tried to sound lighthearted, almost flirtatious. She was playing for time.

"Just a routine check, *North Star*. Just routine."

"All right sir, this is *North Star* standing by on 21."

The patrol boat was about a quarter of a mile away and closing fast when Chen's parents arrived at the helm station, totally confused.

"We were told to bring our passports ..." Chen's father started.

"The Coast Guard is coming to inspect us," Hana said quickly. "You must tell them we are all sailing to Macau for a gambling weekend. It is just the three of us aboard. Understand?"

They got the message immediately. Both of Chen's parents were in their mid-fifties, and while not by any means especially athletic they were spry enough, and young enough to be considered useful hands on a catamaran of that size. Most importantly, they also looked prosperous enough to be on a well-appointed yacht cruising to a gambling mecca. But Hana, afraid the older people might panic or show nervousness said, "Let me do the talking, you just agree with whatever I say." This while she was still trying to fabricate a believable story. *Just me and my future in-laws going to have some fun in Macau*, she repeated to herself.

Moments later the Coast Guard boat moved expertly alongside, the crew tossed out fenders to protect both boats and lashed the two vessels together.

The captain, a somewhat grizzled but still urbane looking sixtyish man with a big brush mustache declined the help of a crewman and swung himself aboard alone. His stern, no nonsense demeanor softened slightly when he saw who was at the helm. He looked bemused at Hana. Her youthful beauty brightened what had been just another boring night of river patrols.

Hana saw his pleased reaction to her and calmed considerably. She became a sprightly ingénue, a part she knew how to play.

"Welcome aboard captain. My name is Li Hana. These are my boyfriend's parents, Mister and Madam Chen."

She spoke to him brightly, as if he were an older uncle and she a favorite niece.

The captain nodded and smiled at the three of them. "Good evening. Please can I see your papers, and the boat registration? And may I ask what you are doing out on the river at this late hour?"

Hana dug out the phony registration, and the three handed over their passports. The captain gave them only a cursory look. They were Chinese nationals after all. Hana started speaking even as he flipped the pages, "We left Guangzhou early this evening. We are going to Macau for the weekend and ..."

Chen's mother interrupted, "My son is meeting us. It is our thirtieth wedding anniversary and my husband ..."

"Yes," it was Mr. Chen's turn to interrupt, "they want to gamble my money away."

Despite the tension Hana had to smile. Chen's parents were staging an impromptu performance. She obviously didn't need to worry about how they would conduct themselves.

"Quite a boat you have here," said the captain, thinking money shouldn't be too much of a problem for these people. Just the sort of wealthy Chinese who would waste time and money gambling.

"Oh, it's a rented boat. We could never afford to buy such a thing," said Mrs. Chen.

"I only wish it was theirs," Hana sighed.

"You can handle this vessel young lady?"

Hana smiled, tilted her head so that her long black hair fell over her right eye and said softly, "Of course. I am a sailing instructor in Guangzhou and," she pointed to Chen's parents, "I do have their help. But if you want to lend us one of your crew for the rest of the way ..."

"I would love to assist you, young lady but must regrettably refuse." He raised his eyes to Hana and smiled. "Not that any of my men would decline the opportunity!"

The captain returned their papers, which they hoped meant he was ready to leave. Instead, he said, "Now about the required safety equipment. May I see where you stow your life preservers." A flash of panic coursed through Hana. I*s he going to inspect the whole boat? Where the hell are the life preservers?* Then she remembered the locker the students had shown her in Hong Kong. Inside were ten PFD's, more than enough for everyone.

"OK very good," the captain said as he strolled slowly around the spacious deck. Moving to the helm station he fingered the computer screen, radios and other electronics. "I wish we were as well equipped," he muttered. Looking back to Hana he asked, "Fire extinguishers? Emergency flares?" *Jesus!* thought Hana, *will he ever quit?*

Hana remembered when the men had to get tools to fix the engine, the tool locker was marked. Thank God all the lockers had stenciled labels on them. A quick glance around and Hana walked to the appropriate hatches and pointed. "Here and here," she said opening the locker doors.

The captain bent down to examine the emergency equipment and checked the expiration dates. All OK. "Very good," he mumbled to himself. Then satisfied all was in order, and that he had been as thorough as necessary, the captain stood and smiled benignly at Hana.

"Very good captain," he said, "all seems shipshape. You run an excellent boat."

By now, Hana had what she thought was a good read on the Coast Guard captain. She surmised he had seen all he needed to and was ready to leave. This might be an opportunity to allay any remaining suspicions, and perhaps guarantee they'd endure no further boardings. It was a gamble, but she thought it worth the risk, so she said, "Do you need to go below?"

The captain glanced toward the steps leading down to the portside pontoon, the berth opposite to where Devlin and the others were hiding. He saw at the foot of the steps Chen's parents' coats which were hanging on hooks. "No that won't be necessary. But I suggest you moderate your speed while motoring during the evening hours or you might be stopped again."

"Oh, absolutely, Captain. Thank you for the advice."

After shaking hands all around the captain wished them a safe journey and returned to his boat. The Coast Guard crew untied the lines, the boats drifted apart, and *North Star* resumed her course, 125-degrees. But at a more cautious seven knots. This time as measured by the GPS.

Once safely away, the Chens went below and brought up Devlin, Marina and Roger. Roger was so proud of Hana he picked her off her feet and twirled her all the while kissing, laughing and hugging. "You were just wonderful." It was a moment to savor, brought the young couple closer, and would make a lasting memory.

Marina, who because of the echoey acoustics of the boat had been able to hear and translate what had been said to Roger and Devlin, joined in the congratulations. "Your performance was worthy of an Oscar," she said. "Though Hana when you invited the captain to go below, I almost died."

Devlin, still a little rattled by that surprise invitation asked with some asperity, "What in God's name were you thinking? Why do that?"

Hana held her ground. "I knew he wouldn't. He was too gentlemanly to distrust what I said."

Devlin shook his head in disbelief but was too relieved to object further.

Hana then pointed to Chen's parents and explained how well they played their parts in the evening's drama. That inspired another round of applause and congratulations. Once Chen's mother understood why they were being cheered she said, "When I saw the captain was about our age, I expected he would respond to us with respect. And he did." Like Hana, she had acted out of an intuition of the man's character.

Devlin, accepting the women's reasoning smiled and said, "I think that's enough work for you tonight, Hana. I'll take the wheel. Next stop, Macau."

CHAPTER 31
SAIL EAST, GO WEST

North Star had successfully passed its Coast Guard inspection, and the crew felt confident they wouldn't be boarded again. Still, everyone was too keyed up to sleep. Roger brewed coffee and tea —something which did not go unnoticed by Hana. Devlin switched on the autopilot and the six shipmates gathered around the table in the main salon to try to relax and decompress.

For the first time, here among allies, Chen's family could ask about their son without fear. "When did you last see Lin? Is all well? How is he?" his mother asked. Roger and Hana could not offer much more information than that he was healthy and a successful, well-liked student at Columbia. Hana added, "We met his girlfriend Wu Yao and like her very much. She's very pretty and must be intelligent since she is working this summer at the New York Times." Roger explained they met her because of a story he was working on about Chinese students in America. "The report was about how well so many of them are doing. Lin is someone I wanted very much to interview." He didn't say it was an interview which never took place. They also said Chen had been working that summer at a ship building company. Exactly where and on what kind of ships could come later.

Marina and Devlin mentioned the evening they all had dinner together, and that the couple even sailed and spent the night aboard their boat. They were also able to speak a little more about his happiness with Wu Yao. "She seems a lovely and very accomplished young lady," repeated Devlin, "and they seem determined to marry soon.

"And have children soon as well," Marina added to the delight of both parents.

The parents knew Chen had done some service for China which opened a path for their escape. The nature of that service was still a mystery to them. As was the reason the American government thought him so important it would initiate this mission on their behalf. Trying to be discreet Roger said the parents were sure to be told everything, and added ironically, "Apparently, whatever service Lin performed, gratified both China and the U.S." All refrained from any discussion of Chen's role as a counterspy. That was for others to explain.

Devlin did feel, despite the limits on what they could say, the parents had a right to know how they would be received in what was to become their new home.

"While you have much yet to learn about your son's accomplishments," he said, phrasing it as diplomatically as he could manage, "We can assure you of an enthusiastic welcome when you finally arrive in America."

Turning the conversation back to the parents Hana asked, "What are you doing about your home in Guangzhou, and all your possessions there?"

"We packed many bags in the last day or so," said Chen's mother, "the most precious, family pictures and jewelry, we brought with us. The bags we sent to the parents of Wu Yao. They run a travel agency and have promised to get everything sent as luggage to someplace where we can redeem them."

Chen's father added, "We have never even met these people, and they have done so much for us. I think it speaks wonderfully about their daughter, and their love for her. It is obviously for her sake they have been so generous."

"And courageous," added his wife. "They have a good life in China and they risked it all. We are not unappreciative of the peril they faced for our benefit."

"Still, you must be very sad to be forced to leave your home, and friends," Roger said with Hana translating.

Chen's father answered, "There is some sadness, but we no longer have living relatives here. At our age we want to spend our remaining years with our son."

"Yes," added his wife, "and watch as he grows and starts his family. Wherever they, and our grandchildren are, will be home to us."

"Besides," said Mister Chen, "we are not the first Chinese to emigrate to America. It is rather common don't you think?"

That got a laugh from everyone. "Yes, said Roger, "I think you could say that."

***

By dawn *North Star* was well into the large bay between Hong Kong and Macau. The sails were raised at first light and the boat and crew joined the other tourist boats plying those waters. A quick satellite call notified Ferrante in Boston of their position and the condition of those aboard. "Fantastic!" Ferrante exclaimed, "Let me know when you're approaching the Macau marina, I will have you met there."

It was a warm, sunny day, a time those aboard could enjoy themselves without fear of discovery. They were just one of hundreds of vessels motoring or tacking back and forth between Hong Kong and Macau. The breeze was a pleasant twelve knots allowing *North Star* to stretch out and skim across the waves at close to that speed herself. Everyone sat outdoors now, no need to hide faces or ethnicities. The boat had outside helm stations located on each side, port and starboard. Roger and Hana took turns at the wheel on the starboard side, their hair flying free, and faces shining with delight.

With Hana at the wheel Roger said he'd shoot more video. Some was of Hana and the others. For their own private use. Never to be seen elsewhere. "I'm just going to pick up more 'real estate' shots," he said. He meant "B roll" video of the scenery; the shoreline and the boats around them. These were like images in a travelogue, beauty shots. But they conveyed what had become the newly relaxed feeling aboard and would be useful in editing.

Two hours later, as they approached within five miles of the Macau city docks, Devlin called Ferrante on the satellite phone. It was eleven o'clock Friday morning; in Boston ten o'clock Thursday evening. After Ferrante had their location, he told Devlin to stay offshore.

"Give the folks I have meeting you another hour to get on site. They need a little time to prepare your welcome." He was referring to getting a plane ready for the Chen family. That delay gave *North Star's* crew and passengers another hour to loll about in the China Sea.

For Chen's parents it was going to be a bittersweet goodbye to their native land. They were subdued, didn't speak much, but rather sat in the stern on a bench outdoors, holding hands and absorbing these final sights of China. Hana and Roger sat on the deck nearby, their legs dangling over a pontoon, the water sliding and swishing by beneath their feet. Watching the older couple, they too held hands and mused over what it must mean to leave your homeland, likely forever. "That has to be so hard," Hana said wistfully.

"Your parents did it," replied Roger. "You and I, and whatever future we might have wouldn't exist if they didn't. Or my grandparents for that matter."

"An ending and a beginning at the same time."

"Never new life without the passing of the old one."

"Wow! Mister philosopher. Where did that come from?" She said tussling his hair.

"Just thinking about how much we both love the life we live now, and how hard it would be to say goodbye to it."

"But?"

"But the chrysalis has to bust out or no butterflies." Roger said with a rueful laugh.

"Well, now a poet!" she said giving his thigh a squeeze. "But we've got time."

"Yeah, I guess. But it's good to be reminded that it ain't endless."

"There comes a time ... it isn't painless, but I think this is the right moment for those two," she said looking at the Chens.

The two young people left to go below, gather their things, and leave the Chen's to their thoughts.

Most on the boat were relaxing quietly but Devlin

was nervous. He tried to hide his old fear that everything could go to hell at the last moment. *It ain't over till it's over.* He stood carefully watching the power boats kicking up big wakes as they blasted by and the many sailboats tacking around them, *no time for a collision*, he thought. Marina sensed his anxiety. She stepped behind him and put her arms around his waist. "Jitters?"

"You know me too well."

"Almost over."

For the two of them this was the climax of a drama that began while sailing on Long Island Sound when a submarine popped out of the sea right next to their boat.

"It's hard to believe two months ago we were preparing for a trip to Maine, and here we are floating in a strange sea half a world away from home, and from the kids."

Marina, nuzzling into his neck, gave him a squeeze, "You sorry?"

"No, but maybe I'm just getting to be an old homebody. I'll be delighted to get back to the States.

Marina slid to his side and leaned into him. With a theatrical pout she said, "We didn't even get a chance to enjoy some Chinese food."

"I know a place on Broadway. Great fried rice."

"You really are getting boring," Marina teased.

The satphone rang just as they kissed.

Devlin answered, "Go ahead."

"It's Ferrante. All's set. Bring her in."

Devlin's last-minute fears were for naught. The hand-off at the casino's dock went without a problem. After handshakes, hugs and warm goodbyes, Chen's parents were ushered into an SUV and whisked to a private jet, ostensibly belonging to a Malaysian high roller. It took them to Tokyo where they were received as guests in transit of the United States.

CHAPTER 32
NEW BEGINNINGS

The Chens spent their first night as refugees in a hotel near Tokyo's Haneda airport. Escorted by two officers they settled into their room at ten p.m. Given the thirteen-hour time difference it was only seven in the morning for Lin in Connecticut. They called and woke him. A sleepy voice answered,

"Hello?"

"Lin, is that you?" said his mother.

"Mom! Oh my God. Where are you?"

"We are in Tokyo. Dad is right here with me. I will put you on speaker."

Emotion got the best of all. There was relief and an outpouring of tears. Chen knew from Ferrante that their exfiltration had been a success, but it became real with the sound of their voices.

"I can't wait to see you. There is so much to say, to explain. And a very special woman I want you to meet."

"Yes, we have heard a little about her." said his mother. "I am sure she is lovely."

His father jumped in, "We are leaving Tokyo for New York at eleven tomorrow morning. I think that is ten o'clock tonight your time."

"That means you should arrive here at about noon tomorrow, Saturday."

His mother mused, "It is strange to think we must fly east in order to reach you in the West."

Chen laughed, "I guess that means it's a small world

after all."

This confused his parents but they laughed nonetheless.

"Have a good flight. I will be in New York to meet you. Love you."

The reunion at JFK was facilitated by the Navy. Chen was flown from the Groton base to the airport where he was met by Wu Yao. They stood at the arrivals portal and greeted his parents, exhausted by their travels but otherwise in good spirits.

Yao welcomed Madam Chen with a bouquet of flowers and received an affectionate hug in return.

"We have so much to thank you and your parents for," said Madam Chen. "We would not be here without them."

"And to think it was all made possible by a squirrel," Yao said to much laughter. "It surely must be the year of the rodent."

"Are you calling me a mouse?" Chen said with mock horror, to more laughter.

"Meeting you," Mister Chen said bowing to Yao, "I think my son is showing what good taste that mouse inherited from his mother."

"The honor is mine xiansheng," replied Yao, using a term of respect for an elder as she bowed in return. She had already won the parents' hearts.

After the hugs, kisses, laughter and tears, a helicopter ferried all four to New London and a meeting with Liam

McCarthy, Bill Roscoe and Nicholas Ferrante.

The mood at the Navy base was congratulatory and cheerful, but relatively subdued. The tension the law enforcement personnel had endured was only slowly subsiding. What remained of paramount importance was to keep Chen's role secret. No one who did not need to know about the fake submarine plans would be told. Chen had been warned by Ferrante, "That includes your parents. It's safer for everyone that way."

At first Chen was shocked to think he was being asked to conceal something so important from his parents; but on reflection he realized Ferrante was right. Their safety was all important. He would tell them someday, but for the present they would be protected from the truth.

As soon as Chen's parents arrived at the Navy submarine base, they understood the kind of ships Lin had been working on. Looking at the submarines at their slips Madam Chen said, "I think I know now why the United States government helped us." Mister Chen agreed, "It has something to do with these boats." But for what precise reason was still a mystery.

Chen Lin, his parents and Yao were ushered into Liam McCarthy's office where some folding chairs had been added, and introductions were made.

"Mister and Madam Chen," Liam said in greeting, "I want to welcome you and say how much I've enjoyed working with your son. He's been a great help in our project."

"And a great help to this country." added Ferrante.

"We must thank you for all the effort you made to bring us here," said Chen's father. "I think, given the kind of 'projects' involved, we can now understand your motivation.

But still a mystery to us is why Xi Jinping agreed to drop the guards around our house?"

Bill Roscoe of the FBI answered with practiced vagueness, "Well Mister Chen, despite all the differences between China and the U.S. there are some things the two governments can agree on. When it suits their purposes of course. All I can say to you is that an understanding was reached with the Chinese authorities and both sides are happy with the outcome."

Mister Chen stared into Roscoe's eyes and understood. They had been told nothing, and nothing more was to be forthcoming. He accepted the opacity as a necessity; a function of the world into which their son had been admitted. The parents felt a glimmer of pride in that understanding.

For the Americans, and the Chen family, it was time to turn their focus to the future. Liam could once again concentrate on the Columbia submarines. And in just two days Chen Lin would return to Columbia with notice that he had successfully completed his internship and would get credit for it.

One of Chen's first contacts when back on campus was Fu Muchen, the leader of the anti Xi protests. He was still suspicious of Chen's quick disappearance back in July.

"We missed you for the filming by WNOW. We expected you to be with us."

"I couldn't do it. I feared it would risk my getting the Navy internship."

Muchen huffed, "Well you got it. How did it go?"

"Very well. And even better, my parents managed to make it to Hong Kong and are now here with me. I'm out from under Xi's thumb."

"Man! How did they manage that?"

"Friends. That's all I can say."

Muchen just nodded. "What about Yao. You guys ok, give her a ring yet?"

Chen laughed, "Not yet but the deal is done. You'll be invited."

"I wouldn't miss it."

Chen felt good. He had managed to explain himself to his friends without any outright lies. Now he could concentrate on getting that all important doctorate.

Chen had earned extra credits for his work at the Navy base and, this being his final year, also gained assurances of help applying for a job. Liam told him of one which was going to become available soon after graduation. "It's up on Cape Cod, Woods Hole. You will be perfect for it," Liam had said. "I will give you my highest recommendation."

Yao still had two years to go at Columbia. The plan was for the couple to marry when Chen graduated the following June, and for her to get a job in journalism in whichever city he found work.

The government, mindful of Chen's service (and excusing his initial deceptions) offered a generous stipend to help settle his parents in their new country. At least until Chen himself could begin earning enough to support them, something which was at least a year away.

***

After they had dropped off their passengers, the catamaran *North Star* returned with Roger, Hana, Devlin and Marina to the Hong Kong marina from which they had left just two days earlier. Again, they were greeted by the students who helped arrange their departure and shuttled to the same hotel they enjoyed on arrival. After a day to shower, relax, and make up for the lost sleep of the night before, they all boarded a direct flight to New York. It was the same day the Chens departed Tokyo, Saturday of the Labor Day weekend.

Marina and Devlin were met in their New York apartment by Marina's mother, and the children Richard and Cynthia. The time away had not been as long as feared, but any thought of sailing to Maine would be forgotten for the year. "Besides we have to go to Disneyworld," young Richard declared with finality. *If that's all it takes to keep peace in the family*, thought his parents, *we're getting off easy*.

After dinner that night, while her mother was in the kitchen brewing a pot of espresso, Marina sat next to Devlin on the couch and took his face in her hands. She kissed him softly and whispered in his ear, "Don't lose your job, you're going to have another mouth to feed." The trip to Disneyland was suddenly elevated to a grand celebration for their growing family.

***

Ma Bai kept his position at the UN. He was held in

very high regard since his successful collection of top-secret plans for the Columbia Class of American submarines. His authority was expanded; he was given more agents to oversee. Unfortunately for him, however, his collaboration with the Russians backfired. The scrutiny it caused meant he was now identified by the FBI as an important Chinese operative and would be closely monitored from that time forward.

Ma Bai's hapless agent Zhang Wei was more successful. He'd been spirited out of the United States ---a blind eye turned by the FBI-- and returned to his family in China as a hero of the State. Someone who orchestrated the theft of Columbia's plans. His wife and son were very proud of him.

***

For Roger and Hana, life resumed much as it had been before the eruption of the "Chen Affair," as they came to call it. Roger was as ambitious and headstrong as ever, and Hana still frustrated with him in many ways, but increasingly tolerant of his "foibles," as she now called them. Despite the objections of her parents, she was sticking with this guy. Maybe he would in
time grow up, and perhaps even move to a network.

As for Roger, his hoped-for "Emmy winning report" as an embedded reporter on a spy mission would have to wait. The government would not allow the release of the video he and Hana shot until it was sure the Chinese no longer believed the Columbia plans were genuine. So far, that was not the case. So the video, and Roger's telling of the story, had to stay unseen and untold. But he did continue, with Gabe Breslin's help, to grow as a reporter and to enjoy his career in local news. The network job could wait. The prestigious "cathedral" could wait. He remained, for a while at least, a happy denizen of the "whorehouse."

EPILOGUE

In June of 2023, two years after the "Aukus Affair" recounted above, there was a terrible accident in the cold waters of the North Atlantic. It happened near the site of the sinking of the passenger ship Titanic in 1912. A submersible boat carrying five passengers and crew descended to view the wreck and was lost. After a long search involving personnel and equipment from many nations, the wreckage of their submersible was found. All aboard perished.

One of the reporters covering the disaster that June was Roger Barnes of WNOW-TV News. His report included an interview with a material sciences expert who was employed by the Woods Hole Oceanographic Institution, which was among those organizations investigating the accident.

One of the millions around the world following the tragedy was Ma Bai, an official with the Chinese Mission to the United Nations who watched the Barnes report in his office.

"What do you think best explains the cause of the accident?" Barnes asked the young scientist, Chen Lin.

"We have learned that the external structure of the lost submersible was constructed of two materials, steel and carbon fiber. Steel has always been the tested and accepted standard for such vessels. Joining it with carbon fiber is very problematic."

"So, do you believe it was the use of carbon fiber that contributed to the implosion of the vessel?"

"Yes. At this point we can't be absolutely sure, but we have known for years that wherever the two materials are joined, bolted together, there is a strong likelihood of failure. Carbon fiber is very strong for its weight, but despite the weight savings, we could not at this point recommend it be used in the external structure of an underwater vessel."

"Why not? What might happen?"

"Well, if a joint between the two sections failed at depth, rather than a slow leak there would be an implosion. The entire submersible would be instantaneously crushed, killing everyone aboard."

Ma Bai froze staring at the television screen. For almost two years his government had been trying to build a prototype submarine using exactly that hybrid steel and carbon fiber technology. A technology supposedly in use for the construction of the latest generation of American nuclear submarines. A technology leaked to Ma Bai by that very same materials scientist now on TV. For many months China had been researching a construction method that this man, Chen Lin, knew at the time was doomed to fail.

Ma Bai's reaction to what he saw on television was recorded by a hidden camera. The FBI had installed it in a ceiling light fixture two years earlier.

As the video showed, the diplomat stood at his desk, pounded his fist down and growled in fury, "Chen Lin, you traitorous snake. I will make you pay."

But even as he said it, the spymaster knew no such thing would happen. He was impotent now. Once Beijing learned how thoroughly he had been duped, Ma would be lucky to save himself.

Robert Ferraro

ACKNOWLEDGEMENTS

Thanks to my ancestors who first came to this country of endless opportunity, the parents who gave life and love, and my family for enduring my various enthusiasms. Thanks also to Jane Murphy, Jordan Rost and Barbara Bonn of the New York Society Library for their patient reading and always helpful comments. A special thank you to the woman at the University of Arizona, whose name I cannot recall but who said, some sixty years ago, "You're pretty good, you should be a writer." Well, I'm trying. Thanks for the encouragement.

ABOUT THE AUTHOR

Robert Ferraro, a television news journalist, won distinction producing news and documentaries. Mister Ferraro is retired and lives with his wife Paula in New York City.

Printed in Dunstable, United Kingdom